THE DEFIANT MAGICIAN

THE DEFIANT MAGICIAN

UNSTOPPABLE LIV BEAUFONT™ BOOK 3

SARAH NOFFKE
MICHAEL ANDERLE

The Defiant Magician (this book) is a work of fiction.

All of the characters, organizations, and events portrayed in this novel are either products of the author's imagination or are used fictitiously. Sometimes both.

LMBPN Publishing
PMB 196, 2540 South Maryland Pkwy
Las Vegas, NV 89109

First US Edition, March 2019
Version 1.01, October 2019

THE DEFIANT MAGICIAN TEAM

Thanks to the JIT Readers

Larry Omans
Angel LaVey
Daniel Weigert
Jeff Eaton
Micky Cocker
Crystal Wren
John Ashmore
Keith Verret
Kelly O'Donnell
James Caplan
Misty Roa
Peter Manis

If I've missed anyone, please let me know!

Editor
The Skyhunter Editing Team

For Kathy.

Thank you for giving me my first fantasy book.

Since then, the world has been a better place.

CHAPTER ONE

Green smoke rose up from the cauldron, partially obscuring Adler Sinclair's pale face. He fanned the fumes to his nose, inhaling deeply.

"It's not right yet."

"Do you think this is wise?" Decar asked, pacing back and forth in front of Adler's work table, which was littered with ingredients—many on the illegal list.

"It will work." Adler's eyes narrowed as he chopped up more chusetor, a rare flower that caused hallucinations and other mental disorders.

"That's not what worries me." Decar halted, the sword on his belt clanking. "If they have the sword, then—"

"We will get it back," Adler stated definitively.

"But why would Olivia Beaufont take it? She must know something, just like her siblings and her parents."

Adler shook his head. "There is no way she can."

"But the sword…" Decar insisted, the stress making his long white face appear suddenly older.

"Don't worry. Turbinger can only reveal the history to a

giant of pure blood, and who will believe them? We've done our job discrediting the giants. We've made them look like brutish, uncivilized creatures."

Decar sighed, agreeing. "Yeah, I guess you're right. It's not like it's a fae or an elf. It's just that the sword was protected, and has been for so long, and now it's out there somewhere in who-knows-whose hands."

A wicked glare crossed Adler's face as he slid the chusetor into the simmering cauldron. "We know who stole the sword. We just have to figure out what she did with it."

"And why? Why would Olivia Beaufont go after the sword in the first place?"

"I suspect she got curious, but who knows why? I thought she'd be an inconvenience, but I never dreamed she'd be a downright headache. She was supposed to work her cases and stay out of this."

"And her magic? Has it normalized?"

Adler shook his head. "No, and that's starting to worry me. It should have by now if it was a surge."

"What does that mean?"

"I don't know," Adler nearly yelled, his face flushing red.

Decar's eyes fell on the small dragon breathing a steady stream of fire under the cauldron. This potion had to brew hotter than most, which would have been a problem to hide from the Council. They would see Adler using a fire spell for such a long period of time, and that could draw suspicion onto him. However, Indikos kept that from happening, and the potion would also keep the magic they were using off the radar. Potions and artifacts and other magical items like depours helped to cover their tracks.

The potion turned a blackish color, its consistency thick like tar. Adler nodded, relief whisking to his face. He grabbed a small bottle from the crammed worktable and filled it with the hot liquid. Setting it down, he showed his brother a victorious expression.

"I don't know why Olivia Beaufont has more magic than she should, or why she's sticking her nose into things she shouldn't, but that's going to change very soon."

Decar nodded, gulping as he stared at the small bottle. "I think this is the right approach. If something happens to another Beaufont, then—"

"It will be very unfortunate," Adler said, cutting off the other magician. "I will do everything that I can to protect Olivia, but if she gets herself into this mess, then there is little that I can do."

"But the potion…" Decar picked up the bottle, his dragonhide gloves protecting his fingers from the heat.

"The potion will restore balance. What we need is to keep a better eye on Ms. Beaufont. Then she won't be off creating extra problems for us."

"And her cases?" Decar inquired.

Adler petted Indikos, telling the dragon to stop breathing fire as he gazed up at his master. "They will also serve to sort the rebellious Warrior out. She's confused, having been out of the House for five years. That's my fault. I underestimated her, but that won't happen again."

"And the sword?" Decar asked.

Adler gritted his long, pointy teeth, new anger flaring on his face. "The sword will be returned. Malcom made a mistake by letting Ms. Beaufont take it."

"I'm still surprised that you didn't punish him," Decar stated.

"I didn't have to," Adler replied. "And I think he can still be of help to us. He's eager to not be punished further."

"But if what you say is true, the cut from Turbinger will drive him insane."

Adler swiped his hand in a small circle, and the contents in the cauldron disappeared. "He thinks there is a cure and will do anything to get it."

"But there isn't, right?"

"Of course there isn't." Adler laughed coldly. "That's why it's one of the most deadly weapons in the world. A warrior doesn't have to kill with it, only mark their enemy. It gives the bearer the option of invoking a fast or slow death."

Decar shuddered, slipping the bottle into his pocket. "I would prefer a fast one if what I've heard about being marked by Turbinger is correct."

"I agree," Adler said with a nod. "I'd rather not lose my mind either. Mental torture is the worst." He pointed to where Decar had put the potion. "You know what to do with that?"

Decar lowered his chin, regarding his brother with impatience. "You mean who to give it to, and yes. I'll ensure that our new lemming follows our plans to a T."

"Good. And then have Malcom report directly to him. I don't need a deranged elf contacting me anymore. It isn't safe."

Decar offered his brother one last curt nod before pivoting and striding for the door. What he had in his pocket was one of the most powerful potions a wizard could make. It didn't kill or heal. Those were simple tasks that magicians could easily do on their own. Controlling another person...now that was an incredibly difficult feat. Yes, mortals could be persuaded. Slightly brainwashed from time to time. But to make them do your bidding? That was a real challenge.

Adler was right. Olivia Beaufont wasn't a problem. She was a nuisance. A rebel who had acted out. Let her curiosity get the best of her. It had only happened because they'd allowed her too much freedom. That was all about to change.

CHAPTER TWO

"Do it again," John encouraged, leaning forward on his stool, his eyes dancing with amusement.

Not as enthusiastic as the older man, Liv twirled her finger in the air, and all the lights in the shop extinguished.

John clapped, causing Pickles to bark and circle on the ground from the excitement, his nails clacking. "Oh, that's just so cool. Now turn them on again."

Liv did as he asked, bathing the shop in light from overhead. "You know, I can do way cooler stuff than turning on and off the lights. Want me to make a windstorm or fix all the appliances that came in?"

John shook his head. "No, I like the small stuff. It's handy."

"But there are apps that control lights."

"Oh, who needs one of those silly things that spy on you?" John gave her a conspiratorial look. "Between you and me, I think that Alicia thing is listening in a bit too much."

Liv laughed. "Alexa," she corrected. "And I find it ironic that someone who fixes appliances for a living is paranoid about new technology."

"That's the thing," John countered. "I like old technology. Like this old mixer." He indicated a vintage KitchenAid countertop mixer that a customer had brought in that morning. He eyed it fondly. "That's the reason I like to fix them—so we don't fill up the landfill with broken junk. And this beauty, well… I can get it working as good as the day it came out of the box."

Liv had always appreciated this about John. Instead of throwing things out, he believed in fixing them. Maybe that was the reason he'd offered her the job she'd inquired about five years prior after having seen the sign posted in the window instead of turning her down because she didn't have any experience. Maybe he saw that she was broken and wanted to help fix her. The day she'd left the House of Seven, she'd made friends with Plato and stumbled across John's shop, landing a job and a place to live. Everything had worked out then, providing a new life she desperately needed. And now her old life and her new one were mixing together like eggs and flour in a bowl. But what would this all produce?

"I thought you wanted *me* to fix the mixer," Liv said. "You can do it, though, if you want to."

He waved her off, coming out of his fond appreciation of the old appliance. "No, you do it. But I do request that you don't use any magic until you've figured out what the actual problem is. We don't need Mrs. Albertson bringing it back, saying it made a cake all by itself."

Liv smiled, thinking of the other appliances clients had

returned because of similar peculiarities. "Don't worry, I've learned my lesson. I'm getting better at incorporating my magic without unintended consequences. However, if it's a problem, I won't use it while I'm in the shop."

John thought for a moment. "A little magic here and there doesn't bother me, as long as you don't get lost in it." His expression grew distant and then dark, as if an old memory was playing in his mind—one involving his ex-wife Chloe, the magician.

"That's been Plato's advice too. I'm learning how to do everything without magic. Then I'm not reliant on it."

John eyed the cat, who was snoozing on the work-bench, skeptically. "Right. The cat told you this."

"How come you believe that gnomes have fireball technology and that I work for a secret organization of magicians, but the cat talking is too far out?"

"I've seen a lot of things in my time. Things that no other mortal would believe. But a talking cat? Come on, Liv. That's a bit far. Funny joke, though."

Snapping her fingers in front of Plato's face, Liv tried her best to rouse him. "Will you say something to prove to him that I'm not pulling his leg?"

Plato cracked open one of his green eyes and shut it again, nestling his face more comfortably into his paws.

"Okay, fine. Be that way," Liv snapped.

John laughed. "Of course, I *did* like that you used your magic to tidy up the shop every evening. I guess it's okay to keep doing that."

Liv shook her head. "I'm not the one cleaning the shop. That's a brownie."

Surprise jumped to John's face. "You mean one of those

little elves? Those are real?"

"Yes, and that one took a liking to you, so keep doing what you're doing, and he'll keep the floors clean."

"Shouldn't I leave him something, like a piece of chocolate or taffy?"

"I don't know how it works with brownies, but I have a book that R…that a friend gave me where I can look it up." Liv looked down at the workstation, trying to hide her worried expression. She'd nearly outed Rory as a giant, which wasn't her place.

John gave her a sideways glance, skepticism strong in his eyes. "Don't worry. I've also suspected that Rory was a giant for a long time. I don't know much about them, but I think he's all right. Chloe mentioned a time or two that they couldn't be trusted, though."

Liv was surprised. John had seemed so innocent that she'd had no idea he saw the magical world as clearly as he did. She realized she shouldn't have underestimated him. He might pretend not to care about other people's business, but that didn't mean he wasn't paying attention. "Yeah, there's a long-standing grudge between magicians and giants, but I'm not sure why."

"But you and he get on well, right?" John asked, striding over to an old unplugged refrigerator and opening the door. It had been for sale for months, but no one seemed much interested in it since it wasn't the standard size. John had faith that the right buyer would find it. Someone with a retro kitchen, possibly.

Presently the refrigerator stored boxes of Girl Scout cookies. He pulled a sleeve of Thin Mints from a box and shut the door.

"Well, Rory and I never even talked much until I nearly destroyed your shop the day my magic was unlocked. Since then, he's been training me."

John's mouth popped open as he slid the cookies onto a plate on the table. "That was you? I thought..." His eyes danced as everything came together. "Yeah, that makes sense now."

"Sorry for lying to you. I didn't know how to explain what was happening, and—"

John waved her off, taking a bite of a cookie. "No, don't apologize. It sounds like it's been quite the adventure for you. And it was only shortly after that when I started to figure out you might have magic."

"How did you know?" Liv asked, taking the sleeve of cookies when John offered it to her.

"Magic has a distinct feel to it that I can't explain," John stated, licking the crumbs from his lips. "It's like it leaves behind a smell or something, although I realize it doesn't. It's like a residue. I felt it when I was around Chloe, and its absence when she left. Anyway, I started getting that strange feeling again recently and suspected it might be coming from you. Then your brother came here and you got that bite, and I knew something bigger than the flu was happening to you." He laughed, neatly arranging the cookies on the plate. "Although, I don't think I would have figured out you were a Warrior for the House of Seven in a million years. That's a big role."

"It's no big deal." Liv took another handful of cookies,

realizing she hadn't eaten enough that day. What she needed was a plate of tacos, but she could settle for a sleeve of Thin Mints. "The Council assigns me lame cases to keep me out of their hair."

John pointed to her leg, which was still bandaged under her jeans where the lophos had bitten her. "Doesn't sound like it's no big deal. What did you say took a chunk out of your leg? A giant snake?"

"That wasn't really Warrior business," Liv admitted. "I was working on an extracurricular project."

John pursed his lips. "Well, I don't know what to say about that, but you're old enough to make your own decisions. And smart enough, too. Just be careful."

Liv smiled. "You're never going to tell me not to do something, are you?"

"I live my life, and you live yours. It really isn't my place. If you think this extracurricular business is worth the risk, you've got to do what's in your heart."

"I've thought since the beginning that something was off about my parents' death," Liv confessed, realizing that she'd never really spoken to John about them. He knew they had died, but none of the details. "I think there's something… Well, I don't want to bring you into it, but I'm investigating. That's all."

"And that's enough. You tell me what you want." John slid the plate onto a high shelf. "Just be careful. But don't worry about involving me. I've been around magic before, and it doesn't bother me."

"Why did you put that up there?" Liv pointed to the plate.

"Well, I don't know what to offer the brownie in thanks, but I thought I'd try some cookies."

Liv laughed. "He's an elf, not Santa Claus."

John chuckled, his eyes lighting up. "I daresay an elf who cleans my shop is more valuable than a fat man who brings me junk I don't need."

CHAPTER THREE

Pausing in the entryway of the House of Seven, Liv checked over her shoulder to ensure she was alone. In truth, there was really no way to be sure of that, since a clever magician such as Sophia could disguise herself or someone could have a spy spell operating. However, it was a chance Liv was going to have to take, her curiosity overpowering her desire for secrecy.

She withdrew her mother's ring from her pocket and held it up in front of the wall inscribed with the ancient language. When she'd been tracking down the canister of stolen magic, she'd learned that the ring could decode the ancient language, and ever since then, she'd wanted to try it here in the House of Seven.

The symbols danced and glowed as they usually did when Liv was near them. This time though, with the ring, they transformed into words she understood, communicating the message of the founders. Liv sucked in a breath, reading the words that materialized:

The Ancient Chamber holds the names of the founding families.

The words faded as Liv read them, returning to symbol form.

Ancient chamber, she mused. That wasn't a place she'd heard of before. Was it in the House of Seven? That made the most sense. But why would it matter that it held the names of the founding families? Liv realized that she couldn't recall all of the founders' names. There were the Beaufonts, of course. And the Takahashis and Sinclairs. For some reason, the ones that had been replaced didn't come to mind, but that didn't make sense. They had to be written in a book or something. They had to be somewhere magicians could reference them. Yet, the harder she thought about it, the more difficult it became to remember any other founders' names. The family that the Ludwigs replaced were the… Nothing came to mind.

Again she raised the ring and ran it past the symbols that covered the walls, glowing gold and sparkling:

The Ancient Chamber holds the names of the founding families.

Okay, maybe that was the only place to find the names. Maybe magic protected them, storing them away. Her mother had once said there was power in the names of the founding families. Spoken aloud, they carried a core strength that could enhance spells.

But where was this Ancient Chamber?

After the words faded, Liv swiped the ring over another set of symbols:

Only two things together open the Ancient Chamber:

the blood of a councilor, and the Founder's ring of a Warrior.

The blood of a councilor? Liv wondered. Clark's blood. She pulled the ring closer to her face, inspecting it for the millionth time. This was a Founder's ring? *A Warrior's ring?* That made sense now, but it also brought with it more questions. Like, why Rudolf, the fae, couldn't bring up the memories associated with the ring? And if it was a Founder's ring, then there were six more just like it out there in the world.

The band of the ring was platinum, and carved on the inside were the words, Together we are strong and balanced.

Those were common words associated with the House. Everything was about balance. That was the explanation for the white tiger and the black crow in the Chamber of the Tree, although Liv suspected there was more mystery behind those strange animals. She still didn't trust the tiger or the crow.

"So this is a key of sorts," Liv muttered. She ran the ring over the wall again, but only the messages she'd already read came up.

"It would seem so," Plato said, suddenly by her side.

Liv jumped, having thought she was on guard. "Damn it, you nearly gave me a heart attack."

"You should run more if your heart is that weak," Plato teased.

Liv grimaced. "I loathe running. But you're right, I do need to up my exercise regimen."

"Speaking of heart," Plato said, nodding in the direction of the words that were about to fade. "Do you think this could have been what Reese was referring to in her message?"

Liv's mouth popped open and her eyes widened. "Plato, you're a genius. Yes, that's got to be it." The words from her sister's message came back to her instantly: Olivia has the key. You have the heart. Together you must finish what we started.

"I guess she could have said blood," Plato reasoned.

Liv shook her head. "No, she couldn't. Reese never called things what they were. She liked to use flowery language and make things cryptic. She also could have said I had the ring, but instead she called it a key."

"But it *is* a key, both to the Ancient Chamber and also to decipher the forgotten language."

Liv slid the ring into her pocket. "And who knows what else it does?"

"Well, it apparently proves you are part of a founding family."

"Yeah, that's a new one for me. So both Clark and I are needed to open the Ancient Chamber. The question is, where is it?"

Plato just looked at Liv. She knew that expression all too well. He'd figured something out and was simply waiting for her to catch up with him.

"The library," Liv said too loudly, her triumph getting the best of her. "That groove in the wall. We suspected that the ring would fit there, but maybe we'll need Clark's blood too in order to make it open or whatever it does."

"And the ancient language is on that wall, so who knows what it says?"

Liv patted her pocket, hope blossoming in her chest.

She needed this win before going to meet with the Seven since that usually derailed her spirit. "Well, it looks like I'll be finding out what's on that wall and opening the Ancient Chamber soon. For now, I'm going to go look up the councilors' noses while they sit looking down at me, silently judging my dress and messy hair."

"Not to mention your defiant attitude and lack of decorum," Plato added.

"Yes, not to mention that." At the Door of Reflection, Liv paused, studying her image in the wavy surface. She had her black traveling cloak pulled up over her head, and wore leather pants and boots. There was no possible way that anyone could know that she had a lophos bite on her leg. Well, except Hester, who had treated her and Clark, who had saved her.

The soaring blackness stole her attention for a moment. Liv knew it was always there, hanging between the Chamber of the Tree and the door to the residential living, although she tried to forget it, as it were a recurring nightmare that haunted her every night.

"Well, I knew there was a good reason I was running late today," a voice said at Liv's back.

She spun to find Raina Ludwig coming out of the door to the residential area. Her soft black hair was sectioned into two sets of braids, which cascaded over her shoulders and rested on the turquoise gown she was wearing. The warm smile she offered Liv was full of sincerity, something she wasn't accustomed to seeing in the Chamber.

"Hello," Liv greeted the councilor.

"I will take the blame for you being late. Tell the Council that I detained you," Raina stated.

"I'm late?" Liv realized she must have spent longer in the entryway than she'd thought. "And thank you. That's very kind of you."

"My pleasure. Adler is in an especially sour mood today. My apologies in advance."

Liv laughed. "You don't have to apologize for that old grump."

The light expression on Raina's face disappeared. "I do, though. As a councilor, I'm responsible for so much, and yet I'm only one of seven, and often outvoted."

That didn't sound good. What did she get outvoted on? Did Liv even want to attend the meeting that day? Maybe she could skip it, saying she was still working a case. She shrugged off her concern and pointed at the blackness. "Since we're already late and I'm definitely not in a hurry to go in, can you tell me what the black void thing is all about?"

Raina gazed at the chasm of darkness, blinking like she hadn't noticed it before Liv pointed it out. "Huh. Yeah, I'm not sure."

"But you wonder about it, right?"

The councilor shook her head. "I haven't before now. But since you mention it…" She blinked at the Door of Reflection, her expression turning neutral. "Anyway, we'd better be off. I'll meet you in there and explain that we were together."

Liv didn't have a chance to thank her before she stepped through the mirrored surface and disappeared.

"Plato, did you get the impression that she was spelled somehow?"

The feline appeared beside Liv, staring curiously at the

swirling blackness. "Yes. She didn't seem to notice this, and forgot about it almost at once."

"But how is that possible, when we pass it every single day?" Liv asked.

"And more importantly, why don't you forget about it, and why do you fear it so much?"

"Oh, good, more unanswered questions. Go write them down," Liv said with a laugh. "*I'm* going to face the scowls of the Council."

"Yeah, I'll get right on that writing business," Plato said as Liv stepped through the Door of Reflection.

Her breath caught in her throat as the image of John lying sick and fragile in a hospital bed blanketed her vision. She wanted to reach out to him but realized that she had no body. As if she were in a dream, she was simply observing the desolate scene before her.

Liv reminded herself that this wasn't real. John wasn't sick or in the hospital. The Door of Reflection was serving up fears from her subconscious; things that weighed her down without her knowing it. She felt stronger suddenly, and less traumatized at the image of John. Of course she worried about him, and constantly harped on him to take better care of himself. That is what friends did for one another.

A nurse entered the room, talking to someone unseen. "Such a strange attack this one endured. Like something out of a movie."

"Has he said anything?" someone asked.

The nurse glanced down at a file in her hand. "He just keeps muttering something about magic."

Liv couldn't breathe, and her knees gave out. She felt

herself falling, doom and guilt wrapping around her as the world went black.

And then she was in the Chamber of the Tree, the councilors all looking down at her, most with disapproving glare on their faces.

CHAPTER FOUR

Taking her spot, Liv observed that there were no other Warriors present that day. They were all off working cases.

As she pushed her hood back, she tried to shake off the images and guilt from the Door of Reflection. Yes, it was bothering her that she could be putting John and the shop in danger, but he'd consented. Taken on the risks, knowing exactly what he was getting into. However, that didn't make it any easier. If something happened to him, it would be her fault.

"Ms. Beaufont, Councilor Ludwig informs us that she's the reason you are late, having detained you earlier," Adler said, peering down at her, the circles under his eyes more pronounced than usual.

"Yes," Liv answered, hiding a grin as she glanced briefly at Raina. The kind smile she'd shown her before was gone, and she wore a stony expression on her face.

Adler looked down the bench at Lorenzo, Haro, and

Bianca. "I'm not sure that excuses her tardiness. What do you all think?"

Bianca leaned forward, her attention directed at Raina. "I agree. And I do wonder what you two discussed at the time we all were supposed to be meeting today."

"I don't believe it's any of your business, Councilor Montovani," Raina fired back.

"Punctuality is important—as we've told you before, Ms. Beaufont," Adler said with an impatient sigh. He picked up the device in front of him, reviewing the notes Liv had provided about her last case. "You were successful at cataloging the locations of all the spring fairies?"

It was a useless job, Rory had explained to her. As soon as their locations were recorded, the information would change. He agreed that they had only given her the case to get her out of their hair.

"Yes," Liv answered, noticing how crestfallen Clark appeared. He usually appeared pretty sullen during these meetings, but today his face looked distraught.

"Are you sure you got all of them?" Lorenzo asked, also reviewing the notes in front of him.

"I am," Liv replied dully.

"Do you have a problem, Ms. Beaufont?" Alder asked, his tone disapproving.

Problem? Well, where was the couch? Liv could stretch out and really unload. "No, no. I'm dandy," she answered.

Haro gave Liv a questioning glance. "I sense that you're not."

She yawned. "Just tired of traipsing through gardens, searching for fairies who are wiping ladybugs' asses."

A sadistic smile turned up the corners of Adler's mouth,

showing even under his white beard. "Well, then I think we have a case you'll enjoy."

Clark flung himself back in his chair. "I really don't think—"

"You've already been heard on the matter," Adler said, cutting him off with a stern expression. "And the Council has voted. You and the others were overruled. That's how this works, is it not?"

Clark's gaze shot to Liv, anger brewing in his eyes. "Yes, I get that this is how it works. It's just that—"

"And Ms. Beaufont wants harder cases, isn't that right?" Adler asked, shooting Liv an inquiring expression.

"Well, yes," she answered. "But if my brother—"

"Councilor Beaufont's concerns shouldn't color your thinking," Adler stated, cutting her off.

"Fine." Liv crossed her arms over her chest, her chin held high. "What is my case?"

The white tiger strode into the middle of the chamber, his green eyes searching the ground as if he were looking for something he'd lost. This seemed to distract Adler from what he was about to say, pulling his attention away from Liv.

"Warrior Beaufont," Haro began, "your next case is to go to the Kingdom of Fae and meet with their queen. We need you to discuss imposing regulations on the Fae for seducing mortals, since it's becoming a more serious issue."

"Wait, what?" Liv asked, catching the flare of anger on Clark's face.

Adler pulled his gaze away from the tiger, who had quit searching and fixed his piercing green eyes on Liv. "We have an agreement with Queen Visa already, so all we're asking you to do is renegotiate the terms. Update them, if you will."

"You're asking her to put her head on a silver platter," Clark nearly yelled.

Adler rolled his eyes, looking down the bench at her brother. "Please don't be so dramatic. The fae are reasonable creatures, whom Ms. Beaufont can, I'm sure, discuss this matter with reason."

"Queen Visa will roast her for even proposing such a regulation," Clark fired back.

"Well, that's not the Council's concern. It was voted upon, and the case passed, four to three," Adler stated.

Liv knew this must have been what Raina was referring to. This was what she'd been outvoted on. Clark, too. And she was guessing Hester was the third, which meant the others wanted her to go on this bizarre case.

"It doesn't have to be Liv who works the case," Clark argued. "She's brand new, and has had limited dealing with the fae. Emilio makes the most sense since he has experience with Queen Visa."

Casually Adler peered around at the chamber before returning his gaze to Clark. "Do you see any other eligible Warriors here to take the case? All I see is Ms. Beaufont—who, by the way, has been begging for more difficult cases."

I wouldn't say I was begging, Liv thought dully.

"Well, this case could wait," Hester offered, her voice low.

"The fact remains that of late, several mortals have gotten themselves into dire situations because of a fae's seduction," Lorenzo stated.

Bianca nodded. "Yes, I agree that something needs to be done. The fae have gone unchecked for too long."

"That might be," Clark began, "but I don't think that my sister should be the one—"

"It's fine," Liv said, this time cutting him off. She was tired of watching the other four Council members roll their eyes at him.

He shot her a shocked look.

"It's fine," she repeated. "I'm happy to negotiate on behalf of the House of Seven." For good measure, she bowed to the Council. "I thank you for giving me a case of this caliber, and promise to not disappoint you."

"Oh, Ms. Beaufont, I have every hope that everything will work out perfectly," Adler said, a giddy purr in his voice.

The white tiger turned to gaze at Liv directly, a warning of sorts in his eyes. Suddenly, she couldn't shake the feeling that she'd just signed her own death warrant.

CHAPTER FIVE

"You can't do it!" Spittle flew from Clark's mouth as they walked to the library, his hair a mess from running his hands through it. "It's a trap. I'm sure of it."

"I've already consented to do the case," Liv argued. "And how is it a trap?"

"You're just going to have to tell them that you aren't going to do it."

Liv halted, slapping his arm. "No. That's just giving the Council more reasons to dislike me."

"I thought you didn't care about being liked," Clark challenged.

"I don't care if they like my attitude or the way I dress, but I don't want anyone thinking I'm a coward."

"Liv, you don't understand. The House of Seven hasn't negotiated with the fae in over a century. The first and only agreement took a long time, and in the process, Queen Visa murdered two Warriors. She's not a stable person."

"What?" Liv asked, continuing toward the library. "How did she get away with that?"

Clark shrugged. "She's powerful. The Council forgave her when she finally committed to the agreement."

"Well, then it sounds like the path has been set for me."

Clark shook his head. "No, you're not getting it. The first Warrior we sent? She killed him on the spot for even suggesting an agreement. The second one didn't get much farther."

"But the third did?"

"Well, he offered her something right off the bat."

"Like what?"

"His first unborn child," Clark answered. Reading the expression on her face, his forehead wrinkled. "No. Just no. There's no way I'm going to allow you to do that."

"Why? I wasn't really planning on breeding anyway so the joke will be on her."

Clark paused outside the library, his face completely serious. "You can't. And it only worked for this particular Warrior because his first child was stillborn. Queen Visa was livid, but the agreement had been signed by then, and you know how the fae stick to those."

Liv nodded, thinking about how she had entered into an agreement with the fae Rudolf without even realizing it, nearly committing herself to ten years of servitude.

"So she's not going to go for your first child, and she's going to be pissed that we're trying to put controls on the fae. It's a trap. She's going to murder you before you get out a full sentence. Then Emilio will swoop in and take over. I'm sure that's what the Council is thinking."

"But why?" Liv asked. "I mean, I get that Adler hates me

and Bianca is a stuck-up jerk, but Haro and Lorenzo want me dead? Do you think they suspect something?"

Clark opened the library door and held it for her. "I don't think so. Warriors are expendable." His face softened. "I'm sorry. You should never have to hear that, but it's a common thing the councilors say among themselves. Well, not me, but you have a difficult job, and we realize you're not always going to return from missions."

"So I'm being used to prime the negotiations?"

"Yes, it seems like it," Clark said in a whisper as they strode through the massive library. "But your attitude definitely hasn't helped, I'm thinking. They did the same thing to Stefan originally; assigned him demon cases. I think Adler was hoping he'd get himself killed since he didn't like his cocky attitude. However, Stefan proved to be particularly effective at fighting demons, surprising everyone."

Liv searched the library, looking carefully in the least expected place for Sophia. "Well, then that's what I've got to do. I'll step up my game and rise to the challenge, surprising them all."

A loud, frustrated sigh emerged from Clark's mouth. "As talented as you are, I don't think there's a way for you to be successful here. Queen Visa will flip out when you propose that the fae cut back on seducing the mortals. The only thing that will soften her up is your death, which will prime the negotiations for when Emilio takes over."

"Can we stop talking about my death, please?" Liv asked with a morbid laugh. "So, it sounds like this is a real case, then? Not just something they are throwing out there to get rid of me."

Clark nodded. "Yes. It's a growing issue. Every few

decades the fae get out of control. The last time was when they started the Make Love, Not War campaign, causing tons of hippies to fall in love with them. Then when they got bored with them, the result was hazardous for the mortals, resulting in brain damage and mental disorders that we blamed on drugs in the seventies. Currently, there's a rise in suicide rates, and we believe the fae are behind it. They get into mortals' heads, making them lust for them, and just dispose of them when they move on to something new."

"Then this is a worthy case," Liv stated matter-of-factly.

"Yes, but that doesn't mean I want my sister's blood spilled for it."

"Speaking of blood," Liv said, pausing in an aisle. "Have you heard of the Ancient Chamber?"

Clark thought for a moment and shook his head. "What's that?"

"I think it's where we'll find answers, and I think it's over here." She tugged him around the corner and pointed to the wall covered in the founders' language. Her hand dropped when she noticed someone sitting nearby, reading a book in a chair.

Akio looked up, studying them.

"We can talk about this later," Liv whispered to Clark. "Will you take over finding Sophia? I know she's close."

"You two are still playing that game?" Clark questioned, disapproval on his face. "I don't think it's a good idea. What if someone figures out that...you know."

It was *a risk,* Liv realized. If anyone knew that the eight-year-old had her magic already, she'd be registered immediately and go straight into rigorous training. Liv wanted to delay that for as long as possible. Sophia deserved to be a kid. Furthermore, if anyone knew how powerful the little magician was, the Council might lock her magic. It was unprecedented in such a young child.

"Will you please just find her for me and tell her I'll catch up with her later?" Liv asked, ushering Clark away.

He consented with a nod, his expression still serious. "Okay, but don't go to the fae kingdom before you talk to me again. We aren't done discussing this."

"Don't worry, I won't run off and get myself murdered without letting you know first."

"Ha-ha," he said with no humor, striding off in the other direction.

Akio was still studying Liv as she approached him. "Are you playing that same game as before?"

"Yes. It's sort of our thing." She took a seat in the chair across from him. "You weren't in the chamber earlier."

"No, I'm doing research for a case." Akio indicated the book in his lap. It was written in Japanese, a language she couldn't read.

"Well, then you don't know that the Council has assigned me to go into the fae kingdom to renegotiate the agreement we have with Queen Visa."

"I heard," Akio said, his face neutral.

"Your brother Haro voted for me to go. Do you know why he would do that? Does he have it in for me?" Liv asked, boldly. There was no point beating around the bush, and Akio, it seemed to her, was a very direct person.

"I don't always know why Haro makes the decisions he does."

"Clark seems to think that it's a death mission," Liv imparted.

Akio nodded. "I wouldn't want to take on this case. However, have you considered that Haro voted for you to take the case because he thinks you can be successful at it?"

Liv shrugged. "Or I'm just setting the stage for another Warrior to take over."

"Being a Warrior is a dangerous business. You already know that. But it's important to remember that it's also a very political job. From what I've observed, you have a fresh perspective. Much like Haro and me, you having not been raised and trained at the House of Seven has offered you advantages. It could be possible that a new face who doesn't act like other magicians is the right person to negotiate with Queen Visa."

Liv hadn't thought of it that way, and it opened up her chest slightly, taking away some of the mounting burden. "Thanks. I think that Adler still wants me out of the way. I'm sort of a pain in his ass."

Akio chuckled slightly. "Stefan was the same way. You two will find a way to work together."

"Speaking of training," Liv began, "if I do return alive from the fae kingdom, I wanted to take you up on your offer of combat training."

Liv had been sparring with Clark in her free time, but that wasn't enough. She needed an expert. Someone who could train her, turning her into a deadly force.

For a moment, Akio didn't say anything, only studied Liv. "I would be honored," he finally said.

Liv didn't know if she could trust Akio, but she needed to be trained in combat, and Rory refused to help with it.

The Takahashis were legendary for their combat skills, so it only made sense to take him up on his offer, especially now that she had Bellator.

As if he'd read her thoughts, Akio asked, "First you'll need a weapon. I can help you pick out the right one."

Liv shook her head. "Thank you, but I already have one."

"Very good, then," Akio consented. "When you return, your training will start."

If I return, Liv thought morbidly.

CHAPTER SIX

Just before Junebug leapt off the crumbling porch into a patch of thorns, Liv caught him. Rory's front yard was drastically different than the back, which was overflowing with lush flowers and vegetable beds and fruit trees. It was sort of ironic to her that the front yard looked so dilapidated in contrast to the back.

She held the chubby kitten above her head, allowing him to paw her nose. "You are just a troublemaker, aren't you?"

He kicked at her hand, trying to free himself. If he had been Plato, he would have answered her, but this wasn't that kind of feline.

She set Junebug down at the threshold of the house. He darted across the living room, tearing up the corner of the rug and sliding around the corner, his feet almost coming out from under him.

"Ummm, what are you doing?" Liv asked, taking in the scene before her. Rory was sitting in his chair, a basket of yarn beside him. He was knitting a blanket.

"I'm contemplating a new security system," he answered, his eyes on the knitting needles in his hands. "Now that I have Turbinger, I think I need better security measures."

"No, I meant, why are you knitting? Are you making blankets for the homeless?"

"It's armor," Rory lied.

Liv plopped down on the couch, lying back and watching as Buxter and Polly played with a ball of yarn in front of Rory's feet.

"You've fattened the kittens up nicely. When do you plan to eat them?"

"In the spring when the zucchini squash is ripe," Rory answered, not missing a beat.

Samson launched himself off the side of the couch, attacking Liv's hair. She sat up, trying to wrestle the cat away from her. "Make sure I get an invite to this dinner party."

"Speaking of food, when was the last time you ate?" Rory asked, gazing at her over his knitting. "You look a bit peckish."

Liv threw herself back on the couch a bit dramatically. "Before I would have loved to have a four thousand calorie diet, but now it just feels like work. I can't keep up unless I'm eating all the time."

Rory whirled his finger in the air, and a huge slice of peanut butter pie covered in fluffy whipped cream appeared on the coffee table beside her. "It's more about what you eat than how much. Choose high-calorie foods. Sweets are especially good for fueling your magic."

Liv took a large bite of the pie, her eyes closing briefly in pure delight. "Wow, this is good. Did you make it?"

"Costco," Rory lied again.

"Yeah, right. I can totally see you shopping next to soccer moms at Costco, stocking up on a hundred rolls of toilet paper and fighting for samples. How long do the jumbo packets of soap last you? One day?"

"Two," he corrected.

Liv wagged a finger at him. "You're a very strange giant, but I'm totally onto you."

"There are better ways for you to spend your time."

"Right," Liv agreed, taking another bite. The whipped cream was definitely homemade and fresh. He'd probably made it that day. "That's why I'm going to the fae kingdom to tell Queen Visa to make her people behave."

Rory dropped his knitting in his lap, giving Liv a deathly serious look. "You're kidding."

"When have you ever known me to kid?" she joked. "And no, I'm not. The Council assigned me this case today. I know what you're going to say, but—"

"You have to do it," Rory interrupted.

"Okay, that was *not* what I thought you were going to say, actually." Liv finished the last of the pie and eyed the plate longingly.

"If you step down from the challenge, you'll lose the respect of the Council."

Liv nodded, picking up the plate and licking it.

"Since they already think you have zero manners," Rory stated, watching her with disgust.

She lowered the now-clean plate, wiping whipped cream from her nose. "Maybe I can get accepted into your

Cotillion school for girls. You run that on the side, right? When you're not feeding the homeless or helping the elderly with rent money?"

"I don't know what you're talking about," Rory stated, sniffing the air. "Do you smell that?"

Liv sniffed. "Yeah, it's fire. Are you barbequing a pig in the back?"

Rory bolted out of his seat, his knitting falling on top of Buxter and Polly, who were still playing. He thundered across the living room, sticking his head out the door.

Liv followed him, identifying the source of the smell immediately. The front yard was on fire.

CHAPTER SEVEN

Rory darted out the front door, moving faster than Liv had ever seen him. He grabbed the hose from the side of the house, directing it at the fire, which strangely was circling the perimeter of the house, quickly spreading toward the center of the yard.

Liv blocked the kittens from following Rory, slamming the door and locking them in. Junebug was on the edge of the property, climbing a stick-like tree that was about to get torched. Pointing her finger at the cat, she muttered an incantation and he flew across the yard, landing safely in her hand.

As fast as she could manage, she opened the front door and gently tossed Junebug into the house, shutting the door before his brothers and sisters could escape. She was about to pitch in and help Rory put out the fire when he whipped around. "No magic! That will only make it worse. We have to put out the fire naturally."

Liv didn't question this, running over to the edge of the yard where the fire was lowest and daring to stomp on the flames. This worked until they were too high and she noticed rogue flames about to lick at the side of the house.

She ran over to a large empty basin beside the house. Using an elemental spell, she filled it with water that was in the ground of the yard. Then she directed it toward the fire by the house, drenching it at once. When she tried the spell again, it produced no water. That was all there had been.

Rory was mostly successful spraying down his side of the yard, but the flames by the sidewalk at the front were growing higher, fueled by the dry grass. Liv looked around, trying to figure out another option. Then she hurled herself back up on the porch, opened the door, and grabbed the large blanket off the couch. She leapt over the kittens, blocked them from getting out, and slammed the door shut again. The smoke from the fire made her cough as she ran over to the flames, whipping the blanket at them, blotting them out. It wasn't easy work, and she was sweating profusely by the time she put the fire entirely out.

She dropped the scorched blanket in the middle of the yard and watched Rory put out the last of the fires on the side of the house. He turned around, surveying the yard, his eyes finding the blanket immediately.

"Sorry about that," Liv said at once. "I'll buy you a new one."

He mopped his forehead with a rag he'd pulled from his pocket. "You can't. My grandmother knitted that from unicorn hair, which is why it was so effective at putting out the fire. Thanks for your help."

Liv swallowed the guilt in her throat, looking around at the smoldering yard. "Who did this to your house?"

Rory gathered his brown curls, piling them on top of his head and wrapped a rubber band he'd pulled from his wrist around his hair, making a tiny ponytail. "It was me."

"What?" Liv asked, sure she'd misheard him. "You set your own yard on fire?"

He shook his head, peering around protectively. "It's part of the security system I just installed. The perimeter catches on fire if an unauthorized person steps onto the property."

"I'm not sure I understand the reasoning here."

"Well, I *did* say I needed a better system. I just threw this one up recently, thinking that I needed extra protection. The reasoning is that it's supposed to scare away thieves. Who is going to walk through fire to trespass on a property?

"So you have a security system that uses fire, but you can't teach me how to throw fireballs?" Liv dared to ask.

Rory let out an impatient sigh. "I already told you: that is gnome magic. This one works differently. The fire would worsen if someone tried to use magic to extinguish it, which I suspect they did."

"It does appear to have worked," Liv stated, looking around and not seeing a single person on the mostly deserted street.

"Yes, and that means my suspicions are correct. Someone is after the sword."

"How do they even know you have it here?" Liv asked.

"There are ways to track down Turbinger," Rory stated. "It's a very magical weapon, and carries with it a strong aura."

Liv remembered feeling it for the brief time she had

held the sword. "Have you had a chance to figure out what memories it holds?"

Rory shook his head, his small ponytail bobbing around. "Not yet. First I have to work on better security measures. Then I will."

"Okay, well, let me know if I can help."

"You've got your own problems," Rory said. "I can't believe I'm suggesting this, but I think you've got to rely on your allies for this new case."

Liv couldn't believe what he was implying either. "You don't mean…"

He nodded. "Yes. You should enlist Rudolf's help."

"But you said I shouldn't trust the fae."

"Yes, but if you *have* to work with them, he's in a good position to give you insights." He drew a deep breath, his eyes suddenly serious. "You need an advantage, or I fear you won't survive the meeting.

CHAPTER EIGHT

Roya Lane was as crowded with magical creatures of various races as the first two times Liv had visited it. She didn't really know how to find Rudolf, the fae, but she'd met him here a couple of times, so it was her best option.

As she slid through the crowd, many looked up at her from their stalls or conversations, shifty expressions on their faces. A gnome who had been showing what looked like a pocket watch to an elf slid it into his jacket and hurried off. Liv remembered that she was like a police officer here. Warriors enforced the law and generally stuck their noses into everyone's business at the Council's direction. Liv was starting to see that some of that was necessary, like with the fae, who were taking advantage of innocent mortals. However, there should be a line. And why was it the House of Seven's responsibility to uphold justice? Why weren't there other organizations that sought to protect?

"Liv Beaufont, Warrior for the House of Seven," a squeaky voice at her back said.

Liv spun to find the brownie who'd helped her at the National History Museum. "Freddy," she called a bit too loud, grateful to find a kind face in the mix of shifty characters who were all regarding her with paranoia.

"What brings you here? Are you visiting Mortimer?" the brownie asked, bowing low to her.

"No, I'm actually looking for someone," Liv said, waving the brownie over to the brick wall and out of the trafficked area.

"I'm great at finding. Who are you looking for?"

"Thank you," Liv said with relief. "I'm looking for a fae named Rudolf."

The happy expression on the brownie's face fell away. "Why would you want to find him? Or any fae? They are very sloppy individuals, never picking up after themselves. They leave mortals' houses filthy, expecting others to clean up."

"Believe me, I know. I'm well aware of their faults. The list of things wrong with the Fae is growing in my mind. However, I need to find Rudolf. Can you help me?"

The tiny elf was nodding before she even got her question out all the way. "Of course. And my apologies. I don't mean to question your business. I only meant to warn you that dealing with a fae usually doesn't turn out favorably for the other party."

Liv sighed dramatically, blowing a strand of hair out of her face. "I really hope you're wrong about that, but I know you speak from a place of wisdom."

"Let's go into this café, and I'll work on some finding spells to track him down," Freddy suggested.

"Finding spells?" Liv questioned. "I hadn't thought of that. Maybe I could try one of those. I don't want to inconvenience you. I know how busy you brownies are."

He shook his oversized head. "It won't work. Fae can't be tracked by magicians, but brownies can find most since we aren't seen as a threat."

Wasn't that just the way? Underestimate the little guy, giving him all the advantages when the time came.

Freddy led her into a quaint shop that looked like it was made for toddlers. All the tables were tiny, the seats like those found in a kindergarten classroom. The shop was decorated with pages from books. They were everywhere, making up the drapes that hung in the front window as well as the tablecloths, and covering every square inch of the walls.

"What is this place?" Liv asked, looking around and realizing she was the tallest person there.

Gnomes and fairies looked up from their tea and pastries curiously.

"It's the Grimoire. They have the best…what are those things called? They have jam in the middle and a fried outside."

"Jelly donuts?" Liv asked.

"Yes, that's it!"

Freddy took a seat at a table by the window, sliding into the chair easily.

Liv stared around uncertainly, pretty sure that she couldn't fit at the table.

"Do take a seat, and I'll fetch you two some waters," a small voice said.

Liv stared around, trying to figure out where it was coming from. Spying her confusion, Freddy said, "It's a pixie. They've already come and gone."

"Say what?" Liv asked, and to her astonishment, two glasses of water with ice appeared on the table.

"They are incredibly fast. Much too quick for your eyes to follow," Freddy explained. "They make wonderful waiters, as well as other things." He indicated the seat across from his. "Now, go ahead and sit, and we can get started."

"But…" Liv didn't know how to tell him that the chair might break under her weight or that the table was too low, so instead, she attempted to wedge her butt into the small chair, keeping most of her weight on her legs as her knees knocked into the table.

A fairy about the size of Freddy appeared beside the table, her pink wings matching her hair. She sized Liv up, giving her a smug expression. "Now, what can I get for you, Freddy, and your date?"

The brownie covered his face with his hands, peeking through his fingers at Liv. "This isn't a date, Zoyla. She's a friend."

The pixie sighed in relief. "Oh, good. For a moment, we feared you'd gone to the dark side."

Liv looked around at the shop and realized that all the patrons were staring at her. Great! She was the cop everyone wanted to avoid.

She laughed, trying to force a smile onto her face. "Don't worry. I'm not as uptight as the others from the House of Seven."

Zoyla harrumphed. "We'll see about that, Warrior."

"It's true," Freddy confided, his face resuming its normal shade of brown.

"What will you have?" Zoyla asked.

"Honeysuckle tea for me, and a jelly donut," Freddy ordered when Liv gave him an uncertain expression, not sure what to order.

"I'll have the same," she said when the pixie looked at her. Zoyla disappeared, and two seconds later two cups of tea appeared on the table with sugar and cream, followed by two donuts.

"Wow, you weren't kidding. She's fast," Liv said, her mouth watering at the sight of the glazed donut, which was steaming like it had just come out of the fryer. The smell of raspberry jam wafted up from the donut, greeting Liv's nose.

"Now to find this fae. Do you have one of his personal effects?" Freddy asked, blowing on his tea before taking a sip.

Liv shook her head. "No. I hardly know him. We've only met a couple of times."

"Hmmm," Freddy said, tapping the side of his teacup with his bony finger. "Has he ever touched you somewhere, like shaken your hand or something?"

Liv picked up her donut, trying to decide where to take the first bite. "No. Otherwise, we'd be looking for a corpse."

Freddy agreed with a nod, nibbling on his donut like a beaver. "Well, then we're going to have to resort to less dependable methods, but they should work." He set down his donut and held out his knobby hands. "I'll need you to hold my hands and think of the person you need to find."

Liv wiped her hands on a napkin covered in words and reached across the table, leaning at a weird angle as she perched on her unstable chair.

"Not your date, huh?" Zoyla asked, materializing suddenly.

Freddy rolled his large and bulbous eyes. "No, but I'm not sure why it's any concern of yours."

"I just find it interesting that you dumped my sister for a rule follower."

Liv gawked at the pixie, who was hovering just above the ground. "I don't follow rules. I'm the worst Warrior the House of Seven has ever seen. Just ask anyone."

Freddy squeezed her hands, which were still in his. "You're the best. And you don't have to respond to Zoyla. She can take her rumors and shove them up her—"

"Will there be anything else?" the pixie asked, her face matching the pink color of her hair.

"Just the check," Freddy said.

When Zoyla disappeared, he directed his attention back to Liv. "Now, it's important that you focus. Think of the fae you're trying to locate. Really dwell on his features. The color of his hair and eyes. The sound of his voice. Anything and everything about it."

"I'm afraid I'll throw up my donut," Liv stated.

"This is important, is it not?" Freddy asked.

Liv thought of her impossible mission: negotiating with the fae queen. "Yes. I'll do it." She closed her eyes and pulled up an image of Rudolf, honing in on his specific features:

the curve of his jaw, the angles of his eyes, the blond of his hair, and his giant wings. He was an attractive man; that was undeniable. Probably the most attractive man she'd ever seen. However, when he opened his mouth, all that changed. As was typical of men, she thought with a laugh.

"I've got something," Freddy told her.

Relieved, Liv's eyes popped open.

"He's close," Freddy continued.

"Oh, like he's here on Roya Lane? That's convenient."

The brownie shook his head and pointed over her shoulder. "No, he's standing right there."

Liv turned to find the fae standing just inside the doorway, his arms crossed over his chest and a dashing smile on his face.

"Well, well, well. Look who can't stop thinking about me?" Rudolf said, sauntering over. He grabbed a chair from a neighboring table and swung it around, gracefully sitting backward on the seat, not looking anything like as awkward as she felt on the tiny chair.

"I wasn't thinking about you," Liv argued.

Rudolf tapped the side of his head. "Oh, we fae always know when we consume another's thoughts. That's part of our gift. I felt your intense obsession with me as I strode by."

"We were trying to find you," Liv explained, motioning to the brownie.

"So you could confess your undying love for me," Rudolf supplied, picking up the donut from her plate and taking a bite. He dropped it again, wiping the corners of his mouth with his pinky.

Liv slid the plate away, a grimace on her face. "No. And seriously? I was looking forward to eating that."

"It tastes better now," he said with a wink.

"I'm certain it doesn't," Liv said, giving Freddy a grateful glance. "Thank you for helping me. It appears you were immediately successful."

"Not a problem, Liv Beaufont, Warrior for the House of Seven," Freddy said humbly.

"Why don't we go somewhere more private to discuss whatever reason you've made up to stalk me?" Rudolf suggested, rising and extending a hand to Liv.

Liv shot the brownie an uncertain look.

"The fae is probably right," Freddy said in reply. "There are many blabbermouths in here, so if you want whatever you discuss to remain private, I'd go someplace else."

"Like the hotel down the lane," Rudolf suggested.

"Eww," Liv replied.

"Don't worry about the check, though. This was my treat," Freddy stated, sipping his tea.

"Thank you," Liv told him, nearly falling over as she stood from the chair and making it topple over backward. That earned her curious expressions from many in the café. "I'll see you soon, Freddy."

He waved as she followed Rudolf to the door. When they were almost through, she heard Zoyla say, "Oh, so she dumped you for a fae. That's karma for you."

CHAPTER NINE

"Stop laughing," Liv scolded Rudolf, who had his head down on the table and was banging his fist on it as he laughed uncontrollably.

They'd found a dark booth at a bistro down the lane called Salem Style. The food didn't look all that appetizing, and in contrast to the Grimoire, the service was slow. But since the place was mostly empty, there was less chance of someone eavesdropping on them, even with Rudolf howling with laughter.

He lifted his head, taking shallow breaths. "I'm sorry," he said between giggles. "Tell me again. You're going to waltz into the fae kingdom and demand *what*?"

"I'm supposed to ask Queen Visa to alter our agreement so that fae don't seduce mortals."

Again Rudolf erupted with laughter, banging on the table and nearly spilling their drinks. "You have a Last Will and Testament, I hope."

"I don't," Liv replied dryly.

Rudolf lifted his head, trying and failing to make his

face serious. "It's really too bad, because I was starting to get used to your face, even with its many flaws."

"Thanks. I think I'd need more to drink to get used to you and your repugnance."

"Ouch," Rudolf said, his laughter falling away completely. "I thought you wanted my help."

"I do. *Can* you help me?"

"Well, not if you treat me like that. I like back rubs and poetry, though."

"No, and hell no. Why don't you do it as a favor, since we're friends?"

"Fae never do favors. You should know that. But agreements? That's another story."

"I'm already in an agreement with you. By the way, have you recalled any memories related to my ring?"

He shook his head. "In most of my healthiest relationships, we have anywhere from six to eight hundred agreements going at one time. I think that means we're on the path to something wonderful."

"I think we're minutes away from needing counseling."

"Fine. I'll help you, but it will cost you. That's how it goes with the fae."

"Well, what do you want?"

Rudolf swirled his red wine, watching as the legs climbed the glass, showing its age. "It's really nothing."

Liv lowered her chin and regarded him with hooded eyes. "I doubt that."

"I'd just request that you accompany me to a shop down the lane," he said, his eyes still on the wine, watching it with amusement.

"What's the catch?" Liv asked.

"There is no catch. You simply go into this store with me, and that's it."

Liv pushed her own drink away, not having touched it. "That's it? Why does this sound too simple?"

Rudolf pursed his lips. "It sort of hurts my feelings that you think there is something deceptive to my request. Why can't it be simple?"

"You don't *have* feelings," Liv fired back.

With a mock look of scorn, Rudolf clutched his chest. "That's not true. I'm very sensitive."

"Fine; you have feelings somewhere under all that ego. But this shop…what's it about?"

"It's just a regular old shop. Nothing fancy."

Liv wasn't buying any of this for a second, but she needed Rudolf's help. That much she knew. "There are no regular shops on Roya Lane. Everything is strange and laced with magic and run by centaurs or elves or whatever."

"You know, Queen Visa and I were once a thing," Rudolf admitted casually.

"Your point?"

Rudolf took a drink, taking his time as he swished the wine around, really tasting it. "My point is that I know her fairly well, and can tell you exactly how to avoid death for the longest amount of time. I can't make any guarantees, but I think I know how you should present yourself for the best results."

"And all I have to do is walk into a shop with you? That's it?" Liv asked.

"Yes. You'll be like my date."

"No," Liv said clearly and loudly on the heels of his statement.

"Fine, you'll be my friend, then."

Liv tilted her head back and forth, her face scrunched. "Let's go with 'acquaintance.'"

"I don't know what makes you so opposed to my affections. Many pine for me and would be grateful for the attention I lavish on you."

Liv shrugged. "I'm just unlovable."

Rudolf regarded her with curiosity for a moment. "No, that's not it at all. You're something, but I've yet to figure it out."

Sighing, Liv shook her head. "I can't believe I've now entered into two agreements with you. I've obviously lost my mind."

"Actually, I think the opposite. You are learning that relying on the fae is the smart approach," Rudolf imparted. "And speaking of the first agreement, I'm going to need something from you in order to have any chance of recovering the lost memory."

Liv raised an eyebrow at him. "What?"

"The ring," he answered.

"Okay, you are insane. Certifiably. Delusional. What's in that wine you're drinking?"

Rudolf laughed good-naturedly. "I don't mean forever. Just for a little while. I need to borrow the ring to find the memory. I've thought about it, and it's the only way."

"How do I know you're not going to do something to the ring or not give it back?"

"Dear, Liv, you have my word, which is the best thing I

could give you." Rudolf winked. "Well, besides a night of ecs—"

"Finish that sentence and I'll puke on you." Liv reached into her jacket and retrieved the ring, holding it in her fingers tightly. "Are you sure you need this?"

Rudolf nodded. "Yes, I believe so. The ring is part of what's blocking the memory. I'll need to do research first, though, to figure it all out. It shouldn't take more than six or seven years."

Liv hugged the ring to her chest. "Six or seven years? I can't wait that long, and you can't have the ring for that long. I need it." She thought of the wall in the library. If she loaned the ring to Rudolf, unlocking the Ancient Chamber, or whatever was there, was going to have to wait.

"Oh, fine. I forget that you magicians don't have that kind of time to spare," Rudolf said with a sigh. "I guess I could push it up on my list."

"To when?" Liv asked skeptically.

"How about in like two or three—"

"Say years, and it will be the last words you speak, fae," Liv threatened, cutting him off.

A seductive smile formed on Rudolf's mouth. "So feisty. I like that."

"Don't care what you like."

"Oh, fine. It's all business with you, all the time. How about I make it my priority after helping you with Queen Visa? I'm not sure how long it will take to recover the memory, but I give you my word that I'll work on it. Hopefully, it will only take a week or so."

Liv regarded him for a long time, uncertainty brimming in her thoughts. "And the ring will be safe in your hands?"

"As safe as your heart would be," Rudolf said, batting his long eyelashes at her.

"If you're trying to convince me, you're doing a poor job."

"Don't worry, Liv. I'll hold it dear, and protect it with my life."

Liv extended her hand, holding the ring. "No one can know that you have it or that it belongs to me, okay?"

Rudolf nodded, holding out his hand. "I promise not to tell another living soul."

Liv hesitated. "Wait, does that mean you'll tell the undead?"

"Oh, she's a clever one," Rudolf said with a chuckle. "I promise to not tell anyone, living or not. With or without a soul. You have my word. No tricks."

"Fine," Liv said with a sigh, dropping her mother's ring into the fae's hand.

CHAPTER TEN

"You know what I don't understand?" Rudolf asked as they strode down the cobbled lane, most groups giving them curious glances as they passed.

"How manners work? How to dress like an adult? How to stop making me throw up in my mouth?" Liv said, a mock look of seriousness on her face.

Rudolf glanced down at the lavender tunic he was wearing and grimaced. "I had this shirt custom-made. The tailor said it really brought out my other features."

"Fire that person. They should have told you that men don't look right in purple tones, even if they have giant maroon wings."

Rudolf smiled fondly over his shoulder at the ornate wings on his back. "You know that fae men tend to be very confident in their masculinity. I realize that's something you're not used to since you surround yourself with magicians who need to overcompensate because they have such little wands, if you know what I mean."

Liv rolled her eyes, moving behind Rudolf when the

alley narrowed. She hadn't been down this part of Roya Lane, which was more crowded and darker, the shops huddled close to one another. "Magicians don't use wands."

Rudolf cast her a disappointed look over his shoulder. "I wasn't referring to wands, hence the 'you know what I mean' part. I was talking about a magician's—"

"I got the point," Liv interrupted.

"Anyhoo, I was going to say that I don't understand why you don't just tell the Council that you were successful at getting Queen Visa to do what they want. You lied to them about the brownie case, didn't you?" Rudolf asked.

"I've lied about the last few cases I've worked on because they were total shit and there was little chance the Council would figure it out. However, this is the first major one they've assigned me. I think they believe I'm going to fail, so it's my chance to shove it in their faces and prove them wrong."

Rudolf gave her a doubtful look. "You might. And you might also get yourself killed. Either way, I'm going to be front and center to witness it." He rubbed his hands together eagerly. "I haven't seen a good show with Queen Visa in a long time. Not since she maimed her younger brother for yawning during one of her speeches."

"Maimed? For yawning? Damn, what a crazy witch! Why has she not been overthrown?" Liv asked.

"Oh, she's loads better than her predecessor. Queen Joy imprisoned all her people for half a century simply because she said she wanted some alone time," Rudolf related, shaking his head. A dark look fell over his face.

"Wow, 'Queen Joy.' How inappropriately named," Liv said dryly.

"I still haven't talked to Arni, the fae I shared the cell with. While Queen Joy was soaking up her alone time, we all were having way too much time with each other."

"The fae are strange creatures," Liv stated. "And I'm going to do whatever it takes to win this case. Everything is riding on it."

"Like your life," Rudolf said with a rude laugh.

Liv shook her head. "No, there are actually some things more important than living."

Rudolf gawked at her, his wings going still. "Like what?"

"Like family," Liv answered as they halted in front of a shop.

"Oh, and if you die, then…"

"Then my family loses their place in the House of Seven. I'm not allowing that to happen. Ever."

Rudolf leaned in close, his nose nearly brushing her ear. "Be careful. You almost looked like you actually cared about something just then." He peeled away, giving her a wink. "Don't worry, though. Your secret is safe with me."

Liv ignored him and glanced at the shop. It was a jewelry store that looked as though it could use a renovation, since the archway of the door was cracked and looked ready to fall in. The display case in the window was covered with cobwebs, obstructing most of the jewelry.

Rudolf placed his hand on the door handle. "Okay, are you ready to stand around and look pretty?"

"This is the shop you want me to accompany you into?" Liv asked, peering into the window. She was unable to see much.

"Oh, yes!" Rudolf said victoriously. "That's good. Pretend to look around out here first. I like that."

Liv straightened, narrowing her eyes at him. "What's going on? What deception are you playing at, Dolf?"

He frowned. "I don't like that nickname. Call me 'Hottie' or 'Abs' or 'Handsome.'"

"Do I have to keep a straight face when I do?" Liv asked.

"And yes, this is the shop. There's nothing for you to worry about. Just come in here and stand inside the entrance. I'll take care of the rest," Rudolf explained.

"Is it safe to go through that door?" Liv asked, eyeing the crumbling frame.

"Usually no, but we'll be okay together."

Before Liv could voice a complaint, Rudolf opened the door, waving her through. The smell of dust spilled out of the store as if trying to escape.

"I'm certain I'll regret this," Liv said, stepping over the threshold and searching the dark shop. Rows of cases lined the store, most of the contents obscured by the thick layers of dust covering the glass. The chandeliers overhead were shrouded in thick cobwebs, and eerie piano music crackled from a speaker at the back.

A gnome wearing a jeweler's magnifying glass strapped to his head looked up when Liv came through the door. "We're closed," he said, hardly noticing her.

Rudolf shut the door and came around Liv, holding his hand back to stop her from moving any farther into the store. "Stay here," he said in a hushed voice.

Liv was about to protest when the gnome yanked the headgear off and slammed it on the counter. "What are you doing in here, you scoundrel?" He shook his tiny fist in Rudolf's direction, a deep scowl on his face. "I told you what would happen if you stepped foot in my grandfather's shop."

Faster than Liv had ever seen Rudolf move, he sped across the dusty carpet, his hands in the air in surrender. "You're going to want to think twice about honoring that promise this time, Subner." He leaned down, speaking in low tones to the gnome.

Subner glanced around Rudolf, giving Liv a speculative glare. She waved from the front of the shop, not wanting to be rude.

"She does resemble her mother, but that doesn't prove anything," Subner said in a terse voice.

"I'm trying to help you out, old friend," Rudolf said loud enough for Liv to hear.

"Help me out? You brought a Warrior into my shop!" Subner yelled.

Liv backed up, glancing around to ensure there were no other gnomes hiding behind the counter or cases. She didn't spy anyone, but a spider the size of a purse dog scurried out from behind the counter and streaked across the floor. Liv threw herself against the door, making it creak painfully, the cracked frame sprinkling dust on her.

Rudolf and the gnome exchanged more terse words. Subner hopped up, looking over the fae's shoulder. "Hey, Warrior, I don't want any trouble."

"Yeah, me either," Liv responded, searching the floor for the spider, which had sharp pincers and more hair than Rory.

"Just get your grandfather," Rudolf encouraged, his voice jovial. "Then we will get out of your hair."

The gnome, who didn't have any hair, scowled at the

expression. "I'm not leaving you alone in the front of the shop."

Rudolf laughed. "I'm with a Warrior. I'm not going to try anything. You think I want her taking me in?" He angled his thumb over his shoulder. "No, thanks. She doesn't let a damn thing go." He leaned down, his words directed at Subner but his eyes staring at Liv. "A real stickler for justice, just like her mother."

"You want to see Papa Creola?" Subner asked Liv, his beady eyes looking her up and down.

"Umm, who?" Liv asked.

"Yes," Rudolf cut in abruptly. "And you know that old gnome can't hear you if you call to him, so go ahead and fetch him. The sooner you do and the more cooperative you are, the better."

Subner hesitated for a moment. "If you mess with anything while I'm gone, fae, I'll—"

Rudolf waved him off. "Hey, have I ever taken anything that didn't belong to me?"

"I'm certain that is a trick question," Subner answered, sliding off his stool and disappearing behind the counter. His footsteps receded as he disappeared through the door at the back.

Rudolf sprinted over to a case beside Liv, brushing off the dust so that he could see what was inside it better. Gems of various colors sparkled to life like they had simply been waiting for the dust to be cleared to shine brightly. "Where are you?" Rudolf muttered to himself.

"Ummm, what are you doing?"

"I'm looking for something," he answered.

"That gnome told you not to mess with anything," Liv warned, still wary of the spider hiding somewhere close by.

"I promised not to take anything that didn't belong to me," Rudolf said, continuing to search the cases.

"Dolf…" Liv cautioned, a warning in her voice.

"Eureka," Rudolf exclaimed in a loud whisper. "Here it is. Now I just need you to place your hand on this case, and we'll be done here."

"What? No!" Liv yelled.

Rudolf jerked around, his eyes frantic. "Shush. Not so loud. All you have to do it stick your hand on the case and we're out of here."

"No. You said all I had to do was accompany you to this shop, and I'm certain that more is going on here than you let on," Liv said, and then amended her statement. "Actually, I know it for a fact, but whatever."

Rudolf kept looking over his shoulder at the door in the back. "Look, do you want to know how to survive Queen Visa and get her to sign the new agreement? Because I know how, but I'm not telling you until you put your hand on this case."

Liv rolled her eyes. It was a small request, but something told her that it was filled with deception. Still, she had her own goals, and as far as she knew, Rudolf was in the best position to help her. And what was the big deal with sticking her hand on a dirty jewelry case, besides it probably being covered in centuries of bacteria and germs?

With an annoyed sigh, Liv trudged over to the case and slapped her hand on the grimy glass. To her surprise, the floor rumbled under her feet as sparks shot out of the cabinet beside her. Liv jerked her hand away and shielded her face, but the commotion quickly died away, and the shop went quiet.

Liv peered around her arm. Rudolf reached into the now-open case, removing a purple gem. He grabbed her by the wrist and tugged her toward the exit. "All done here. Let's be gone."

"What just happened?" Liv asked, looking at the cabinet that had opened like a box at her touch. She tugged away, wanting to study the scene further even as Rudolf encouraged her out the door.

Thundering footsteps resounded from the door at the back. The fae's eyes shot in that direction, panic on his face. "We've got to go."

"Why?" Liv asked.

Subner appeared in the doorway, murder written in his eyes. "You deceived me, fae, and you're going to pay!"

CHAPTER ELEVEN

Rudolf grabbed Liv by the arm, yanking her toward the exit with more strength than she'd known he had. Bolts that hadn't been there seconds prior materialized over the rickety door, locking them inside the shop. Subner disappeared back down the hallway behind him, which didn't make Liv feel any better. She didn't think for a second that he was going to go cool off and forget this whole mess.

"What the hell did you do?" Liv yelled at the fae.

"I took what rightfully belonged to me," Rudolf responded, swinging around, frantically searching for something. "Did you see where the spider went?"

"What? Are you serious? This isn't the time for pest control."

Roughly, Rudolf shook his head, dropping to his knees to look under the cabinets. "The spider has the key to the locks."

Liv rolled her eyes at this. "Of course, he does. Silly me for thinking this was a Brinks security system and we just needed the code. Of course, we need to hunt down a furry man-eating spider and steal the key from him."

Reaching blindly under the cabinet with his face pressed to the floor, Rudolf grunted. "The spider won't eat us, but it's a bitch to catch."

"Well, I realize all you have are your looks and lack of personality to rely on, but I have magic." Liv pointed her hand at the locks and was just about to mutter an incantation when Rudolf launched himself off the floor, diving into Liv.

"No!" he yelled, knocking her into a dusty case.

With his face too close to hers, she read the seriousness in his eyes. "Let me guess, magic only makes it worse?"

He nodded, gulping in a breath. "Yeah. Unless you want the spider to turn into a man-eating dragon, don't try to magic our way out of here. Believe me, I've done that, and it's not fun."

Liv pushed him off her, looking around the shop. It was strange that Subner had simply locked them in and disappeared. Strange in a foreboding way. She sort of wished he would have stayed and thrown fireballs at her. At least then she wouldn't be panicking, waiting for whatever was supposed to show up to make them pay, as he had promised.

Rudolf was back to searching the floor for the spider when Plato casually showed up and perched on a case. He looked like he'd just awoken from a long nap and was amused by the scene.

"Looking for a spider key, are you?" he asked Liv.

Letting out a heavy sigh, she nodded. "Yes. Any ideas about how to catch the sucker?"

"Do you have a bolt of silk fabric on you?" Plato asked, watching as Rudolf scurried behind the counter, grunting the entire time.

Liv patted her jacket. "Shucks, I left that at home in my sewing den."

"Oh, too bad. Hindsight would have told you to bring it," Plato said.

Loud noises echoed behind the closed door at the far side of the shop, orange light illuminating the cracks around it.

"Anything else we can try?" Liv asked, in a hurry.

"Do you have any small live rodents on you?"

Liv couldn't stop herself from rolling her eyes. "Do you count?"

"Come on, Liv, that thing can't eat me. I was thinking more about bait for the spider key."

"Well, since I don't have any rats on me, can you offer a more practical solution for how to catch this thing?" Liv asked in a rush, the thunder growing louder.

"For starters, your friend needs to stop making so much ruckus. It scares the thing," Plato offered.

"Right," Liv said, drawing out the word. "Hey, Jerkface, will you stop banging around over there? Apparently, you're making the spider nervous."

Rudolf's red face popped up on the other side of the cabinet. "I realize that, but I don't really have time to quietly draw the thing out. Papa Creola is going to be up here any second now."

Liv was guessing that was a bad thing. "Later I'm going to kill you, fae. For now, I've got to figure out how to get out of here, so stay quiet." She spun around to face Plato again. "Okay, I made the bane of my existence quiet down. Now what?"

"Well, it so happens that the best hunter of the spider key is the lynx," Plato said, not at all in a rush.

Liv's eyes widened, and she motioned toward the cabinet. "Then go! Seriously, what are you waiting for?"

"For you to ask," Plato stated. "I can't secure a key for someone unless they specifically request it. You would have known this if you had read that book the giant gave you."

Liv was seriously planning to kill both Rudolf and Plato when they got out of this store. She waved him away. "Yes, yes. Will you go and get the spider key for me?"

Unhurried Plato hopped down from the counter and disappeared around the cabinet where Rudolf stood. He shot her a frantic expression.

"You're relying on a lynx to get us out of this? They can't be trusted," he screeched.

Liv couldn't help but laugh. "Says the fae who is the master of deception."

"Seriously, if Papa Creola gets up here, we're screwed," Rudolf nearly yelled, whipping his head between the locked door and the one on the other side of the shop which was vibrating from the ever-growing thunder behind it.

"Is he your papa?" Liv asked, unable to keep her curiosity quiet even if they were minutes away from death.

Rudolf shook his head. "No. I mean, yes. He's sort of the father of us all."

Liv's face scrunched with confusion. "Say what?"

"He's the father of time," Rudolf explained, jumping up

on the sill of the window at the front and working on getting the curtain rod down.

"Then why doesn't he reside in a clock shop?" Liv asked, directing her finger at the rod and breaking it in two using magic. One of the pieces flew down to her open hand. The other landed with a thud on Rudolf's head, making him stumble off the ledge. He rubbed the top of his head where he'd been hit, picking up the rod off the ground.

"Ouch. We're supposed to be working together, not hurting each other," Rudolf informed her, still massaging his head. "And it would be sort of obvious if he ran a clock shop, don't you think? Especially because he's in hiding."

Liv swung the makeshift weapon, noticing how different and mediocre it felt in contrast to holding Bellator. She should have brought the sword with her, but she hadn't expected to be fighting the father of time, and she'd thought it best to leave it behind until she was formally trained.

"Why is the father of time in hiding?" Liv dared to ask as the thunder got even louder.

"Nobody knows," Rudolf stated, putting his back to Liv's and holding the rod like a baseball bat.

"And you stole his gem, is that right?"

"I took back my property," Rudolf countered.

The thunder ceased, making Liv feel like she'd suddenly gone deaf. She glanced over her shoulder. "Is there a possibility that Papa Creola forgot about us or decided to let us go?"

Rudolf backed up a step. "Not a chance. It's been nice

knowing you, Liv Beaufont, Warrior for the House of Seven."

Liv tensed. "I hope this was worth it, dipshit."

Rudolf coughed. "Another nickname I don't approve of."

The door at the back creaked. Liv squinted, trying to make out the dark figure in the distance. A scurrying noise behind the counter stole her attention.

When she looked up, she was not prepared for what appeared in the doorway.

The father of time was simply adorable.

CHAPTER TWELVE

Unlike Subner, who had a face full of wrinkles and a sour expression, Papa Creola had smooth skin and rosy cheeks. His long white beard hung in loose ringlets, and on his head was a cone-shaped hat, and to Liv's surprise, he started whistling as he strode forward.

"Is it possible this was all a misunderstanding, and he's come to talk it out?" Liv asked Rudolf from the corner of her mouth.

"No, it's worse that he's acting so nonchalant," Rudolf answered, pressing more firmly into Liv, nearly making her topple over.

With his hands behind his back, Papa Creola swayed, his eyes on the case from which Rudolf had removed the purple gem.

"I figured you'd be back, Rudolphus," the little man said, his voice as cheerful as if he'd just thought of a joke.

"It's mine," Rudolf argued, gripping the rod tighter.

Papa Creola halted, his sparkling blue eyes connecting with the pair. He chuckled and rocked forward on his toes and back on his heels. "Of course it is, Rudolphus, but you should know as well as anyone how a thief works. It was yours and then I stole it, which makes it mine now." He held out a stumpy little hand and wriggled his fingers. "Give it back, and I'll let you go."

"No!" Rudolf yelled. "And you'd never let us go from here unharmed. Not after what we did."

The gnome's eyes flickered to Liv, and she suddenly felt a chill. A thousand years had passed in a tomb. Her body lay cold in the ground. Winds swept across the desert, stirring up sand and creating a new landscape. Ages later, the planet was different, and yet time remained the same. A constant ticking.

She had the urge to clap her hand to her chest and ensure her heart was still beating. To look in a mirror to check that she hadn't rapidly aged. To lie down and rest in a bed where she might one day die.

Shaking off the strange thoughts that didn't seem like her own, she straightened, not breaking eye contact with the gnome.

"Olivia Beaufont. I should have known you'd be the one to rouse me from my slumber," Papa Creola said, sounding amused.

"Ummm, have we met? And by the way, my name is Liv."

He nodded. "Yes, my apologies. Only for the first seventeen years did you go by your given name. And this one you'll keep for...well, I mustn't offer spoilers. That's gotten me in trouble a time or two."

His eyes slid back to Rudolf. "Clever, bringing a

Warrior from the House of Seven in here. You aren't as stupid as you look, Rudolphus."

"Thank you," Rudolf said proudly, a half-smile forming on his face.

"It sounds like this has all been a misunderstanding," Liv said, trying to see where Plato was. "Would you mind opening the door, and then I'll be on my way? You can kill this fae if you'd like."

"Hey!" Rudolf protested.

Papa Creola laughed. "I do plan on getting rid of Rudolphus. He has really been on this planet for too long. But I can't permit you to go, Warrior Beaufont, for fear you'll tell others about me. It is *so* tiresome moving about." He looked around fondly at the shop covered in dust and cobwebs. "I was starting to take a liking to this place, and will miss it."

"Don't worry, I don't talk to anyone," Liv said at once. "I won't tell anyone I saw you or that you're here. You can go about your business or whatever you do."

The jovial expression fell away from his face. "I do nothing. That's the point."

"Right, sounds lovely," Liv said pleasantly. "Well, that secret is safe with me. Just open this door here, and I'll be on my way."

"Yes, I don't plan on killing you. I might steal and cheat and deceive, but I keep my word. No Warrior will die by my hand," Papa Creola stated. "I'll just wipe your memory clean of everything, and you can be on your way." He chuckled, scratching his belly. "Well, you won't know your way, because you'll be forever lost. But you'll be alive, as I promised."

"That doesn't sound like a good deal," Liv said in a muffled voice over her shoulder to Rudolf.

"No, I think death is probably better," he agreed.

"Give him back the gem you took," Liv encouraged.

He shook his head. "Not a chance. There are some things worth fighting for. Yours might be family, but this is mine."

"I took that stone from you for a reason," Papa Creola cut in. "It should belong to me." He swept his arms wide at the cases all around the room. "These objects are better kept away from greedy fae and disillusioned elves and whatnot. The House of Seven agreed with me, which was why they helped me to round them up."

"What?" Liv asked, not expecting this. "Warriors stole these for you?"

He pointed at Rudolf's pocket. "Your own mother took that gem from Rudolphus, which was why you could open the case."

"What?" Liv repeated, having a hard time keeping up with all this strange information.

"Oh, but my dear boy Rudolphus would have known that, wouldn't you?" Father of time asked the fae with a quizzical expression on his face.

"I-I-I never got a good look at the perpetrator," Rudolf stuttered.

"Yes, only the back of her head as she fled, her long blonde hair flying behind her." He hugged himself, smiling. "Oh, I do so love long-ago memories. Show me more of them, lad."

"Why would my mother steal this gem for you?" Liv asked Papa Creola.

"Because," he began, rocking forward and backward again, "these objects aren't safe out there. These things—they don't agree with the passage of time."

"What do you care about the passing of time?" Rudolf fired back, his face pinched with anger. All his normal lightness was gone, replaced by a bitter expression. "You abandoned us, hiding yourself away here."

Papa Creola shook his head and clicked his tongue. "You're selfish, fae. You don't get it, and I don't expect you to. Several millennia of watching over things have changed nothing. The winds fluctuate, sometimes blowing hard or diminishing to a tiny breeze. The oceans change with the tides. Even the seasons are varied. All the other fathers and mothers on this planet have jobs, but time?" He yawned loudly, drumming his hand over his mouth. "It is always the same. Each second is the same length. Each minute is equal to the next. What you young'uns fail to see is that there is nothing for me to manage." He laughed as if suddenly thinking of something. "Well, I had to keep you all out of trouble, putting away all the artifacts one could undo time with, creating problems for the continuum." Fondly he looked around. "Now that this has been done, I'm really not needed, which makes for a well-deserved retirement."

"But you're the father of time," Liv argued. "You can't simply retire and disappear."

He nodded. "Spoken like a true Warrior. Yes, that was what your mother told me. I regret not wiping her memory, because she stalked me for many years. I finally found this place, safely hidden from even the best detective, which she happened to be. I won't be making the same mistake with you, Warrior Beaufont, which is why I've taken it upon myself to tell this story, which few have heard." He smiled, rubbing his hands on his arms like he was suddenly cold. "It's been nice to recount the story to someone. Makes me remember why I did it in the first place. But the time is approaching for me to wipe your memory and banish Rudolphus to the underworld, where he shall burn for… Well, honestly, I've got no clue where you all go when you die. That one still eludes me."

Papa Creola raised his hand, pointing at Liv. "It sort of pains me to do this, although I know it is for the best."

"Rudolf," Liv said in a whisper. "Do something."

"I think I'm about to wet myself," he answered. "Will that work?"

Three things happened simultaneously. Liv's hand instinctively shot into the air. Plato's black and white head poked out from under the counter, a rusty key clenched in his teeth. A wisp of white smoke drifted from Papa Creola's fingertips.

A shield shot up between the pair and the father of time. His memory charm bounced off it, shattering like glass in the air. Rudolf sprinted forward, taking the key from Plato and going to work on the many locks on the door.

"Oh, just as clever as Guinevere Beaufont, and I dare say a smidge faster," Papa Creola said. "But we all know a Warrior's shield won't hold against a gnome's secret weapon."

Actually, some of us didn't know that, Liv thought. Her eyes cut to Rudolf, who only had one of the locks undone.

When she turned back around, Papa Creola was

winding up his arm as if he were about to pitch a ball at a batter. In his hand a spark materialized, building hotter and faster until it formed a fireball.

"Are you serious?" Liv mumbled. "F-ing fireballs. This isn't fair."

Like a major league pitcher, the father of time released the fireball, which headed straight for Rudolf. Liv couldn't believe herself when she darted in front of the fae, knocking the fireball toward the back wall with the wooden rod. It crashed, knocking over a set of jars.

The gnome relentlessly launched three more attacks at them one right after the other. The rod broke in half on the third hit, and Liv dropped the smoking stick and ran over to one of the nearby cases.

Reading what she was about to do, Papa Creola shook his head, his brow furrowing. "Don't you do it, Warrior Beaufont."

She placed her hand on the case, and as it had before, it opened like a box. Hardly taking a moment to look, she reached in and grabbed the first object she could find. It was a mirror. She held it up, giving the father of time a challenging look. "Let us go, or I'll break it."

He laughed, but there was no joy in the noise. "Like I care."

"You care, or you would have destroyed these objects already," Liv stated, hoping her observation was correct.

Apprehension crossed Papa Creola's face. She was right.

He released another fireball, throwing it at lightning speed. She had almost no time to react, swinging the hand mirror like a makeshift bat. The fire dissolved almost at once after making contact. Amazed by the reaction, Liv lifted the mirror up to stare at it in awe, but she saw an image that nearly caused her to drop it. The mirror hiccupped in her hands, but thankfully she kept hold of it.

Looking back at her from the mirror was her own face, but no longer smooth and young. An old woman stared back at her, her eyes dripping with wrinkles, ancient wisdom in her blue eyes.

"Damn it, Warrior Beaufont, now you've done it," Papa Creola growled. "I vowed that no one would see the future again or play with time. I should have known you'd be just as much trouble as your mother. No more Mr. Nice Father of Time."

Rudolf swung around, horror in his eyes. "Duck!" he yelled as a barrage of fireballs rained down from overhead.

Liv dove under the nearest counter as the fireballs crashed, singeing her cape as she yanked it to her. The scorching heat from the flames made her face feel as if it were on fire. It was too much. The fireballs were getting too close. She was about to admit defeat when a blast of icy wind rushed across her face.

A hand reached down from the other side of the counter, a brute force that she couldn't resist. Liv was yanked out and upright. She hardly had a chance to make out the scene around her before Rudolf pulled her out the unlocked door onto Roya Lane.

Over her shoulder she spied the father of time, frozen in a small patch of ice, his hand extended as a small fireball ignited.

CHAPTER THIRTEEN

Liv kept running once they were on the cobbled path but quickly realized that Rudolf wasn't beside her. She turned around to find him doubled over, his hands on his knees as he gasped for breath.

She went back, staring frantically at the open shop door they'd just exited. "Hey, let's get out of here. He'll thaw out any second now."

Rudolf shook his head as he lifted up. "No, he won't dare come out on the street. One sighting of him and his precious retirement will be over."

Liv shivered at the thought of nearly getting burned to death and tugged Rudolf forward. "Doesn't matter. I don't want to chance it."

He gave her a sideways smile as they ambled down the crowded path, their clothes still smoking in places.

"Why are you smiling at me, Liar Pants?" she asked, searching the upcoming area with new paranoia.

"You're not as mad at me as I thought you'd be. You are pulling me along with you," Rudolf gloated.

"I'm still livid, and I'm planning on taking you to an abandoned warehouse so I can kill you slowly. Someplace no one can hear you scream and the body won't be found for ages."

He laughed. "No, you're not."

Liv sighed. "No, I'm not. You saved my life back there. I don't have a lot of rules I operate on, but one of them is that you don't punish someone who is the reason you're still alive."

Rudolf gave her an affectionate smile. "Then I probably shouldn't tell you that Papa Creola wasn't going to kill you. He was trying to kill me, and simply disarm you long enough so he could wipe your memory."

"No, you definitely shouldn't have told me that. Now all the goodwill I felt toward you is gone."

He shrugged as they walked. "But I did save you, in a way."

"Yes, the ice magic was handy," Liv admitted. "Why didn't you just do that in the first place? Ice magic is a gift of the fae, correct?"

"Yes." Rudolf sighed, suddenly looking exhausted. "As you could have probably seen, it didn't last long enough. As soon as I froze him, he began to melt. Furthermore, that spell cost me a great deal of energy. If I'd done it before we had the locks off the door, I would have passed out before we could get out of the shop."

Liv nodded, understanding. Her own reserves were quite low. "Where can I get some frozen yogurt or candy that won't cause me to hallucinate?"

Rudolf gave her a repulsed expression. "Why would you waste your time on fake ice cream and cheap candy when you can have double-Dutch twelve-layer ganache cake topped with vanilla bean ice cream?"

"Excuse me for not having an answer to that," Liv stated, feeling her feet starting to drag more with each step they took. "Just take me to this place and ensure there isn't poison in it, or whatever strange stuff the magical creatures lace into their meals on Roya Lane."

Rudolf pointed at a restaurant up ahead. It had two pillars out front that looked like they were sculpted out of marshmallow. "This is my favorite place," the fae said, leading the way.

Liv read the sign above the door and instantly cringed: The Sugary Nipple.

"This place better be legit and not have pole dancers," she warned.

"Don't worry. It doesn't. Today is Wednesday," Rudolf stated, opening the large door for her.

Neither of them spoke until they'd finished half their dessert. The ice cream had partially melted, creating a moat of vanilla around the crumbling tower of cake. Liv licked chocolate syrup off her fingertips and regarded Rudolf with a disgusted stare. "You tricked me."

He gave her a rueful expression as he licked whipped cream off his spoon. "That is most regrettable, but it was unavoidable."

"I wonder if any fae anywhere has ever tried just telling the truth and being straightforward," Liv mused.

Rudolf blinked as if contemplating this question. "I

don't think so, but in my defense, you wouldn't have accompanied me if I had given you the full details."

"That you were going to get me locked in the father of time's shop, where he'd wipe my memory and make me watch your murder?"

"Well, I never saw my death as a part of the equation. Honestly, we could have gotten out of the shop if you would have moved a bit faster."

Liv gawked at him. "How dare you!"

"I dare." Rudolf stuck the spoon into his cake, leaving it sticking straight up. "And quick thinking on using the shield to protect us. I'd say everything worked out perfectly."

Liv tapped her fingers on the table, giving him an impatient stare.

"Okay, fine," he admitted. "So your cape got a bit charred. I think I did you a favor. That thing is atrocious. You should finish burning it and go buy something short and see-through." He whistled. "Yes, a Warrior dressed to impress would get the job done every time."

"Dumbface, when are you going to address the real issue here?"

He gave her a blank stare. "Your lack of fashion sense isn't the problem? I'm confused."

"What's the gem do?" Liv asked.

"Gem?" he asked, giving her his best confused look. "What gem?"

Liv sighed dramatically, forcing herself to take another bite although she wasn't sure she could handle much more. The cake had been easily the size of her head when she started. Now it was more like the size of Plato's head.

The lynx had disappeared after obtaining the key, as usual.

"The gem you risked my memory and your life for," Liv prompted.

"Oh, that." Rudolf waved his napkin at her before wiping the side of this mouth. "That's nothing. Just a little trinket I lost."

"That my mother stole," Liv corrected. "Have you simply been keeping me around for this mission?"

Rudolf lowered his chin and pursed his lips. "You'll remember that you're the one who asked for my help. Twice, I'll add. You asked me to bring up the memory associated with the ring."

"Which, by the way, I don't trust in your possession, since it appears you have things stolen from you," Liv said.

"By your mother," he countered. "She's the only one who has ever successfully stolen anything from me. A very clever magician, and so hot in—"

"Finish that sentence, and I will shove your face into your cake," Liv threatened, cutting him off.

Rudolf nodded, believing the threat at once.

"The ring," Liv began. "Could the memory be connected to when she stole the gem from you?"

He shook his head. "No. I remember that, and she wasn't wearing it. The memory predates your mother. It's...well, I can't remember, which was the reason we made a deal."

Liv remembered agreeing to get whatever it was that Rudolf wanted that was at the bottom of the fountain in the House of Seven. She didn't look forward to battling what lived in the fountain to fulfill her end of the bargain, but she knew that unlocking those hidden memories was the key to learning the truth. It had to be.

"Why did you make me go with you to Papa Creola's shop?"

Rudolf took a long sip of water. "Isn't it obvious? I couldn't have stepped foot in there, but you, as a Warrior for the House of Seven, can't be turned away by the father of time. The House of Seven apparently made an agreement with Papa Creola at some point. I knew that much, but not the extent, which he disclosed to us." As if a new thought had occurred to him, Rudolf's eyes flitted to the side, lost. "Are you going to tell the Council that you discovered his location?"

Liv considered this and shook her head. "Not right now. I don't see the point or the benefit, and then I have to explain a whole host of things, namely that I'm associating with a rude fae."

He scoffed. "I'm not rude. I hardly ever call you names."

"'Hardly ever?'" Liv questioned. "I didn't know you did it at all."

"Only behind your back," Rudolf admitted.

"Why did the cases open when I touched them?" Liv asked.

"Oh, that one is easy," Rudolf explained. "Again, that's part of the agreement the House set up with Papa Creola. I wasn't sure if I was right about it, but it was a chance I had to take."

"So you could get this gem that does what, exactly?"

Rudolf folded his hands in his lap, giving her a calm expression. "That information will cost you. Do you want to be indebted to me for something else?"

"No, but I do want you to pay up on your end of the bargain." Liv held out her hand as if expecting him to give her money. "Tell me how I get Queen Visa's cooperation?"

"Wear something slutty," Rudolf answered, not missing a beat.

Liv rolled her eyes. "No, this isn't about how to give you what *you* want. It's about Queen Visa."

He rolled out his neck, stretching. "Yes, I know. And as I said, wear something slutty."

"I don't think so," Liv replied.

"Well, if you want to make a good impression on the queen and her court, you better dress slutty. Actually, the sluttier, the better," Rudolf imparted.

Liv pushed away from the table. "I risked my life and memory to help you, and in return, you tell me to dress provocatively? Have I mentioned lately that I'm looking forward to your funeral?"

He nodded as if he understood. "Yes, I get it. But the truth is that Queen Visa views the Warriors and Councils from the House of Seven as a bunch of uptight do-gooders. She loathes their conformity. If you want to make a good impression, you've got to set yourself apart from the rest, including the ones that she's had dealings with in the past. Be bold. Stride into her chambers wearing something fabulous and smoking a pipe. Do the drugs she offers you, and make her laugh. Once you have her disarmed, offer her your immortal soul."

Liv shot forward. "Wait, what?"

Rudolf held up his hands. "Well, even if you soften her up with a bit of cleavage, you don't think she's going to give you the agreement for nothing?"

"Well, why don't I offer her a purple gemstone coveted by the father of time?" Liv asked.

Rudolf shook his head, his eyes frantic. "No, she won't want that. And no one should know that I have this. It's not a big deal. Silly, really. Actually, it's super boring."

"Yeah, you seem really bored right now." Liv observed how his pupils had dilated and breathing intensified.

"You must have something the queen wants. Your soul, your mortality, maybe even your lynx."

Liv threw herself back, gawking at the fae. "Are you insane? I'm not giving her Plato."

"But your soul is on the table, is it?"

Liv shook her head. "No. I'm not giving her any of those things."

"Well, suit yourself, but without a bartering piece and showing a bit of thigh, you're going to get slaughtered. It's your choice," Rudolf said, eyeing his melting ice cream with disgust.

"What if I offer her something that only I have?" Liv said, formulating a plan as she spoke.

Rudolf's brow furrowed. "She's not interested in possessions. Queen Visa owns the entire Las Vegas Strip. She can have anything she desires."

The passages Liv had read of the ancient language of the founders repeated in her head, reminding her of an advantage she might have. It also meshed with something she'd heard growing up, something her father had mentioned a few times. She wasn't sure it would work, but she had to try.

Slapping her hand on the table, she made Rudolf jump.

He still appeared to be a bit on edge after the ordeal in the shop. “I think I know what I can offer her.”

“Well, what is it?” he asked, his curiosity piqued.

“I’ll tell you, but first I have to go read a book.”

Rudolf shook his head. “No, you’ve misunderstood everything I’ve tried to tell you tonight. First, you need breast enhancements and stiletto heels. Queen Visa isn’t interested in anything you can find in a book.”

“I beg to differ,” Liv said, standing victoriously. “Knowledge is power, and that’s inevitably what she wants most.”

CHAPTER FOURTEEN

One of the main reasons Liv loved tinkering with electronics was that it always got her mind off her problems. From the start, the pain of the loss of her parents and her frustration had fallen away when she focused her attention on fixing something.

As she turned the alarm clock over in her hands, she appreciated that the fear of potential impending death wasn't staring her in the face. Queen Visa and what she might or might not do to her was a distant idea that was almost boring to consider, like a rerun of an old television show.

"Oh, there you are," John said, smiling at her as he bustled into the shop carrying a box full of broken devices. "I wasn't sure if I'd see you today."

Liv sighed. "Sorry that my schedule has been off lately. I plan on staying late tonight to make up for it."

He pursed his lips as he slid the box onto the workbench. "You'll do no such thing. There's no reason for you to do that, and getting rest or doing whatever it is that you need to accomplish is just as important."

"But, John, I don't want you to think—"

"Shop is getting fumigated. End of discussion," he said, cutting her off.

"No, it's not," she argued, looking around the nearly pristine store. The brownie who was cleaning it was doing an impeccable job.

"No, you're right. It's not. But it's absolutely not necessary for you to stay late," John stated. "The quality of your work is more than satisfactory, which means you get to work fewer hours. I can't expect more efficient help to stay the same number of hours as someone who is inept and takes forever to fix a vacuum cleaner."

"Well, you *could*," Liv countered. "That's the beauty of owning your own business. You get to do what you like."

John sniffed the air around Liv, giving her a curious expression. "Do you sort of smell like a bonfire, or is that just me?"

Liv nodded. "Nope. I smell like I was roasted over a campfire. Sorry. It's stuck in my clothes, but I plan to get new threads soon. Just have to get my younger sister to order me up some."

"Sophia, you said her name was, right?" John asked.

Liv nodded affectionately. "She's brilliant. You'd love her."

"Well, I hope to meet her at some point, then. Maybe I can take y'all out for ice cream."

Liv laughed. "That's adorable. She'd probably like that, but I have to get clearance to take her out of the House of Seven, and I don't even know how that works."

He waved her off, sorting through the box. "No rush. Seems like you've got your hands full with nearly being roasted alive. Everything was all right after that, I'm guessing."

Liv eased his worry with a nod. "Totally fine. It was just this gnome known as the father of time. He's in retirement, now that he thinks he controls all things that alter time, but I'm thinking there have to be loopholes he's missing. Poor guy looked like he needed a break. Maybe he feels marginalized in a world where the passing of time never changes. I'm not supposed to tell anyone about this, but you're sort of different since you're mortal and all. Anyway, that's what I did last night. You?"

John thought for a moment. "I regrouted my bathroom. Wanted to test my skills on my own shower before trying it on yours and everyone else's in the building."

Liv smiled. John Carraway was what was right about the world. He was simple and pure and unconditionally thoughtful.

The door dinged as a customer entered, but immediately, Liv realized he wasn't an actual customer. Their patrons didn't wear three-piece suits and scrunched expressions or have their hair slicked back tightly or carry briefcases.

The guy who had entered the shop didn't appear at ease as he strode through the front aisles, headed for their back workstation. As Clark had when he'd first entered the shop, he eyed the devices with repugnance. No, this wasn't a man who came into an electronics shop to have his worn-out device fixed. He simply threw it away and bought a new one. Liv was certain of this.

Without asking permission, the man pushed many of the parts and wires on the workstation to the side, making room for his briefcase.

John didn't grimace at this, although Liv did and nearly snapped at the stranger. However, she caught herself when John flashed her a look that said, "Be nice." Being nice wasn't something she was good at, but for John, she'd try.

"Are you Mr. Carraway?" the man asked John.

"No, I am," Liv spouted, unable to control herself.

John smiled at her, offer the stranger his greasy hand. "Yes, I'm John Carraway. Call me John, please."

"Thanks, John," the man began, shaking his hand, but not looking too pleased about it. "My name is Wayne Grimson. I work for Usher and Usher law firm. You might have heard of us."

"I haven't," John admitted at once.

Plato appeared beside Liv, jumping up on the worktable and eyeing the man.

Mr. Grimson paused, seemingly unnerved by the feline's sudden appearance.

Pulling his attention back to John, he unbuckled his briefcase, opening it. "I'm here because I represent a client who has an interest in acquiring your shop for a new retail outlet."

"It's not for sale," Liv said at once.

John shot her a look but nodded along. "She's right. Although I appreciate the interest, the shop isn't for sale."

The man forced a conceited smile. "I misspoke, Mr. Carraway. My client is a very influential developer and has actually already acquired all of the shops on this block.

Yours is the last, and it's really only a matter of some paperwork."

"Wait, you can't do that. This shop belongs to John," Liv argued, standing up and pushing her stool out behind her. The tools she'd been working with began to vibrate on the workbench, a result of her anger flaring up. She took a deep breath, and they settled.

The lawyer glanced at the tools, a curious expression on his face.

"It's a tremor," John said at once, covering for Liv. "And she's right. I'm the legal owner of this shop. Had it almost thirty years."

Mr. Grimson gave another disingenuous smile. "The thing is that the city of West Hollywood wants promising retail that nurtures the community, helping it evolve." He looked around the shop with a disapproving glare. "I'm afraid that the planning commission doesn't see this place as doing that."

"Are you out of your mind?" Liv fired. "John's shop is a staple of this community. We save citizens thousands of dollars by repairing their devices. No one gives back more than he does."

Liv would have kept going but quieted down when John held up a hand.

"I don't understand. The city planning commission can force me out?" John asked.

"I'm afraid so," Wayne Grimson said, not looking at all apologetic. "There have been a series of petitions, and at this point, the commission has voted for you to sell to make way for other ventures they see as fitting their model better."

"This is total bullshit," Liv blurted, catching the revolted look in Plato's eyes.

Mr. Grimson didn't even glance at her, almost as if she were invisible.

"There has to be something I can do," John argued, his voice cracking, and along with it, Liv's heart. "Can't I appeal to the commission? Or talk to your client? Maybe we can find a compromise."

Mr. Grimson handed John a large envelope with a frown. "I'm afraid not. You have thirty days to vacate the shop, and after that period you'll be paid a suitable amount for the property."

"'Suitable?'" Liv argued. "How do you decide what is suitable?"

Again, he ignored her, keeping his eyes on John. "Please review that file and call my firm with any questions. I think you'll find our offer more than fair. If you don't, then we will have to take more severe action."

At the conclusion to his words, the lawyer turned and strode from the shop, arrogance in every single one of his movements.

CHAPTER FIFTEEN

The library wasn't cooperating that day. Liv remembered frequenting mortal libraries the last several years. They were so easy. One walked right in there and did a search for a book, then went and found it. That simplicity didn't exist at the House of Seven library.

The book Liv needed to locate apparently didn't want to be found. There was no handy-dandy computer with search capabilities or a librarian who could help her find the book she was looking for. Honestly, she didn't even know the title of the book, only that it must exist somewhere in the maze of the House's library. And really, titles weren't that important when searching. It was about putting out the right intention. That was the way Liv's father always described trying to find a book in the library.

"When you think the right thoughts and stay attuned to them, the library will lead you in the right direction if it desires," her father had often told her.

Liv really hoped it desired. Otherwise, her clever plan

for dealing with Queen Visa was going to hell, all because a library didn't want her to have that particular book.

"So he's just going to give up?" Sophia asked. She was trailing behind Liv, pulling out books and adding them to her stack.

Liv sighed, closing her eyes and thinking intently of the book she needed. When she opened her eyes, her hand rested on a volume. *Everyone in LA is an Asshole*.

Liv grunted. Yes, they are, she thought, seething at the thought of that smug lawyer she wanted to put in a headlock. But that definitely wasn't the book she was looking for. She continued searching, glancing back at Sophia.

"No, he says it's not worth fighting them," Liv explained. "He thinks it's a sign that he needs to move on."

"But how can he just let the shop go?" Sophia asked.

Liv didn't have a good answer for that. She knew that the repair shop meant everything to John, yet one tiny conversation with an uptight lawyer and he was surrendering.

"I think he's scared," Liv related. "I offered to use magic to help save the shop, and he was adamant that I couldn't. He said that some things weren't worth fighting over, and he didn't want me risking myself to help him."

"But that's what friends do for each other," Sophia protested.

Liv faced her sister, a proud smile on her face. "That's exactly what friends do for each other. But John is highly protective of me, and he also loathes conflict."

"So he's just going to walk away from the shop?"

"Well, he says that it's the universe telling him to retire

in Mexico like he always planned," Liv said, a stone in her heart. She couldn't imagine John leaving. He'd talked about it for years, but she had never taken him seriously. And now the day was upon them, forced on John in the most unexpected way.

"You did say he was getting older, and you were worried about his health," Sophia murmured thoughtfully.

Liv nodded. "Yes, and he does deserve to retire. More than anyone I know. I'll just miss him painfully."

"Where will you live?" Sophia asked.

"Yeah, he plans on selling the apartment building." The melancholy in her voice was palpable. When that lawyer with the shiny suit had entered the shop, he had changed everything for a lot of people. Kicking John out of the store created a ripple effect, one that would displace Liv from the home she'd built for herself. Defeated, she said, "I guess I'll move in here."

Sophia didn't beam as Liv would have expected. Instead, she shook her head. "You won't like it, and we both know that. Most of the magicians are uptight and cranky, and mealtimes are super-big bore-fest. It's also hard to have privacy. I'm constantly finding spying spells, which I disable, but that never lasts long."

"So you *don't* want me to move in here?" Liv asked, surprised.

"I do, but more than that, I want what you want, and that's sort of obvious." The little magician slid her books onto a table when they came to the end of a row. She'd found more than enough books on the subject she was researching: fae fashion.

Liv regarded her thoughtfully. "You're pretty much the best person I know. A cut above John, and that's saying a lot."

Sophia looked up from the book she'd cracked open and smiled. "Maybe I can meet him before he goes to Mexico."

Liv nodded solemnly. "Yeah, maybe."

"And hey, you could always get an apartment somewhere else, couldn't you?" Sophia asked.

"I could, but it takes time to find a place, as well as credit, which I don't have," Liv related with defeat. "John never cared about that kind of thing. And it's hard to prove income when it comes from a secret magical organization. No, the easiest option is just to move in here, at least for the time being."

"Well, on the bright side, we can have slumber parties," Sophia said, lost in thought as she flipped through the book, studying the images.

"So, do you think you can conjure up something from the subscription service that will work?" Liv asked. She'd been working on honing this part of her magic, but she still didn't have a subscription to the service where magicians got their clothes. Without that, she'd have to manifest the garments from nothing, or from raw materials, which was a lot harder.

Sophia glanced up, a spark in her eyes. "Yeah, I see what your friend meant. The fae like their necklines low and their slits high."

Liv grimaced. "Rudolf isn't really my friend. Let's call him a business associate."

"What do you think he wants the gemstone for?" Sophia asked, checking over her shoulder that they were alone. She then verified by using a spy-reveal spell.

"Some selfish gain, I'm sure," Liv related. "The fae mostly care about themselves, it seems."

"No wonder their kingdom is in Las Vegas," Sophia stated, flipping through the book again. "They'd freeze anywhere else wearing clothes like these."

Liv squeezed her eyes closed, scrunching her nose like she was preparing to get a painful shot. "Okay, dress me in something sleazy."

The warm jacket and pants she'd been wearing disappeared, replaced by cool silk fabric, but not a lot of it. Liv felt a chill run down her arms as she opened her eyes.

"This color is burning my eyes. What is it?" Liv asked, staring at the dress Sophia had put her into. It really didn't qualify as a dress. More like a worn-out sleeve on one of Rory's shirts.

It was a halter dress that was entirely too short and too tight, but that wasn't the worst part. The thin piece of neon-green fabric had holes all over it, exposing her hips, thighs, waist, and back.

Sophia snickered, checking the books she'd been referencing. "It's called 'neon ivy.'"

Liv fake-gagged. "I think it should be called 'puke green,' since that's what it makes me want to do."

"I can try a different color if you'd like," Sophia suggested. "How about pink?"

Liv lowered her chin and regarded her sister with an impatient stare. "Do I look like a pink kind of girl?"

Sophia giggled, covering her mouth. "Well, I think you look really edgy and cool."

"I look like I'm going to freeze," Liv countered.

Sophia agreed with a nod. "You're right. You need something." She circled her hand in the air, and around Liv's neck materialized a silk scarf that provided nearly zero warmth.

"Thanks," Liv said dryly.

"Oh, and before I forget, I've been studying up on makeup and hair. Let me fix that up for you."

"When do you learn this stuff?" Liv asked, closing her eyes as if Sophia was going to apply eyeshadow by hand.

"YouTube," the little magician answered simply. "Okay, you're all done."

Liv opened her eyes, not feeling any different. However, her hair wasn't resting on her shoulders anymore, but rather was in a high ponytail, the strands curled and hanging down on one side. "Do I even want to look in the mirror?" The question brought back the memory of looking into the hand mirror in Papa Creola's shop. She couldn't shake the image of herself as an old woman.

"I think you look rad," Sophia gushed, producing a regular hand mirror.

Tentatively Liv held it up, not recognizing her own reflection for a moment—again. "Wow! If this whole magician thing fails, I can just go into prosti—"

"Liv, is that you?" a voice called from behind her.

Liv froze, recognizing Stefan's voice and wishing she could make a portal and escape. However, portal magic wasn't allowed in the House of Seven. After giving Sophia a frustrated look, she turned around to face the Warrior.

"Yeah, it's me," she said, keeping her eyes low and checking to ensure that her boobs were hidden. Well, mostly hidden.

"What are you wearing?" he asked, his eyes wide as he studied her. Stefan was wearing his usual long traveling cloak and black boots. His dark hair was extra disheveled, and his pale face was splattered with mud in places.

Liv wound her fingers in the silk material around her neck. "It's a scarf," she replied.

A laugh burst out of Sophia's mouth.

Stefan cracked a smile. "Yes, I see that. I was referring to the rest of the…" He raked his finger through the air. "I was mostly referring to whatever it is you're wearing."

"It's my costume for the Kingdom of Fae," Liv said, finding it hard to talk with the amount of lip gloss covering her mouth. She resisted the urge to wipe it off with the back of her hand.

Stefan nodded at once, scratching the side of his head and staring at the carpet like he had found something of sudden interest there. "Okay, well, that makes sense."

"Actually, I'm glad I ran into you," Liv stated, thinking of the book she was looking for. "Do you have a second?"

"Liv, I've got to run to a lesson," Sophia cut in, gathering up the books. "Do you need me for anything? I mean, am I done helping you pick out clothes?"

The little magician had almost dropped her guard and revealed that she was the one who had manifested Liv's clothes. They both suspected that Stefan was well aware of the girl's talent from hints he'd supplied.

"Yeah, no problem, love," Liv said, giving her sister a

side hug, afraid of smearing makeup on her pristine white dress. "Thanks for helping."

"I'll get to work on clearing out drawers for you in my room if you want," Sophia said.

Liv nodded. "Thanks. That's nice of you."

She watched the young girl hurry away with her arms full of books.

"You're moving into the House of Seven, it sounds like?" Stefan asked.

Liv turned, sighing. "Yeah, unfortunately, I have to."

"'Unfortunately?'" Stefan questioned.

"Yeah, I'm sort of a loner who prefers to live by myself," Liv explained.

Stefan's mouth popped open. "What? Not really! I'm shocked."

"Ha-ha," Liv said as her eyes searched Stefan, remembering something Hester had let slip. "Hey, did you by any chance get bitten by something?"

The light expression on his face disappeared. For a moment, he looked incapable of speech. Then he pointed at the bandage on her leg, recovering. "I guess I could ask the same thing of you. What got you?"

"What got *you*?" she countered.

His eyes darted briefly to his arm. "I'll show you mine if you show me yours."

Liv shook her head. "No. I'm not that curious, but nice try."

"So, you wanted my help on something," Stefan redirected.

"Yeah," Liv began, striding forward, finding it hard to

walk in the platform shoes Sophia had put her into. She'd been so repulsed by the dress and the makeup that she hadn't noticed the ridiculous contraptions on her feet. "I'm looking for a book, but the library doesn't seem to be providing any options."

Stefan nodded. "Yes, you have to be singularly focused, and if I may be so bold, you might be a little distracted with your wardrobe planning and this relocation business."

Liv thought about that for a moment. Her mind *had* been reeling at the thought of John being booted out of his shop as she searched, hence the book she'd found about LA assholes. That author had it spot on the money. Most people in LA *were* assholes. Well, not John. Or Rory, but she wasn't going to tell the giant that. It might go to his already overly large head.

"Yes, I think you're right," Liv stated. "I might have been a bit distracted. Still, do you know of a book that talks about how Warriors' blood is most valuable when the person is alive?"

The idea had occurred to Liv when she'd read the ancient language of the founders and it had spoken of councilors' blood being needed to open the chamber. It was implied to her that the councilor should provide that blood, meaning that someone couldn't kill them and use it. That idea had first been proposed to Liv by her father, who had related one of his cases to her. He stated that it wasn't widely known that the magical properties of a royal's blood changed based on whether they were living or dead. Furthermore, the blood was incredibly useful, since royalty had certain access to things. When Liv recalled this lesson from her father, she wondered why it had taken her so long to realize that Reese had meant that Clark's blood was part of the riddle. Inside and outside the House it was common for royal blood to open things since they were elite and few.

"I do know a few books like that," Stefan related. "But first, is this involving one of your secret missions, like how you got that bite on your leg?"

Liv rolled her eyes. "I don't know what you're talking about. How would I have time for secret missions when I'm busy preparing to be murdered by Queen Visa?"

"Valid point, Warrior Beaufont," Stefan said, bowing slightly. "My apologies. Please follow me." He spun around and strode down a narrow aisle of books, breezing past all of them before coming to the end of the row. Liv had a hard time keeping up with him, afraid with each step that she was going to trip on her heels.

Stefan slipped a leather-bound book from the shelf and handed it to Liv. She took it, reading the cover aloud. "The Royals." She looked up at Stefan, adrenaline rushing through her veins. "Does this detail who the original Seven were?"

Stefan's face scrunched with confusion. "No. It simply explains how the House is set up, and why. The history is a bit abbreviated, in my opinion. I read it many times when we were invited into the Seven."

Liv's elation dissipated as fast as it had come on. "Okay, well, thanks. This sounds like it will be helpful."

"For?" Stefan asked, drawing out the word.

"For saving my life," she joked.

"Oh, well, then I daresay you owe me big for helping you with this request," Stefan teased with a roguish smile.

"Totally, and I'll pay you back by not telling anyone that you have a mysterious bite."

Stefan winked at her. "Same, Liv Beaufont. Your secret is safe with me."

CHAPTER SIXTEEN

"Hot daaaaamn," Rudolf hollered with a whistle, looking Liv up and down about three times longer than was necessary.

Liv nearly swung her purse at his face, but she remembered that it held something fragile and refrained. "You sincerely have a death wish, don't you?"

"I didn't know you would clean up so well," he said. "Seriously, if you dressed like this more often, you wouldn't be such a sour old maid."

Liv clutched her purse and shook her head. "I'm not an old maid. I'm a Warrior for the House of Seven."

"Yes, yes, I, as well as everyone in the magical world has heard about that. She's Liv Beaufont, Warrior for the House of Seven. Blah, blah, big shot material."

"Would you shut up so that I can focus?" Liv wove between drunk tourists who held giant plastic glasses and gawked at her like she was a showgirl. She sort of wished that Queen Visa would put her out of her misery and kill her on the spot.

"Which casino do the fae own?" Liv asked, looking up and down the sprawling Strip.

Rudolf laughed. "Which one? We own them all. The Kingdom of Fae is the entire Strip, but the Queen's chamber is there." He pointed to the Cosmopolitan hotel. It towered beside the Bellagio's fountains, which were presently quiet, the tourists lining up for the show that would soon begin.

"Okay, so I just have to go to the top floor and request a meeting with Queen Visa?" Liv asked.

Rudolf shook his head. "I have a better idea." He hooked his arm through hers and nearly dragged her in the direction of the building.

"Am I going to like this idea, or will it involve having a fight with Mother Nature or some other powerful entity?" Liv dared to ask, nearly slipping several times.

"Knowing you, you're absolutely going to hate this idea, but I guarantee that it will stall your death for a few minutes, at least."

"I don't want my death stalled if I have to smell your cologne any longer," Liv said, holding her nose.

"What? I'm not wearing cologne. That's a fae's natural scent," Rudolf said, offended. "Calvin Klein and all those other designers pay big money for our pheromones."

"Ewe. I heard that stuff was full of cat piss and whatnot," Liv commented.

"Speaking of cats," Rudolf began, "where's your lynx?"

Liv looked around, never knowing when Plato was there or not. "I guess he hates Vegas as much as me. Must have stayed home for this one."

"Well, maybe he'll show up to bail you out again."

"Honestly, I don't think there's any bailing me out this time. I have to rely on your advice and my cunning, which means I'm screwed."

Rudolf led the way into the Cosmopolitan. Ladies and men stopped, not hiding their reactions as he passed. One woman dropped her giant plastic cup, spilling beer on the ground, her mouth hanging open like she couldn't believe such a man existed.

"Do you ever get tired of people gawking at you?" Liv asked, turning around to take in the crowd staring at them.

Rudolf flashed her a toothy grin. "What do *you* think?" He reached out and touched her chin. "And baby, they are looking at you, too. You're wearing that dress like a champ."

"So you want a broken nose. Cool. I'm on it." She cocked her fist, ready to launch at his pretty face.

Rudolf simply smiled. "Save your angst. We're going to need it for the bar."

"Bar? That's where you're taking me? It's too early to drink, and I need my wits about me."

"It's never too early to drink. I always think better when I drink," Rudolf stated, stopping and holding his arm out.

Liv hadn't seen such a beautiful bar in all her life. The Chandelier was several stories tall, and it dripped with thousands of beads like they were inside an actual chandelier. Couples sat on the posh sofas and at the bar, sipping cocktails and making out.

"Wait, I get that it is Vegas, but those people are going at it," Liv said, feeling the need to shield her eyes from the public displays of affection happening pretty much everywhere.

"Take a closer look," Rudolf whispered in her ear.

Liv searched the bar and realized at once what she was seeing. "Those are fae?"

He nodded. "Yes, and the Cosmo is the place they come to hunt most often. The Bellagio is where they perform most often. The Venetian is where they indulge in their drugs of choice. You get the idea. Each of the casinos seeks to meet one of their needs."

"Why aren't you including yourself in that?" Liv asked.

Rudolf raised an eyebrow at her. "Haven't you figured out by now that I'm not like the rest of the fae?"

"How so?" she inquired, unable to take her eyes off a couple as a fae ran his hand up a woman's leg, kissing her neck.

"I have class."

A laugh burst out of her mouth.

"Hey, now," Rudolf fired back, offended. "I do. You won't find me in here seducing mortals. I don't even like Vegas. Notice that I'm always in Roya Lane when you're looking for me?"

"Yeah, and why is that?"

Rudolf glanced around, searching for a spot. "I have my reasons."

"Oh, ever the man of mystery. What do I have to do to get you to spill that information? Fight a gnome? Wrestle a centaur?"

Rudolf grabbed her by the hand and tugged her to a pair of stools at the bar. "You have to make out with me."

Liv jerked her hand away. "Left or right?"

He spun around, a quizzical expression in his eyes. "Left or right what?"

"Do you want your left or right eye blackened?"

He grinned. "Right, for sure. It's my better side." Then he leaned in faster than Liv could fully react and slammed his lips onto hers, kissing her with so much force that she nearly toppled backward. She grabbed him by the shirt and pushed him back, and before she could stop herself, she launched her fist at his left eye.

Rudolf stumbled backward clutching his face. Guards swooped in from all directions, pulling weapons. Three seized Liv's arms, and another caught Rudolf as he stumbled backward, checking him over. The entire bar turned into complete chaos as the couples broke apart, yelling and trying to figure out what was going on.

Liv tugged at the restraints being forced onto her but found it impossible to break free. She caught a smile on Rudolf's face as he shook the guards off of him, telling them he was fine.

"Why did you do that?" Liv yelled as the guards pulled her away from Rudolf.

"So that you'd do exactly what you just did," he answered with what looked like a painful wink. "I'll see you up on the top floor, Dollface. You're going to do great!"

Liv shook her head at the fae as the guards marched her away, taking her to a set of elevators.

"Where are you taking me?" Liv asked the man beside her, who she realized at once was a fae.

He gave her a serious expression. "To see management. She prefers to deal with troublemakers directly."

CHAPTER SEVENTEEN

The top floor of the Cosmopolitan looked out on the Strip, providing what was undoubtedly the best view in town. Below, Liv could just make out the Bellagio's fountains, which were cascading in perfect unison.

The guards led her through a hallway dripping with the same kinds of beads as in the Chandelier bar. Eerie music played from unseen speakers. The windows were floor to ceiling, sunlight spilling through and making Liv squint.

"Your management deals with troublemakers directly?" Liv asked. "Seems like she needs more to do. That's a job that should be outsourced."

"She specifically deals with magicians who assault fae in her kingdom," the guard answered.

Oh, so they were dropping all pretenses now. They knew who she was, but the question was, did they know what? She was going to have to reveal that at the right time.

Liv was unprepared for what she saw next. The guards led her into a room that put the Chandelier to shame.

Queen Visa's chamber was a wide-open office, the wall shimmering with light as if it were made out of diamonds. The carpet was solid white and instantly made Liv feel like she was walking on a cloud. Overhead hung dozens of chandeliers, their crystals reflecting the light, sending rainbows all over the room.

I'm in heaven, Liv thought, her mouth dropping open.

"What the hell have you brought me?" Queen Visa called from the far end of the room. She was sitting behind a large modern desk. Behind her the wall was entirely glass, displaying the view of the Las Vegas Strip.

Various groups of fae turned to look at Liv as the guards led her to the front of the room. They were dressed similarly to her, although none of the women was wearing anything as skimpy as her dress.

"We apprehended her in the Chandelier bar," the guard said, releasing Liv finally. "She punched a fae."

Behind the desk sat the most beautiful woman Liv had ever seen. Queen Visa's blonde hair hung in loose ringlets, perfectly framing her heart-shaped face. Her topaz-blue eyes narrowed, and that somehow made her even more attractive. The curves of her pink lips were flawless, drawing Liv's eyes to them. When she stood, Liv could see that she was wearing a solid white blazer fastened at the waist with no shirt underneath, her boobs barely covered. The white pencil skirt was snug, hugging her narrow hips and stopping just short of her upper thighs. Her pink stilettos made a gentle noise as she strode around the desk, a murderous expression on her face.

So this is the woman who is going to kill me, Liv thought. *At least my last sight will be a good one.*

"You, magician, stroll onto my territory and assault one of mine? You must have a death wish," the queen said, walking around Liv and sizing her up. "I don't get it, though. You don't dress like your kind. Where's your oversized cape and bad sense of style?"

"I left it at home. When in Rome..." Liv said, her voice only slightly unsteady.

At her back, there was a commotion, but Liv didn't dare turn around.

"You? The magician assaulted *you*?" Queen Visa asked, looking away from Liv.

A moment later, Rudolf was escorted to the front a safe distance from Liv. He was still clutching his face where Liv had punched him.

Bowing low, he forced a smile. "Yes, my queen. I was working on seducing her, and out of nowhere, she punched me in the eye."

Queen Visa scrutinized him with a stare that could melt ice. "You don't play the seductive game, and you know better than to try it on a magician. What are you playing at, Rudolphus?"

He shook his head. "Nothing, my queen. I've been trying to get back into the game. Maybe I'm a bit out of practice, and I didn't know at first that she was a magician."

The queen studied him for a moment, softening slightly. "My poor, dear Rudolphus. You're still broken from her death, aren't you?"

Liv's eyes cut to the ground. She tried to not look interested.

"Yes, my queen, but I'm on the mend. Which is why I'm here," he answered.

"I sure hope so," Queen Visa answered. "It's been well over a century. Move on, already."

He nodded, not at all looking like the fae Liv knew. "You're right. Of course, you're right."

She reached out, brushing her hand across his cheek, cold affection in her eyes. "We did have fun together, didn't we, my darling Rudolphus? Which was why I had to kill her. You'll always be mine. Always."

He pressed his hand to the one holding his face and forced a smile. "I realize that now, and I'm extremely honored."

Queen Visa's hand dropped at once, and she spun to face Liv. "Now, the question is, what do I do with you, magician?"

Not kill me, Liv thought. Instead of saying that, she hitched up one hip and smacked her lips like she was chewing gum. "You can start by telling me how you got that ass. Do you do Pilates?"

The collective gasps of the fae around the room made Liv stiffen.

Queen Visa traced her pink fingernail over her perfect lips, regarding Liv with an unreadable look. "You look familiar. Where do I know you from?"

"I work at a repair shop in WeHo. Did you bring a blender in last week?" Liv said casually, although her heart was racing.

Queen Visa cracked a smile that nearly made Liv faint. It somehow made the impossibly beautiful woman even prettier. "I like you, magician. What's your name?"

"Aren't you going to punish her?" Rudolf complained. "She gave me a black eye."

Queen Visa shook her head at him. "You know as well as I do that a few bruises and scars make you more attractive. You maybe should be thanking Ms…" She gave Liv an expectant look.

"Liv," she answered.

"Now, Liv, why are you in my casino? Magicians don't like gambling or drinking or anything fun, really. Just libraries and other boring things," Queen Visa said.

Liv swayed her shoulders to the music playing overhead. "I'm not like other magicians."

"I see that. But what brings you to the Cosmo?" Queen Visa asked.

"A simple request," Liv said, her throat starting to constrict. The moment was nearly upon her. She didn't think she could go through with it.

Queen Visa raised an arched eyebrow at her. "For me, I gather."

"Or whoever is in charge here," Liv dared to say.

Again the crowd at Liv's back gasped, many exchanging whispers.

To her surprise, Queen Visa didn't kill her on the spot. Instead, she laughed. "I haven't been spoken to like this in…well, never. You amuse me, magician. Not only are you not like your kind, you're not like the fae." She waved a hand at the people behind Liv. "You all are a bunch of boring dimwits who only tell me what I like to hear and rarely say anything of interest."

"That's because they have free rein and not enough respect for mortals," Liv said.

"I'm not following your reasoning, Liv."

"Well, a bit of humbling goes a long way. Your fae gallivant, making mortals do everything they desire and seducing them without concern."

"And you think that if they didn't do this that they'd have better personalities?" Queen Visa asked.

"I think that if they weren't obsessed with love and sex, they'd find other hobbies, which would make them more interesting to you."

Queen Visa considered this for a moment. "It makes sense. You all have become even more lustful lately, and then you have nothing to talk about. You're so scared I'm going to remove your privileges that you suck up to me, never telling me what you really think. After a few hundred years, it's quite tedious reigning over you all."

From around the room came several protests. Queen Visa shook her head. "No. I've made up my mind, thanks to my new friend, Liv. I want you all doing other things besides seducing mortals all the time. Get hobbies. Go on adventures. Leave the mortals alone for a while."

"But, Queen," many around the room said.

Liv couldn't believe it was working, but the hardest part was almost upon her.

The floor rumbled under their feet as Queen Visa's beautiful eyes flared red. Her gaze narrowed, and steam seemed to rise from behind her. "I have decreed. Who dares to defy me?"

"Not I," many of the fae said, their protests immediate.

"That's what I thought," Queen Visa said confidently, her demeanor returning to normal. "Now, Liv, why don't you join me in the spa? It's time for my afternoon massage."

Liv gulped. Her eyes darting briefly to Rudolf. He was pale, and seemed to understand the severity of the moment. "Can't do a massage. I've got to return to the House of Seven in a sec." She opened her purse as Queen Visa's face transformed back into one of pure vengeance.

"You! You're a Warrior for the House of Seven!" Queen Visa boomed, her voice making the chandeliers overhead shake. "How dare you come into my kingdom and assault one of my own?"

Although she was trembling inside, Liv remained outwardly steady, withdrawing a vial of her blood from her purse as well as an ancient scroll, the one where the first agreement with the Fae had been written. "Oh, you didn't know I was a Warrior? Shucks, I totally forgot to mention that part. Anyway, here's a vial of my blood. Thought I'd offer it to you in exchange for an update to that little contract you signed ages ago with the House."

Queen Visa was momentarily thrown off, her eyes focused on the vial in Liv's hand. "Why would I want that? And what update to the contract?"

"Well, you just stated that you weren't going to allow your Fae to openly seduce mortals anymore, so that should probably go in the contract, just so we cover all our bases." She dared to wink at the queen. "Keep them accountable, you know. Make it legit."

"You came here to get me to update the contract?" The queen's voice was filled with so much hostility that it felt sharp enough to saw Liv in half.

"I came here to give you this." She waved the vial in the air. "And then there's the boring contract business. Just wanted to get that out of the way so I can catch a show. I have tickets to see O, and don't want to be late."

Liv knew from dealing with Rudolf that the fae were

bound by exchanges. They couldn't give anything without taking, and vice versa. This was how she was getting the contract signed, which would be binding…if she survived.

"Again, what do I want with a Warrior's blood? I could simply kill you here and now and have as much of it as I like."

"You could," Liv said tentatively. "However, blood that is freely given is more powerful. Not only that, but when the giver of the blood is still alive, the magical properties are tenfold. Did you know that?"

The queen looked to the side, uncertainty on her face. "I didn't, actually."

Liv shrugged. "It's true. But you know how useful a Warrior's blood is, right?"

Queen Visa regarded Liv with a thoughtful stare. "I know that it grants access to certain things. Opens portals otherwise closed to other magical creatures, and in essence, acts as an extension of you."

Liv nodded. "It would allow you to read the ancient language or enter the House of Seven or attend one of our boring-as-hell meetings."

The queen released the smallest of smiles, which made her look even more wicked. "You *are* a clever Warrior. What are they doing with you?"

"Mostly killing me slowly with their dumb bureaucracy," Liv imparted.

The queen reached out and took the vial, watching its contents spill back and forth as she tilted it. "What is your last name, Liv?"

"Beaufont."

Queen Visa's eyes widened slightly. "Yes, now I recognize you. You look just like your mother. She wasn't a horrible magician. A bit of a rebel, too."

She closed her eyes, still holding the vial in her hands. Liv watched breathlessly. When Queen Visa opened her eyes, she wore a victorious smile. "You're smart not to have deceived me. This is in fact Beaufont blood."

"I had no plans to deceive. Just for doing a job. You get it." Liv held out the scroll and checked her wrist, although she wasn't wearing a watch. "So can you sign this with the amendments? My show starts soon."

Queen Visa considered her. "So the House of Seven wants my fae to stop seducing mortals, is it?"

"I think it's a frequency issue, honestly. They are probably just jealous because they can't get dates," Liv said.

To her surprise, the queen laughed. "If they dressed more like you, they would."

"Yeah, but that's not helping them."

The queen hesitated for a moment before directing her finger at the scroll. "I don't know why, but I like you more than any magician I've met, and I've met many of them. Killed many of them, too."

"It's probably the hair extensions. People always love that I have long hair," Liv lied, holding up a piece of her hair, which was real.

"You're not boring. That's the reason I like you. I'm tired of boring fae and magicians."

Liv tapped her foot. "Show starting. Can I get the scroll signed? Then I'll be on my way, but I'll come back for a massage and general debauchery later."

"If anyone else had attempted what you just did with

this amendment business, they'd be dead right now. You realize that, don't you?"

"I'm actually new to this business, so I don't know much," Liv stated, acting bored.

"Well, Liv Beaufont, I look forward to seeing what you do for the House of Seven," the queen stated, circling her finger in the air. The scroll glowed for a moment, and then faded to its original color. "I'll honor your request in exchange for the blood. The contract has been amended."

Liv kept her relief hidden and nodded. She could hardly believe she'd done the impossible and survived. She couldn't wait to see the councilors' faces when she shoved this at them.

CHAPTER EIGHTEEN

"I told you the right eye," Rudolf said, still nursing his swelling left eye. He and Liv had split up and met a bit off the Strip, taking a portal to Roya Lane from there.

"I don't take direction well. Just ask the Council," Liv answered.

"I can't believe you gave her your blood," Rudolf said.

"Oh, hell no," Liv said, realizing she should have changed before coming to Roya Lane. They already gawked at her there, but now they had even more reason, with her wearing a neon-green dress that was full of holes and hooker heels. "You don't think I'm insane? I gave her Sophia's blood, which is why she knew it was a Beaufont's. It doesn't have the same magical potency as mine. She won't be able to find out that it's Sophia's though. I'd never put my little sister in danger."

"No, she won't figure that out, but she's going to be livid when she realizes you fooled her."

"If I gave her my blood then she could enter the House of Seven and go in to the Chamber of the Tree or a whole other hosts of places," Liv said, thinking of the ancient chamber.

Rudolf gave her a sideways look. "You realize that if she figures that out, you're dead that very minute."

"Oh, I've already bought my coffin."

A group of gnomes dared to point at Liv and heckle her. She held up her fists, narrowing her eyes at them. "Keep it up, and I'll show you how I can shove these heels up your—"

Rudolf hooked his arm through Liv's, steering her away. "Keep that up, and they'll never teach you fireball magic."

"I'm pretty sure I've sullied my reputation with the gnomes for a long time."

He shook his head. "Still, it would be good to preserve things as much as possible. They can hold a grudge longer than any other race, but they also hold a unique advantage over some. You never know when you're going to need to make nice with them."

Liv untangled her arm from Rudolf's noticing in the dim light of Roya Lane how badly his eye was swelling. She gazed at her hand, which to her surprise didn't feel injured from the assault—not like his darkening eye. "Hey, I'm sort of sorry for punching you. I realize in hindsight why you kissed me."

He beamed, his blue eyes still lighting up despite the swelling. Bowing low, he said, "You're welcome, my lady. I figured that if you made the right kind of entrance, Queen Visa would find you interesting. She loves rebels and a bit of drama."

Liv smiled, thinking she was glad she enlisted Rudolf's

help. Without it, she would have been doomed, strolling into Queen Visa's casino wearing magician clothes and being all business. The Council had told her that she needed to enlist more diplomacy on her cases when she had upset some dumb goblin tribe. She could safely say that she'd used a great deal of diplomacy on this case.

Liv patted the handbag she was tired of carrying around. She changed her clothes in a darkened alley off Roya Lane, feeling instantly better with her body fully covered and the scroll safely hidden in her cape.

Rudolf grimaced. "I had hoped that you'd changed your evil ways and were going to start dressing more appealingly."

"Never have such disillusions about me," Liv replied as something occurred to her. "When we were in Queen Visa's chamber, she mentioned something about you not getting over something. What was that about the woman she killed?"

A shadow moved behind Rudolf's eyes. "I don't think you heard her correctly."

"I think I did," Liv fired back. "And you don't hang out with the fae, do you? Why is that?"

He sighed. "After several hundred years, they bore me. Maybe in a century or so I'll be lonesome for my kind."

Liv looked around at the always-bustling Roya Lane. Various races were hurrying in different directions, talking in languages she didn't recognize. "Is that why you hang around here?"

Rudolf followed her gaze and shrugged slightly. "Yeah, I guess."

"Well, maybe you will like the fae better now that they have to diversify and get hobbies," Liv said.

"Yeah, maybe," Rudolf stated, but there was no enthusiasm in his voice. He seemed suddenly lost, like a shell of his former self.

"Are you okay?" Liv asked, surprised to find herself worried about Rudolf.

He closed his eyes for half a beat and let out a breath. "Yeah. I'm just thinking about what an awful kisser you were. It was a real disappointment."

Liv slapped him on the arm. "Hey, that was an uninvited and disgusting attempt on your part. Of course, it wasn't any good."

Rudolf leaned away, gripping his arm. "No more abuse. Keep your brutish fist away from me, Warrior. All you know is violence."

Liv couldn't keep herself from laughing. Rudolf joined in, letting go of the stress that had built while they were in the queen's chamber.

"I can't believe it worked," Liv said with elation.

"Honestly, I can't believe it did either. Not in a million years did I think you could pull it off, but you, Liv Beaufont, Warrior for the House of Seven, have this weird charm. It's almost like an anti-charm that somehow endears you to people."

Liv shook her head. "Take that back, or I'll blacken your other eye."

He shook his head. "No, go ahead and make your threats. I'll take your abuse. But you should know that despite your attempts to be atrocious, I still like you."

Liv shook her head, pulling her hood up. "Well, I like

you like one does a garbage truck. You're glad they exist, but you don't want them to stick around."

He puffed out his chest and bowed low. "Thank you, my lady. I'll take that as a grand compliment."

"I wouldn't," Liv said dryly.

He offered his hand, probably hoping she'd give him hers. When she didn't, Rudolf pursed his lips. "I'll work on finding the lost memory. You try to keep yourself out of trouble."

"No promises," Liv said, creating a portal to the West Coast entrance of the House of Seven. "And don't lose my ring, or I'll make Queen Visa look like a docile puppy."

Rudolf nodded. "I have no doubt, Liv Beaufont."

CHAPTER NINETEEN

Again the image of John lying helpless in a hospital bed assaulted Liv's vision when she stepped through the Door of Reflection. She hadn't figured out how to get out of these visions. They seemed to release her when they were done, spitting her out into the Chamber of the Tree.

If she could squeeze her eyes shut and not see the man before her suffering, she would, but that wasn't an option.

The nurse entered the scene, just like before, talking to someone unseen. "Such a strange attack this one endured. Like something out of a movie."

The Door released her. Liv shook off the strangeness of returning to the real world, blinking at the chamber and trying to clear her vision. Her mother's words rang in her head, making her throat prickle with guilt: "Our magic doesn't fit into their world."

That was what Guinevere Beaufont had said on more than one occasion about mortals, having her own heartbreak over the matter. Liv had thought she'd done the right thing by telling John about magic, but what if she hadn't?

She reasoned that he already knew about magic since he was married to a magician. But what if the truth she shared with him was going to put him in more danger? He accepted magic better than most, but did that mean he needed to know? She wasn't sure, and now he was about to lose his shop and the life he'd built. Maybe things would be better when he retired to Mexico. At least she wouldn't have to worry about him, although she'd miss him painfully.

Adler was in the middle of one of his dumb lectures when Liv stepped into the light.

"Mr. Ludwig, your excuses are of no concern to the Council," he stated, his attention distracted by Liv taking her spot between Stefan and Decar, who, as usual, wasn't present.

The relief that flooded Clark's face was palpable. He actually cracked a smile, but it vanished when Liv made the tiniest of gestures with her hand.

"As I was saying," Adler continued, looking completely thrown off by Liv's sudden appearance. Many of the councilors exchanged whispers, glancing at her curiously.

Adler cleared his throat. "As I was saying," he repeated, but shook his head. "Actually, Ms. Beaufont, do you want to tell the Council what you're doing here? You're supposed to be meeting with Queen Visa."

"Yes, I understand that," Liv said, pushing her hood down and shaking out her long hair.

Adler lowered his chin. "Have you come to ask for a different case? Mr. Beaufont hasn't been successful at getting you removed from the case, if that was your hope."

Liv smiled inside. "Get a different case? Oh heck, naw."

Bianca grimaced at her causal language. "It's understandable to be scared of Queen Visa, but unfortunately there are no new resources we can provide you for the case. We've already voted and decided on the matter."

"Scared of Queen Visa?" Liv asked. "She invited me to have an afternoon massage with her. Hopefully, she doesn't get my number, or she'll probably never stop texting me."

"Wait, you met Queen Visa?" Bianca leaned forward, her tall, pale forehead wrinkling.

"For sure, and that is one hot woman," Liv replied.

Adler let out an annoyed sigh. "Ms. Beaufont, the Council doesn't have time for your games. If you're not going to take this case, you'll be removed as Warrior, and the Beaufont family replaced in the House of Seven."

Liv turned and looked at Stefan, who appeared to be hiding an expression of amusement. "Playing a game? I didn't think that was allowed here. I thought the rule book specifically said no fun could be had in the Chamber of the Tree."

If he had been trying to hide his expression before, it was close to slipping to the surface now.

"Ms. Beaufont, this behavior will absolutely not be tolerated!" Adler yelled, making the crow on the far end of the bench squawk and take off, flying up to the rafters. Liv sort of hoped the white tiger would eat that pesky bird, but he wasn't in sight. She remembered that they were part of the balance of the chamber, although she wasn't sure entirely how.

Seemingly disarmed for a moment by the crow's disappearance, Adler took a calming breath and closed his eyes. When he opened them, he didn't appear much less hostile than he had moments prior. "Ms. Beaufont," he began, his tone brimming with frustration. "You've been asked to amend the agreement with Queen Visa. Under no circumstances are you to return here until that's been done."

"Right, I totally get it," she said casually.

"Very good, then," he said, obviously restraining his anger.

"Totally great," she fired back.

He blinked at her, his eyes narrowing. "You've been dismissed."

Liv didn't budge.

Adler tried again to return his attention to Stefan, but Liv's continued presence was too much for him. To Liv's relief, Clark was doing an excellent job of covering the laughter she was certain he wanted to burst into.

"Ms. Beaufont, why are you still standing there when you've been assigned your case and dismissed?" Adler asked, each of his words careful like he might explode with anger at any moment.

Liv slapped her forehead. "Oops, I'm such a ditz. Totally slipped my mind. I'm done with that case."

Adler's eyes rolled up in his head. "Councilors, I call for a formal disciplinary action for Ms. Beaufont."

"Discipline?" Liv asked. "That's what I get for risking my life and successfully completing the death mission you assigned me?"

Adler's nostrils flared, but it was Lorenzo who spoke next. "You were successful in the Kingdom of the Fae? You got Queen Visa to agree to the amendments?"

Liv laughed. "Agree? She thought it was her idea." She

pulled the ancient scroll from her robes, earning her gasps from everyone on the bench save Clark and Haro.

Adler snapped his hand impatiently, making the scroll fly out of Liv's hand and soar through the air, landing in his long fingers. Impatiently he unrolled the scroll, his eyes darting over the words.

"What does it say? She really got the queen to agree?" Bianca asked, leaning over to read.

Adler's fingers tightened on the parchment in his hand, lowering it slightly to look over it at Liv. "How did you do this?"

"You *did* ask me to get her to agree to minimize the fae's seduction of mortals, right?" Liv asked.

"You know full well that was the case you were assigned," Adler answered.

"Is there a reason that you appear so angry that I've done what you asked?" Liv questioned.

"I think," Raina cut in, "that Councilor Sinclair is simply surprised that you completed the case so quickly." She was smiling with unbridled relief, as was Hester next to her. Clark had also finally let his elation shine.

"How were you able to get Queen Visa to agree?" Lorenzo asked.

"It involved clocking a fae and wearing way too much makeup," Liv answered.

Haro laughed at this, his usual serious expression cracking. "It is generally the unconventional methods that work in these situations."

Liv nodded, studying the magician. Maybe Akio was right, and his brother did have faith in her. She'd have to question the other Warrior on that later since he wasn't in the Chamber.

Adler chewed his thumbnail, his eyes continuously running over the scroll in front of him as if he couldn't believe it was real.

"Anyway, I'm ready for my next case," Liv said, reaching into her pocket and retrieving the codex to which notes on cases were sent by the Council.

Bianca looked up and down the bench. "Case? Do we have another case lined up for Olivia?"

"I do believe you know that I prefer to go by Liv, but it's cute that you keep using the wrong name," Liv said, feeling brand-new confidence. At least three of the councilors hadn't expected her to return alive, and her presence in front of them was throwing them off.

"We actually don't have anything for Ms. Beaufont at the moment," Adler said, continuing to study the scroll. "We… Well, we expected it to take you a little longer to finalize the agreement with Queen Visa."

You expected me to be murdered, Liv thought proudly to herself.

"I think Warrior Beaufont has earned a day or two off," Hester said, smiling. "And when you return rested and refreshed, we will have a new case ready for you to tackle."

Liv nodded, grateful to have her support, especially with Adler, Bianca, and Lorenzo giving her less-than-accepting looks. "Okay, sure thing. I'll brush up on my Warrior skills in the meantime."

She turned, noticing the white tiger at her back. How long had he been there, standing so close to her? He tilted his head to the side, regarding her with a mystified expression, like he too was surprised she'd survived the Kingdom of the Fae.

"Oh, and Ms. Beaufont?" Adler called as Liv strode toward the exit.

She turned, holding her chin high. "Yes?"

"I do hope that you displayed a new level of diplomacy while interacting with Queen Visa," Adler stated. "That would be best for long-term relations."

Liv decided against sharing that she had complimented the queen's ass. "Yes, no worries. As I mentioned before, Queen Visa was quite taken with me."

And she'll stay that way until she realizes the vial of blood she holds isn't mine.

CHAPTER TWENTY

Walking into the training studio brought back memories Liv couldn't deal with just then. Her mother used to bring her up to these rooms, encouraging her to train. When Liv hadn't shown a lot of interest in learning combat magic, her mother had never pressured her, saying there would be time later for such things.

"Your job right now is to be a kid," Guinevere Beaufont would say to her daughter, her beautiful blonde hair up in a messy bun on her head.

"But will you get in trouble with the other Royals if you don't train me?" Liv would ask, having overheard conversations between her father and mother at night when she should have been asleep. It hadn't gone unnoticed by the Sinclairs and others in the House of Seven that the Beauforts didn't abide by the same rigorous training practices as the other families.

Her mother simply smiled, her blue eyes sparkling. "Whose job is it to worry, Olivia?"

"Yours," Liv answered, reciting what her parents had told her a hundred times since she was old enough to fret.

"And what's your job?" Guinevere asked her.

"To be a kid," Liv replied.

"That's right," her mother answered. "There will be time for your training. You can never recapture the freedom of your youth."

In truth, her mother had probably never thought that Liv would need the training. It was unlikely that she'd become a Warrior. Guinevere was the strongest Warrior the House had seen in a century, and if anything happened to her, Ian would take over. He was incredible, driven from a young age. No one expected that something would happen to them both, making Liv the Beaufont Warrior for the House of Seven.

She stood in the middle of the training studio, feeling the surreal aspect of this all. It kept hitting her, sometimes making it hard to breathe.

I'm a Warrior. The one for the Beaufont family, she thought, turning to face the mirror, suddenly feeling very much alone. *I'm all we have left. That doesn't quite feel like enough, but it will have to be.*

"I see you survived Queen Visa," Akio said from the entrance.

Liv had known he was there moments prior to him materializing. Maybe it was being back in the studio that made her more aware of her surroundings. Maybe it was because she realized that more than ever her combat skills were going to need improvement if she was going to survive. She'd been studying the book *Mysterious Creatures* every night, training with Rory on the side, and working on her combat skills on her own. But it wasn't enough. She needed Akio's help if she was going to improve radically.

The Council wasn't going to let up on her, not after the stunt she'd pulled as she revealed her success with the Kingdom of the Fae. But she couldn't help herself. Adler had deserved to learn the truth in a way that put humiliation and surprise on his face. Also, Liv was making her fair share of enemies and would need to know how to defend herself. That was why she was there.

"Against some of the Council's better wishes, yes, I survived," Liv answered, nodding to Akio as he swept into the room. He was wearing the decorative kimono he often sported, his sword strapped to his hip.

His brown eyes smiled even though his face remained placid. "I'm glad to see you return, Liv. I can't say that I didn't worry about your safety. It seems you are full of surprises."

"I'm tactless. That's all," she replied.

Akio looked around the studio, searching for something. "You said you had a weapon you'd chosen?"

Liv withdrew Bellator from the sheath across her back, delighting in the way it felt in her hands. She hadn't spent much time with the sword yet, but looked forward to getting acquainted; bonding with it in a way that would create loyalty between them. That was how Rory had explained it, anyway.

"Where did you get that?" Akio asked, his eyes widening as he stumbled back slightly.

Liv drew in a breath. "I found it," she lied.

His eyes darted between the sword and her face. "Don't tell me. It would be better that way."

"I found it, seriously," she continued, remembering what Rory had said. No one could ever know that he'd made it for her.

Akio nodded. "Yes, 'found it.' That's fine. What is it called?"

Liv hesitated, her eyes running over the smooth hilt and the blue gems adorning it. "It's called Bellator."

Akio did smile then, wrinkles forming around his eyes. "Appropriately named."

"Why? What does Bellator mean?" Liv asked.

Akio's head tilted to the side. "You don't know?"

Liv shook her head.

Akio reached out, hesitating when his fingers were close to the sword. "May I?"

Liv relinquished the sword to him, missing it as soon as it was out of her grasp. His eyes filled with delight when he wrapped his hands around the hilt. He sliced it through the air, its blade making a sharp whizzing sound. He spun around, swinging Bellator with a grace Liv had rarely seen. It looked more like a dance than anything else—a deadly one. When he'd spun back in her direction, he straightened, holding the sword horizontally and presenting it to her.

"I've never held a giant-made sword," Akio stated.

Liv pretended to look surprised. "Giant-made? Well, I'll be."

The glint in his eyes betrayed the expression he was trying to suppress. "And Bellator simply means 'Warrior.'"

Liv's mouth fell open. *That cunning giant,* she thought.

Akio pointed to the sword in her hands, an impressed expression on his face. "I don't know where you 'found' this, but if you hone your skills, you and Bellator will be a formidable force."

"Goodwill," Liv supplied.

"Excuse me?" Akio asked as if he hadn't heard her.

"I picked it up at the Goodwill in WeHo," she explained. "You can find all sorts of treasures there."

"Indeed," he said with a wink.

"Where did you learn to fight?" Akio asked after their third sparring bout.

"I didn't, really," Liv answered. "I always declined the lessons when they were offered."

He shook his head, leaning on his sword, which was thinner than hers and made in the style of the magicians. "It doesn't matter if you were taught or not. Growing up, someone always teaches us how to fight, and usually informally. It's in the passion or integrity or lack thereof that they pass along. I sense a unique boldness in you, Liv, and it comes out when you spar."

Where would that come from, Liv wondered. She didn't know. Her mother was brave and her father opinionated, which was an obviously deadly combination she'd inherited from them.

"I guess my parents taught me how to fight," she stated, holding Bellator but unable to look Akio directly in the eyes.

That was probably why he leaned in to get her attention. "Then focus on them. It is our greatest teachers we must hold in our hearts when we fight. Combat is demoralizing. It's scary facing adversaries. We rarely persevere for self-preservation alone. However, when we remember the ones who made us who we are? Well, we become unstoppable."

Liv had trouble swallowing for a moment, as if her throat had been cut. She managed a nod. "Do we go again?"

Akio sheathed his weapon, nodding at her. "Yes, but I'm going to try to disarm you this time."

"Without a sword?" she asked.

He offered her a sideways smile. "Yes. I think I'll be okay, and your enemy will rarely tell you what they are about to do, so consider yourself at an advantage."

Liv bowed when he did, then straightened. She was ready when Akio darted forward, coming at her like a bull released from a pen. His hands were around her waist. She swung Bellator above her head but suddenly felt disoriented. The other Warrior moved faster than she could follow, like a phantom. She blinked, wondering where he'd disappeared to. Shaking, she spun around, but he was already at her back again, his arms constricting her. Grunting, she tried to overpower him but knew it was useless almost from the start. Bellator clanged to the ground from the pressure of his grip.

Liv stumbled back, shaking her head. "How did you do that? How do you move so fast?"

"It's a perk of not holding a weapon," Akio admitted. "We gain and we lose when we hold a weapon. They make us deadly, but often slow us down. Never forget that wielding a weapon isn't always the right approach. It depends on the battle."

"Will you teach me how to move like that?" Liv asked.

Akio nodded. "Yes, but first let me teach you how to hold your sword." He picked up Bellator and extended it to her. "This time, don't think of yourself as carrying this sword. Rather, believe it is an extension of you. When you swing Bellator, see it as part of you."

She didn't want to tell him that sounded like hippie crap, but that was exactly what it seemed like to her. However, she'd never seen anyone move like Akio Takahashi. He was fluid like water and unrivaled in his agility. The way he moved was almost unbelievable. This wasn't a competitor she wanted to go head to head with.

"Okay," Liv agreed, taking Bellator. "An extension of my arm."

"Once you conquer that idea, you'll unlock any benefits that sword can offer you."

"How do you know it will?" Liv asked.

He gave her a skeptical glare. "A sword like this, that was seemingly made for you, has many ways to aid its bearer. However, you have to prove yourself worthy of the power it would lend you. It's important to remember that a Warrior and her sword should be partners in battle. Currently, you're acting like you're in charge, and it is your tool."

Liv worked to cover the tension his words had unearthed. "I found the sword," she lied.

He nodded. "At the Goodwill. I remember." He bowed again, signaling the start of another sparring match.

This time she didn't react to his first attempts to pin her. Instead, she allowed Bellator to lead her like they were a couple on the dance floor. Again Akio disappeared behind, but instead of swinging around, she felt the sword urge her backward. She threw herself in that direction, knowing that Akio was there. Slamming into him, she took him by surprise, knocking him to the ground. Swinging Bellator over her head, she brought it down, stopping inches from his face.

"Very good," he said in a raspy voice, sweat beading on his forehead. "I think that's good for today."

CHAPTER TWENTY-ONE

"You did promise me you'd tell me before you set off for the Kingdom of the Fae," Clark said, leaning against a bookcase in the library, his arms crossed.

"I said I'd tell you before I went off to get myself killed, and I didn't do that, did I?" Liv retorted, sitting on one of the oversized couches and flipping through the book Rory had given her, *Mysterious Creatures.*

"Liv," he said in that warning voice he always used.

"There was nothing you could have done, and you know full well that I had to complete the case," Liv reasoned. "So I figured out a strategy and executed it."

Clark released a tight laugh. "The Council is still stumped by how you did it. Your notes said you dressed like a fae and appealed to Queen Visa from a different angle."

Liv nearly snorted. "Yeah, I sort of left out some details."

"Well, how did you get the queen to agree?"

Liv looked around, catching Sophia's eyes on the other

side of the sitting area. She was curled up with several books, her attention mostly on her sister and brother, although she pretended to be reading most of the time.

"I've got the spy-finder spells operating," Sophia stated. "You should be safe."

Liv nodded. "I enlisted the help of a fae."

Clark sighed. "The same one you gave the Warrior's ring to?"

"I didn't give it to him," Liv countered. "He's borrowing it so we can discover the lost memory."

Clark motioned to the wall covered with the founders' language. "However, if we had it right now, we could try to open the ancient chamber or whatever is behind this wall."

Liv reluctantly agreed. "Yeah, it's the first time I've been here in a while that Stefan Ludwig isn't hanging around."

Clark dragged in a breath. "Between the three of us, I don't know about him."

"Why?" Liv asked, leaning forward and thinking about the time Stefan had tried to follow her.

"I don't know," Clark replied. "I'm certain he's hiding something from the Council."

Liv was sure he was, but what she hadn't determined was if it was something good or bad. Not all things Warriors kept secret from the Council were bad. She could attest to that.

Sophia squeezed her eyes shut and waved her finger through the air. In front of them, a round pillow materialized on the table, frilly pink ribbons and lace adorning it.

Liv and Clark watched with curiosity as the girl referenced one of the many books beside her. Then she closed her eyes again and stroked her finger through the air as if she were writing in cursive. On the front of the pillow, the letters P-L-A-T-O stitched into place.

Liv laughed. "You made him a bed?"

Sophia shook her head. "It's not supposed to have so much lace."

"He's going to love it," Liv stated.

"Do you think he'll stay with you here at the House of Seven?" Sophia asked.

Both Liv and Clark answered at once, her saying "yes," and him replying the opposite with a sharp, "No."

Liv cast him an annoyed stare. "Of course, he will."

"Come on, Liv," Clark argued. "We can't have a lynx staying with us. What if the Council finds out?"

"They won't," Liv retorted. "He's a master at hiding himself. No one has ever caught him."

Clark lowered his chin. "Which is exactly why you have to be wary of that creature. He's not normal."

"Says the magician born with royal blood that can open ancient chambers," Liv stated dryly.

"This is different, Liv," Clark stated. "You're involving yourself with lynxes and giants and fae and mortals. It isn't safe."

"Why?" she countered.

"We've already been through this," Clark said with a tired sigh, pushing away from the shelf.

"Yes, and all you can offer me is prejudice that explains nothing," Liv countered. "What if we're all separate, but that's not how it was meant to be? What if we forged bonds, and I'm not referring to those stuffy little agreements the Council makes me negotiate."

"Liv, I'm all for being open-minded, but you can't

delude yourself into thinking they are the same as us," Clark explained. "Magicians were put on this Earth to protect magic. We're the civilized race that has always craved justice with magic. We will sacrifice freedoms to ensure that powers aren't abused."

Liv flipped through her book, thoroughly tired of having this conversation with Clark. She was surprised when the book stopped on a random page that didn't feel so random. She sat up, clearing her throat. "Magicians are one of the least understood creatures. Considered to be more civilized than the other races, they've been governing since the beginning, with the inception of the House of Seven. However, their practices are often seen as arbitrary by outsiders, and their methods unchecked. Many wonder how they became the constabularies of the magical world without question. Is it that the elves simply don't care, and the giants prefer anonymity, and the gnomes like having a governing body that does their dirty work? There is no consensus on this, and the history doesn't tell a straightforward story. It is clear that the one magical race cloaked in the most mystery is the magicians."

Liv shut the book, giving Clark a victorious look.

"Written by a giant," he said, having spied the name of the author: Bermuda Laurens.

Liv rolled her eyes. "It's not just in this book. I can't find the names of the founding families anywhere."

"They are in the ancient chamber," Clark reasoned.

"But why? Why isn't there this giant history book that explains exactly how the House of Seven was formed?" Liv argued.

"Because that would undoubtedly detail our weaknesses," Clark fired back.

"You say that in an almost rehearsed manner," Liv said. "Is that one of Adler's lines?"

"No," Clark said, biting off the word. Then he shook his head. "Yeah, fine. But he's right. If we put our history out there for everyone to read about the magic that formed the House of Seven, that would put weapons in our enemies' hands. They might find out how to enter the House. They would know how we are governed. They would know more than they should."

"And yet, we keep it such a secret that even the royals don't know the history," Liv countered.

"It's for the best," Clark said, rubbing his knuckles into his forehead the way he did when he was frustrated.

"I'm not so sure." It was actually Sophia who communicated her dissent.

Clark shook his head at his little sister. "I agree there is something going on. I still haven't figured out what the deal is with the canisters, but that's separate from what you're talking about."

"Maybe," Liv said, uncertainty in her tone.

"And despite my digging, I can't find anything nefarious about the storage area you discovered in the monastery," Clark stated.

"How so?" Liv inquired.

"Well, those canisters of magic are rare—"

"Not if you were in the room I was in," Liv interrupted. "There were several hundred. It was almost blinding."

"Right, but in the scheme of things, they are considered rare," Clark said dismissively. "From everything I can learn from doing research, storage units of magic like that are dangerous because there are no controls on them. Anyone, like unregistered magicians, can use them to do anything they want and get away with it. You'll remember that Valentino was ready to use the power for his own selfish gains. It's not a safe form of magic, so maybe they are being stored in that place to keep them away from those who would abuse them."

"Maybe," Liv said, reluctance in her voice again. She saw a figure materialize at the far end of a row. Stefan's image might not have even registered, except that he'd poked his head into the light of a neighboring row. Once he caught sight of the three in the reading area, he'd disappeared back into the row. Why was he always hanging out in this area? Had he been trying to spy on them and realized that charms had been used to prevent that?

Liv leaned forward. "Hey, Soph, will you put a disguising spell on me?"

"For sure," the young magician squealed, hopping up to her feet, her pink dress and curls bouncing with the movement.

"Wait, why are you having her do it?" Clark questioned. "You know how to do it, right? Please tell me the giant hasn't neglected your training that badly?"

Liv wanted to ignore him, but not at the expense of Rory's good name. "Of course he hasn't. I daresay you couldn't find me in a game of hide-and-seek."

Sophia giggled. Clark scowled. It was the new family dynamic that Liv was becoming accustomed to, and sort of enjoying.

"I want Sophia to do it so that it's not trackable, since

her magic isn't registered yet." Liv waved in a "hurry up" fashion. "Will you please? I'm going to follow someone if I can catch up with him."

Sophia nodded, pressing her finger to her chin, thinking. "Here, how about this?" She waved her hand in the air, and the next thing Liv knew her form had disappeared.

"Did you make me invisible?" Liv asked, impressed. She had expected Sophia to make it so she blended into her surroundings or took on an image another person expected to see. There were literally hundreds of disguising spells, but invisibility was rare and took an extraordinary amount of energy.

Sophia nodded with a suddenly tired face. "Do you like it?"

"I love it," Liv said, wanting to rush forward to scoop up the little girl, who looked like she might pass out at any moment.

To her surprise, Clark stepped forward, looking in the direction he'd last seen Liv. "Go on, then. Do what you were going to do. I'll take care of this little one. She'll need a nap now."

Liv smiled. "And a cookie."

"Three," Sophia said, sounding a bit delirious.

Liv didn't look back as she hurried off, hoping to catch up with Stefan before he got away.

CHAPTER TWENTY-TWO

The streets of the city were strangely deserted when Liv stepped through the portal Stefan had created. Rory had recently taught her how to stall a portal from closing by, in effect, throwing her foot in.

The chilly air next to the canal was a stark contrast to the weather in Santa Monica where they'd come from.

Stefan had already traveled quickly down the cobbled street by the time Liv snuck through the portal, slipping through just before it closed. She slid into the shadows of a building, its windows decorated with planters overflowing with flowers. In the distance, she heard laughter and jazz music. This place was cheery, even with the sun setting and the lamps flickering to life.

Liv peeked out of her hiding spot as Stefan disappeared around a corner. The invisibility cloak that Sophia had put on her had worn off, but it had gotten her this far. "What are you up to, Stefan?" Liv muttered to herself.

"This is Amsterdam," Plato said, who was now at her side.

"What's that supposed to mean?" Liv asked, peering down at the cat.

"Well, there are a number of things the Warrior could be doing. For instance, in that direction is the famed red light district." He tilted his head toward where Stefan had gone.

"Eww."

"Or he could be working a case for the Council," Plato reasoned.

"He might, but something tells me that he's up to something or working a rogue case," Liv stated, coming out of her spot and hurrying down the lane.

"Why, because that's what you do in your spare time?" Plato asked.

Liv ignored him. "Stefan followed me. Logic would prove that he was suspicious of my activities because he's also hiding something."

"Oh, so you mean a liar is the first to think someone is lying? A sneak is always paranoid that someone is spying on them? It's like a form of reflection?"

"Yes, that's the idea," Liv answered.

"Or maybe he was just following you because you *were* in fact up to something: stealing treasures from museums and breaking into monasteries," Plato mused.

"Yeah, I don't think so. Stefan Ludwig is up to something too, and I'd like to figure it out."

"It seems that many in the House of Seven have that mystery and secret cloaking them," Plato stated.

"And the only way to find out the secrets Ian and Reese alluded to is to investigate," Liv stated.

"So, do you think that Stefan is tied up in their deaths?" Plato asked.

"I'm not ruling anything out, but if he is, I'm going to shove Bellator straight down his throat and make him wish he'd never met Liv Beaufont."

Plato smirked. "That should be your motto."

"It totally should be," she agreed. "I think most people wish they'd never met me, but that's mostly because I'm sort of a pain in the ass."

"Sort of?" Plato questioned.

"Watch it, lynx, or you'll wish you'd never befriended me."

He shook his head. "I never regret a decision. Call it my expert foresight."

Liv regarded him with a curious stare. "Right. And how is it that you found me that one day on the streets five years ago? You've never mentioned it."

"Haven't I?" Plato countered, his eyes focusing up ahead. "Looks like Stefan is getting away. We should continue this later."

"If I know you, that means 'never.'" Liv doubled her pace before coming to a halt at the corner where Stefan had disappeared. The glow of the red lights reflected along the road there, giving a hint of what could be found around the bend. She didn't know what she'd find Stefan doing, but she hoped it wasn't visiting a brothel. Then again, that was more innocent than the other horrid possibilities going through her mind. Could he be behind the missing canisters of magic? Was he helping to cover up the secrets about the House of Seven? Did he know what happened to her parents? She had so many questions, and the only way she was going to get answers was to pursue every lead.

Peering around the corner, Liv found a row of shops, their 'merchandise' dancing in display windows. People strolled by on the sidewalk, but to her disappointment, Stefan wasn't around. *Damn it, did I let him get away?* Liv wondered sourly.

Plato's ear twitched to the side.

"You hear something?" she asked him, noticing the movement.

"I hear a lot of things, but there's one sound in particular that I haven't heard in quite some time."

"Which way?" Liv inquired.

"Around the back of that shop." Plato indicated the store in front of them.

Nodding, Liv edged along the wall, trying to not move too quickly but also not look like a sneak following a magician. It was a balancing act. Most of the people on the street at that hour didn't seem to pay her much attention, too entranced in conversations with the person beside them or the moves of the women under the red lights.

Liv hurried through the alley between the shops, which was mostly in darkness. She negotiated around puddles and over anything that would make a noise and give away her presence. Then she heard it—the noise Plato must have picked up on. A slow screeching, like metal scraping against metal.

Liv slid up next to the wall, a violent shiver rippling down her back. She knew for a fact that whatever that noise was, it wasn't as innocent as someone pushing a metal cart over a metal incline or whatever it was. In her core, she knew the noise was connected to evil and darkness the likes of which she'd never met.

"What is that?" she mouthed to Plato.

He blinked at her, seeming to deliberate. *Pull out your sword,* he answered in a voice she heard in her head, as if they'd suddenly forged a telepathic link.

Pulling Bellator from its sheath, Liv continued down the alley, the sound growing fainter as she neared it.

Ragged breaths that sounded like cardboard being sawed in half replaced the screeching. Liv halted at the corner, preparing herself, or at least attempting to do so. When she peered around the corner, she almost gasped, nearly exposing her presence.

Nothing in the world could have actually prepared her for what she saw.

CHAPTER TWENTY-THREE

Stefan never got used to the smell. How could anyone? It haunted him at night, lingering in his nostrils, reminding him of what he'd become if he didn't find the cure to that which plagued him.

He'd kill himself first, though. He'd already made up his mind about that one. But he still had time. Not much, but hopefully enough.

The demon he'd clutched in his hand wasn't the one who had bit him. Stefan knew that. It had the same red, slimy skin, veins running down the side of its face like its insides were on the outside. However, this demon had several horns around its cheekbones and many more on its head.

Sabatore, the demon who'd sunk his rows of razor-sharp teeth into Stefan's arm, marking him with a curse, had two prominent curved horns mounted on his head and a silver ring through his nose.

"Tell me where I can find him?" Stefan urged in a tight

whisper, holding the demon up higher on the wall and pressing the sword deeper into its torso.

The sound that spilled over the demon's quivering lips was not intelligible.

"I know you speak English, you good-for-nothing piece of shit." All the demons spoke every language—Stefan had learned that—although they preferred to communicate through howls and screeches that haunted mortals long into the night. These were the beasts who corrupted good people, filling them with greed and paranoia, making them commit horrible acts and perpetuating evil in the world. Yes, evil would exist without demons. It always had, but as they spread, so did hate so vicious it sought to take over the world.

Stefan knew it was about balance. And achieving that balance, helping maintain it, had been his job. Now his mission was personal: to hunt down the beast who had marked him, trying to make him just like Sabatore. The irony that the demon hunter might one day become the very thing he hated wasn't lost on Stefan.

If Raina knew, she wouldn't think it was ironic, though. His sister would be devastated if she knew he'd been bitten, which was why she didn't know. Besides that, she might not be able to keep the news from the Council, and Stefan would be gone at once. That was the rule, and there were no exceptions. Those bitten were contaminated by evil, the venom surging through them, ready to take over at any point, the corruption starting from within.

I have more time, he told himself. *I have to.* The alternative was unfathomable, and yet, Stefan knew how demons spread, marking magicians or elves or giants, spreading their disease and the evil they symbolized.

For most of his career as a Warrior, he'd studied and trained for how best to track and kill demons. It wasn't until it got personal that he began to research in the library how the virus was spread and how to stop it. He needed Sabatore's blood. That was the only way to form the antidote. Hester had told him that much but hadn't promised it would work. She'd given him one final warning before promising not to tell the Council.

"Your secret is safe with me for a little while," the councilor had told him in an aching voice. "However, when the time comes, you won't be able to fight it. The demon will take you over, and Stefan will be lost forever."

He shook his head. "I won't let that happen. I'll end things first."

With pain in her eyes, Hester looked away. "I'm sorry to say that many as strong as you, have had the same intention, but it was too late by that point. It happens fast, sometimes with no warning. One moment you're you, and the next… Well, you're changed forever and also gone forever. Once the demon takes over, there is no coming back."

Stefan had realized what she'd meant when the voices started in his head; the echoes of the demon he would become. It wanted to swallow him whole, taking over his life and making him haunt this world for eternity. Stefan battled that demon presently in his head, shaking away the chanting that often woke him at night.

"Tell me where Sabatore is and your death will be

swift," Stefan threatened the demon he had pinned against the wall.

"You can't kill me," the demon said with a gurgled hiss.

Stefan laughed morbidly. "That's what they all say."

With one hand still on the hilt of his sword pinning the demon to the wall, its hands and legs restrained, Stefan pulled a red depour from inside his cape.

The demon began to squirm more furiously, thrashing its head forward, trying to impale Stefan. He held it steady, though, used to how they freaked at this stage of the game.

Pressing the sword more firmly into the demon, Stefan began to recite the magical text that released the demon from the Earth, but more importantly released that which was trapped within it. "*Metuendas Dcemonis violentias, dimittere unam animam de amicae tuae involasti, permittens eos tandem.*"

The words he spoke had a new meaning for Stefan now. A personal one: *Demon, release the soul of the one you stole, allowing them to finally rest.*

A scream that would haunt Stefan's dreams spilled from the demon's mouth, filling the night air with a sound most would dismiss or not hear at all. Metal on metal: that was how best it was described. A sharp noise that cut at the demon within Stefan, begging him not to continue. Not to murder the demon before him. He shook off the urge wrapping around his insides.

In one swift movement, Stefan pulled the sword from the demon, launching his other hand into the gaping wound, inserting the red depour, which was the size of a rose petal, into the demon.

"*Ad infernum, a quo factum est tibi in sempiternum in ipse comburetis,*" Stefan finished, dropping the demon and striding away.

As the words he'd spoken streaked across Stefan's mind, the demon burst into flames, consumed by the fire that would finally end it: *Return to hell, from which you came, where forever you shall burn.*

Stefan turned when he was a safe distance from the demon, which was quickly reduced to ash. He pulled his handkerchief from his cape, wiping the blood from his hands first and then his sword.

At his back, he heard a noise and spun around at once, finding only shadows and darkness.

No, all was safe in Amsterdam for now, he told himself.

The sounds of life on the nearby streets were suddenly more peaceful, as if the knowledge of the demon's death had spread at once through the city. However, no one knew when a demon was slain, only that their nightmares had been given a respite.

However, that wasn't the case for Stefan Ludwig. His nightmare was only getting worse.

CHAPTER TWENTY-FOUR

None of it made sense.

Liv tried dismissing what she'd seen in the back alleys of Amsterdam as purely House business, but it didn't seem right to her. Plato had remained quiet for a long time, allowing her to talk things through as she tinkered with an alarm clock that should have been past repair. However, magic made many things possible, if she could just figure out all the things that were wrong with it. The clock was about like Stefan Ludwig. Liv couldn't figure him out.

"Hunting demons is one thing, but interrogating them?" Liv said for what felt like the hundredth time.

Perched close by, Plato simply nodded again, still not offering any insights.

"Who is Sabatore, and why is Stefan looking for him?" she mused, turning the alarm clock over in her hands, not really looking at it, but rather, lost in thought. "And why question a demon? They aren't trustworthy in the least. It's like asking Adler Sinclair for advice. Whatever he says is total bullshit and probably only serves his greedy, mysterious agenda."

"And here I thought you and Adler were starting to get along," Plato joked.

Liv shook her head. "I just don't get it. Sabatore. Have I heard that name before?"

"I don't think so," Plato stated with confidence.

Liv looked up. "How do you know?"

"I just know," he said smugly.

"You're not with me all the time. I do have a life away from you, you know?"

"Do you?" he challenged.

She shrugged. "Yeah, you're right. I probably don't. Even when I'm alone, I'm pretty certain you're spying on me somehow."

"Have you worked out the Latin he was speaking?" Plato asked.

She sighed. "You know I haven't, not all the way. Are you ready to fill in the rest for me, or are you going to pretend that you have no idea?"

"How would you like me to proceed with this one? Give you hints? Tell you everything? Act like I don't know?"

Liv couldn't help but laugh. "Well, I know it was an incantation, but a bit more complex than the ones I'm used to." She pointed to the book, *Mysterious Creatures*. "I can't find anything like that in that book, but I'm going to search the library, too."

"It's a banishing spell," Plato said with a yawn. "It's meant to trap demons in the underworld where they supposedly came from."

"I got that bit about hell when he mentioned *infernum*,"

Liv said. "I just didn't understand the first part. Shockingly, my Latin is a little rusty after five years of hardly using it while working in a repair shop."

"Yes, I'm not sure I got the entirety of the message either," Plato related.

"Well, tell me what you think you heard."

"Something, something. People talking on the streets. Gurgling noise. Shallow breathing. A siren in the distance—"

"I meant the bit Stefan said," Liv stated, interrupting Plato's attempt at bad humor.

"Oh, that," Plato said. "Roughly, I think he said, *Demon, release the soul of the one you stole, allowing them to finally rest."*

Liv raised an eyebrow at the cat. "Oh, is that 'roughly' what you heard? Sounds pretty exact, and maybe a bit rehearsed."

He shrugged. "What can I say? I used to know a demon hunter. The verse sort of came back to me."

Liv gave him a conspiratorial look. "And this incantation…it's used to kill the demon?"

Plato shook his head. "No, there are several ways to kill a demon. The way he did it was one of them, using fire. But the incantation is supposed to trap the demon, and more importantly, release the soul they leech onto."

A shiver ran over Liv's arms. "So demons are actually people?"

"Yes," Plato affirmed. "Trapped souls are the vehicle the demons use."

Liv sneered. "Like renting a car."

"Yes, but there's no steep insurance or new car smell," Plato joked.

"That's so sad," she related. "I had no idea that demons were so awful. Just the look of that thing was enough to haunt my dreams forever."

"Not to mention the smell," Plato added.

"Yes, I'm guessing that demon hygiene is pretty awful. And I bet they never floss."

Plato lowered himself to the workbench, making Liv look up at once. That was what he always did just before someone entered the shop, trying to make himself inconspicuous.

Liv pushed the alarm clock to the side, ready to greet the person who walked through the door, expecting one of her usual customers.

The person who staggered through the door wasn't anyone she'd expected.

Liv bolted up, every inch of her body tense and ready to fight, but she didn't know why.

The man who entered the shop didn't have a familiar face, but there was definitely something about him. She couldn't remember where she'd seen his long face or shifty eyes, but something told her that she had, and it wasn't good. Plato had disappeared, which didn't make her feel any better as she reached behind her on a nearby shelf for a screwdriver. It wasn't Bellator, but it was going to have to do.

The man pretended to look over the contents on the front shelf, his eyes cutting over to Liv every several seconds. The more she studied him, the less certain she was that she actually knew him. Maybe she was being paranoid. There were tons of shifty characters in WeHo. That was actually part of the charm, she thought with a mental laugh.

"Can I help you find something?" Liv asked, noticing that he didn't have an appliance in his hands, and therefore probably didn't need anything repaired.

The man shook his head roughly, his hands pressed into his jeans pockets.

She could have sworn she knew him, but where from? His head was bald, and...his ears. They flickered, like a picture on television.

She blinked, trying to decide what she'd just seen.

"The Santa Ana winds picking up out there?" Liv asked, trying to make conversation or do anything to reveal more clues.

The man shook his head, not giving anything away. He was wearing a loose-fitting t-shirt and knit pants with sneakers. There really wasn't anything out of the ordinary about him. Holding the screwdriver behind her back, Liv tried to make sense of what she'd thought she'd seen. Had it been a figment of her imagination?

Barking from the back made both the man and Liv start. She spun around, momentarily putting her back to the man. John was here. Maybe that was a good thing. Then she'd snap out of all this pondering and actually get some work done. It was only making her crazy.

Feeling something stir behind her, Liv turned around to find the man closer than before, just on the other side of the workbench. She forced a smile, holding up the screwdriver. "Sure I can't help you find something? What brings you in today?"

He sneered, showing a mouthful of yellow teeth. Instantly she was sure she'd seen this man before, but where?

"I don't think you have what I'm looking for here," the man said, his voice bringing with it familiarity.

"What are you looking for?" Liv asked, her fingers tightening on the screwdriver.

"It's old," the man answered, a haunting quality to his voice.

Liv searched the space around the man, taking in the obstacles between them in case a fight broke out. She wanted to be prepared for anything.

"Old? Like a vintage record player?" she asked.

He shook his head and again his ears flickered, for a second appearing much more pointy than they appeared most of the time.

He was an elf! She knew it at once.

"Is it an electronic device?" she questioned, buying time.

The man shook his head again, stepping to the side, his eyes intent on her.

"I've got your coffee. Want me to bring it up there?" John called from the back.

"No!" Liv answered at once. "I mean, no, thank you. I'll be back there in a minute. Stay where you are."

The elf took another step in her direction.

"What do you want?" Liv dared to ask. His glamour was fading, and with it any pretenses.

"You know," he sang, his voice raspy.

Liv didn't know, but she felt that she should.

"I'm not a mind reader. Why don't you tell me what you want?"

The deranged look in the man's eyes was unlike anything Liv had seen. He appeared more scarred from the inside out than any homeless person she'd seen on the streets. At her core, the man frightened her; not because of what he might do to her, but rather for John and the shop.

"Give it to me," the man said, his voice almost pleading as he stepped forward. "All you have to do is give it to me and they'll end my suffering."

Liv stumbled back as the man lifted his arm. Reacting instantly, Liv leaned to the side, throwing her foot into his chest and knocking him across a display case. The sound of metal crashing to the floor assaulted her ears. The elf had gone down faster than she'd expected, but he'd also gotten back into position quicker than he should have.

"What the heck is that?" John called from the back.

"Nothing!" Liv yelled. "Stay back there!" She raised her hand, directing it at the man, but it was too late; she saw that at once. He released a blast of water, and it was like being hit by a firefighter's hose. Water blasted her so hard in the midsection through her clothes that it burned her skin.

It pushed her back hard into the shelf behind her, making a loud noise. Her spine hit the edge, making her fall to the floor.

"Liv!" John called.

There were rushing footsteps as the man stepped closer to her. This was Liv's chance to attack him as he reloaded, ready to assault her again. She rolled over and took this opportunity to direct her hand at the door to the back, locking it so John couldn't get through.

The elf attacked her again, this time throwing himself

at her. His fists missed her face as Liv dove over the fallen appliances, grabbing the man by the back of the shirt and tossing him into a different display case. He went down hard, seeming to have lost a great deal of energy. Liv was just about to throw another attack at him when he wailed like a child and cradled his arm.

This gave her pause. She didn't know how to deal with someone who reacted with such emotion. Allowing him to climb to his feet, Liv noticed that a wound had opened on the man's arm and was pouring blood. Everything slowed down in her mind as she spied the black spider-like veins radiating away from the wound, reaching around the man's arm, crawling up his shoulder, and then from under his shirt up to his neck.

"You," Liv said in a hushed voice, recognizing the elf she'd cut with Turbinger.

He shook his head as he held his arm, the spider veins now covering his face. "This isn't over," he warned, and turned and raced from the shop.

CHAPTER TWENTY-FIVE

Liv was shaking so violently from adrenaline and anger that she let the elf get away. It had happened so fast, and the shock that he'd come back for her—for the sword—had given her momentary pause.

In her mind, she should have stopped him. Detained him. Taken him to the House of Seven. But what was she going to say? "This is the elf I stole the giant's sword back from when I broke into the National History Museum. Oh, and by the way, that was me. Surprise!"

And there had been John to worry about. He was currently beating on the door to the back that she'd locked to protect him. With a wave of her hand, the locks disappeared and the door released, John stumbling through it immediately.

With wide eyes, he stared at the chaos, his eyes finding Liv at once. "Are you all right? What happened?"

She nodded, trying to will a full breath into her lungs. "I'm fine. And I'm sorry about this." She motioned to the front of the shop, which was destroyed, shelves knocked over and appliances and their parts strewn across the floor.

He shook off the apology. "I don't care about the shop." He looked her over, his brow furrowing before he pulled off his leather jacket and offered it to her. "Here, you're shivering. Take this."

It wasn't until then that Liv remembered she was drenched in the water the elf had sprayed at her. She declined John's offer, using a drying spell to evaporate the water. That didn't help with the pain where the water had burned her skin.

"Do you want to tell me what happened here?" John asked, looking at the wreckage.

"Would you believe that Plato got spooked and made this big mess?" Liv said, noticing when the lynx materialized on the other side of the workstation and jumped up so John could see him too.

"And the water?" John asked, pointing to the puddles on the concrete floor.

"Oh, yeah, well, he knocked over the water dish I had just given him when he got spooked," Liv lied. "I think he saw his own shadow or something. You know how touchy he can be."

"Liv," John said, crossing his arms and drawing out her name.

"Okay, fine. It wasn't Plato," Liv said, going to work picking up the broken devices. She would have used her magic, but it felt weakened from the battle.

"Who was it?" John asked, then shook his head. "No, never mind. You don't have to tell me."

"John, I think I need to move into the House of Seven

early," Liv said, and couldn't believe the words had fallen out of her mouth.

Apparently, John couldn't either because he looked up suddenly, the broom and dustpan in his hands. "What?"

"Well, I mean, I was planning on doing it at the end of the month when that horrid lawyer forced you out of here," Liv began. "However, I think I need to quit and move before that. Like in the next hour."

John set the broom down and gave Liv a serious look. "Are you in danger?"

She nodded, then changed the direction of her head to shake it. "I'm always in danger. That's the nature of the job. But more importantly, you're in danger. And look at what that jerk did to your shop!"

John actually laughed at this. "I've done worse things to it after a night of whiskey. For the life of me, I don't know why I think I can repair a damn thing when I'm drunk. Then I end up tripping on a cord and knocking over an entire shelf of stuff."

Liv didn't laugh. "John, I'm serious. That deranged elf is going to be back. He all but promised it."

"Well, then go to the House of Seven so that you're safe," John stated. "You said they had security measures. Lord knows I can't protect you very well. The locks on your apartment are a bit of a joke, but in my defense, you won't let me put any more on there."

Liv quit cleaning up and gave John her full attention, feeling the weight of the situation like a great burden on her heart. "John, this is serious. If that elf had gone after you? Well, I don't like to think about what would have happened."

"Don't..." John said his voice cracking. "Don't leave here and quit just because you're worried about me. We don't have that much time before...well, before it's all over. Before I move and the shop is gone. If you need to quit because you have to focus on your Warrior duties or you need to be in a place that's safer, then do that. I'll support you. I'll help you pack. I was planning on it anyway. But don't you do anything because you're worried about me. I know you locked that door so I couldn't get out here and help."

He pointed at the back door, his arm shaking.

"John, I had to—"

He cut her off, shaking his head. "I may not be a Warrior with magical powers, but I can take care of myself, Liv. I've been doing it for a long time, and I won't have you thinking you have to protect me."

This was the same argument he'd thrown up when she'd offered to fight the lawyer and whoever else was forcing him out of the building. There was a pride in his eyes that she hadn't questioned then, and something told her not to argue with now. He looked strong, and also close to breaking, like all she had to do was walk out that door in the name of protecting him and it would undo him. They didn't have much time left together, and she understood that he didn't want it tarnished with his safety and magic.

"John, I'm sorry," Liv said, looking at the wreckage. "I'll clean all this up."

He waved her off. "It isn't a police officer's fault when a criminal breaks into a house, and it isn't your fault when the bad guys come after you. It's a part of the territory. And

Liv, I'd much rather have you around and criminals tearing up my shop than the alternative."

She didn't know what to say. Nothing seemed adequate in her mind. Thankfully the door clanged as someone entered, interrupting the moment.

Liv spun, ready to jump in front of John and defend him. She softened with relief at the sight of Rory.

He stood stock still, his eyes scanning the shop. "What happened?"

Liv gazed at John and Rory. This was going to create a new level of complexity for everyone. Looked like it was about to be Honesty Hour.

"The elf came back, looking for Turbinger," Liv explained.

"Turbinger?" John asked as Rory seemed to process.

"Yeah, it's a—"

"Book," Rory lied, cutting Liv off.

Liv shook her head. "No, it's a sword."

Rory shot her an angry look.

"He's already in this," Liv argued. "The least he deserves is the truth. He already knows that you're a giant, so we might as well put everything on the table."

"Liv, it isn't safe," Rory began, keeping his gaze off John.

"Not safe?" Liv questioned. "An elf came to John's shop and tried to blast me through the wall. The sword is doing strange things to him. I think John deserves our honesty at this point."

"It's better if you just stay out of this," Rory said, still not looking at John.

"I'm already in this," John stated. "Until the last day of

the month, I'm all in. And if you two don't like it, you can just…well, eat Pickle's turds."

The laugh jumped out of Liv's mouth without her expecting it.

Rory laughed too, the tension broken by John's ridiculous sense of humor.

John stepped forward, looking up at the giant. "I might be a mortal and not understand the magical world." He scratched his head. "I admit that it doesn't always look right to me, like I'm not seeing it clearly. Hell, some of the things Liv shows me I forget later, as if I hadn't seen them at all. Who knows why? However, I'll tell you what I told her, and that's that I don't want the people I care about running away in order to protect me. I'm already involved, so don't shut me out now."

Rory thought about that for a moment and then nodded his head slowly. "Okay, but we just don't want anything bad happening to you."

"You two are like a broken record player." John chuckled. "Of course, give me a chance to tinker with that record player and I'd have it as good as new."

Liv laughed, but Rory remained stoic, his eyes searching the wreckage.

"You say it was the elf from before?" he asked Liv.

She nodded. "And he promised to return."

Rory shook his head. "He won't have much longer. You cut him with the sword, right?"

John looked back and forth between the two, following the exchange.

"Yes, and the wound appeared to be infected," Liv answered.

"No, it's not infected. You don't have to fatally stab someone with Turbinger unless you want their death to be immediate," Rory explained. "Simply cutting them with the blade will eventually lead to death. It's why it's the most deadly weapon on Earth, and therefore in my protection."

"But I got the impression the elf thought if he got hold of the sword he'd be okay," Liv stated.

Rory dismissed this at once. "That's a false rumor. There is no cure for a mark from Turbinger."

"Then we won't have to worry about the elf for much longer," John said, injecting cheerfulness into his words.

Rory's face didn't display the same hope. "I fear the elf will grow even madder before his end. They usually do. Desperation will set in."

"That means he'll be back," Liv said, thinking. "And the sword…is it safe?"

The sigh that fell out of Rory's mouth didn't fill her with confidence. "It's safe enough, but after this, I'll have to increase security measures. I knew someone wanted to get to the sword, but this complicates things."

"What can I do?" Liv asked.

Rory looked her over in that way he had, concern spilling from his eyes. "You can eat. How much magic did you use fighting him?"

"Not much, but I guess it was enough to deplete my reserves," Liv answered.

John clapped his hands, stepping between them. "That settles it. I'm taking you two out for pizza."

Liv rolled her eyes. "We need to clean up the shop and figure out how we're going to deal with this."

John dug into his pocket, his change rattling. "I see no

better way of doing that than over an extra-large pizza." He withdrew a handful of quarters. "And how about a few rounds of pinball?"

Liv couldn't help but laugh. She might have been putting John in danger, but he was absolutely one of the best things for her morale. "Okay, but I think we'll need two extra-large pizzas." She leaned forward, cupping her mouth as if she were trying to hide what she was saying from Rory. "Remember, he's a giant."

"I heard that," Rory stated. "And I'll stick with a salad."

Liv gave him a sideways look. "What, are you on keto and watching your figure?"

He shook his head. "I'm lactose-intolerant."

CHAPTER TWENTY-SIX

Liv couldn't believe it, but she was actually looking forward to getting assigned a case from the Council. As they'd ordered, she'd taken a few days off after her successful completion of the fae case. It had been nice to clean her apartment and have extra time with John and work on her sparring skills with Akio, but she wanted a case, even if it was something ridiculous like grooming a centaur or telling gnomes they needed to bathe every fortnight. She figured that since Queen Visa hadn't killed her, she'd go back to getting lame cases, which she didn't mind so much.

What she wanted most, besides for John to stay and his shop not be sold to dumb investors, was to get her mind off things. He wasn't going to allow her or Rory to interfere, although they all but begged him while they were eating pizza. The giant had picked over his salad like a dainty southern debutante who was afraid to eat in front of a potential suitor, grimacing as Liv stuffed greasy pizza with double pepperoni into her mouth.

What he'd liked even less was her insistence that they find a potion that cured him of his lactose problems. Apparently, giants were against such things as potions, preferring to go the all-natural approach with their digestive systems.

When Liv entered the Chamber of the Tree, she was surprised to find she was the only Warrior there that day. The white tiger was standing next to her spot as if waiting for her, his eyes focused on the councilors. Thankfully, the black crow was absent. Or maybe he was off chasing Adler's small dragon around somewhere, the two plotting world domination at the Sinclair brothers' insistence.

"You're late, Ms. Beaufont," Adler said, his eyes low as he studied something in front of him.

She wasn't; Liv knew that. But what was the point of arguing with the sour old man? She'd simply take her case and get out of there. The less arguing, the sooner she could be trimming trolls' toenails or whatever else they wanted her to do.

Liv took her spot and forced an "I'm a team player" smile. That was when she noticed the melancholy look on Clark's face. He was probably horrid at poker. He had to be, based on the expressions he couldn't keep under wraps.

She tilted her head to the side, studying her brother. Was he still mad about her going to the kingdom of the fae without telling him? Had he learned something about the canisters? Was he angry that she had followed Stefan? The worries streamed through her head as she tried to focus.

Liv cleared her throat as the councilors looked around nervously, many of them focused on Adler, who didn't seem to care. He continued to study the screen in front of him, unhurried.

After a long minute, he glanced up. "Right, well, we have a new case for you."

"Cool. Throw it at me," Liv said, trying to inject enthusiasm into her voice.

The disapproving look that graced Bianca's face was totally worth saying dumb shit, Liv thought. She straightened and made her face serious. "I mean, very well. I patiently await the assignment."

Adler leaned forward to look down at her. "Ms. Beaufont, you do realize that being a Warrior isn't a game one should take lightly, don't you?"

What was the right response here? Liv wondered. Something sarcastic? Or she could ask Bianca to give her lessons on how to take everything too seriously? However, Clark's expression broke her resolve. She simply nodded. "Of course, it isn't a game. I take my role seriously."

"I have yet to witness that," Adler replied with a smug look.

"Olivia, the Council has voted on a new case for you," Bianca said, her eyes blazing with evil delight.

"Can't wait to hear about it, B," Liv replied.

Bianca's face contorted with annoyance.

"Oh, you don't like my little nickname for you?" Liv asked, mock seriousness on her face. "I rather like it. Get it? B for Bianca, and also because you're a real bi—"

"You're being assigned to hunt demons," Clark said in a rush, interrupting Liv.

Her playfulness evaporated as her mouth popped open. "Wait, what?"

Adler looked down the bench at Clark with a sinister glare. "I do believe it is my role to announce the cases, Mr. Beaufont."

"Actually, I don't think that there is any assignment on the matter," Haro stated. "The Council is about balance and equality."

Adler released a frustrated sigh. "Although that is true, for efficiency's sake, we've always had me make the announcements."

Liv was hardly listening. She could hardly believe what Clark said. She was being assigned to go after demons. The image of the red devilish-looking monster in the streets of Amsterdam was engraved into Liv's memory. The sounds and smells that radiated from the beast weren't something she could easily forget, and now she was being ordered to hunt them down and slay the monsters?

Clark held out a hand. "By all means, please do the honors, then. I didn't mean to disrupt efficiency." Liv could hardly believe the rebellious tone laced into his words.

Adler brushed off his shoulder as if whisking away Clark's gesture. "Ms. Beaufont, you're being assigned—"

"Demons?" she asked, cutting him off, unable to believe this turn of events.

Adler made a sound of frustration and nodded. "Yes, demons. If you'd let me fin—"

"Although I appreciate the Council's confidence in my combat skills, I think I need more training before tackling such dangerous beasts," Liv said, realizing that she was probably only making things worse for herself at this point. *Oh well, might as well swim all the way to bottom since I'm already halfway there,* she thought.

"It's not a matter of confidence," Adler stated through clenched teeth. "It has more to do with necessity."

Oh, good. For a moment she thought the Council was starting to view her as a capable warrior. "I don't understand. I thought it was Stefan's job to go after demons," Liv argued.

"Do you see Stefan here?" Adler asked.

Liv looked around just to be a smart ass. She really couldn't help herself. "Unless he's hiding, I don't think so."

"Demonism is spreading," Lorenzo explained, his hands steepled, his fingers touching his lips lightly. "It's a growing problem, but recently it has become worse."

"I still think that putting a more experienced Warrior on this case would be better," Clark argued.

"And I've already explained to you that they are all busy," Adler said with an impatient sigh. "The outbreak in Florida is especially bad right now."

"Although we'd like to offer you a case that suits your skillset better," Hester began in a small voice, "there is an undeniable need to address the demons in that area of the United States."

"'Skillset?'" Liv questioned.

Loudly, Adler tapped his hands on the table in front of him. "Some on the Council think that one of your better qualities is negotiations."

Liv smirked. "But you don't agree?"

Adler rolled his eyes. "I think that you've had beginner's luck."

"So why not send me after demons? That will teach me a lesson." She couldn't help herself. Liv had to say it. It was obvious what Adler was trying to do. Queen Visa hadn't murdered Liv as he had hoped, so was sending her off to battle demons in the swamp. He was probably already planning her wake and had picked out the family who would replace the Beaufonts.

"I didn't assign you this case," Adler said in a low voice. "The Council voted on it, and the majority won."

Liv studied Hester, Clark, and Raina. Their reactions said enough for Liv. They had voted against this, but the other four wanted to throw Liv in the demon pit and see if this time she'd come out ahead. Then she remembered something she'd heard about Stefan. Adler had assigned him demon cases in the beginning too, hoping to get rid of him, but the warrior had surprised him. Liv wanted to believe she'd rise to this challenge just like with Queen Visa, but this somehow felt harder because there was no way to negotiate with a demon.

"I'm just confused why I'm getting assigned this case now," Liv began. "Before the cases were trivial, but it sounds like this demon problem has been going on for a while."

"If you don't want the case, all you have to do is decline it," Adler stated.

"And then my title will be removed, and I'll be swiftly kicked out of the House of Seven," Liv said, staring down at the white tiger.

"Oh, so you *can* remember rules," Adler fired back.

She wiggled her nose, enjoying this more than she should. "Depends."

"There are roughly three demons in the lower part of the state of Florida," Adler said in a bored voice, reading from his tablet. "Your case is to track them down and slaughter each one."

"Do I get a *Killing Demons for Dummies* book?" Liv asked.

Clark slapped his hand to his forehead, embarrassment written on his face.

"Ms. Beaufont!" Adler said, warning in his tone.

Liv stuck her hands on her hips. "What? Demon hunting is advanced. I might not know a lot, but I know that much. It's not something they cover in the first year of Warrior training, am I right?"

"If you'd taken the House's training, this wouldn't be an issue," Bianca dared to say.

"Really? Then tell me, B, how *do* you slay a demon?" Liv challenged.

She blanched, her mouth slamming shut. "I'm not a Warrior, and therefore it's not my job to know such things."

Raina nodded. "It's true that it's more complicated and undeniably dangerous. And although some of us might have voiced our doubts about you being assigned this case, the Council has voted that you should be assigned to it."

"And we act as one," Adler reminded her.

Raina nodded. "Of course. And I'm sure you will find resources to assist you." Liv could have sworn she'd winked at her.

"Ms. Beaufont, the Council does not have all day to wait for you to make your decision on this case," Adler said.

Liv looked around at the chamber floor, which was empty save for her and the white tiger. She stopped herself from pointing out to him that there were no other Warriors in need of the Council's attention.

"I'm going to do it," Liv stated confidently. "Of course, I'll do it. I simply think that giving a newbie Warrior such a dangerous case might speak of certain prejudices."

"Ms. Beaufont, would you like to speak more plainly about what you're implying?" Adler fired.

Liv thought for a moment. "Absolutely. Right after I return from killing those demons."

CHAPTER TWENTY-SEVEN

Akio didn't interrupt Liv as she explained what had happened with the Council the night before. He simply ran his eyes over Bellator, which was resting in her hands, the gears turning in his mind.

"When I was a boy, I had a falcon," Akio began, his tone thoughtful.

"Who didn't?" Liv joked.

His eyes lit up, apparently appreciating the joke. "The bird of prey kept rodents and other smaller birds away from my family's estate. One day he flew off and didn't return, and within the week, the mice and other animals had invaded our yard."

"I'm not sure I'm following you here," Liv said, sheathing Bellator and deciding to stretch before they started sparring. "How does that relate to the Council's assignment?"

"I actually don't know why the Council is assigning you such difficult cases," Akio explained. "However, if Haro voted for you to take the case, that tells me there is a real problem with demons. Could they have assigned the case to a more experienced warrior? Yes, I think so, but there's little reason to worry about that now since the case is yours and there's no going back on it."

"It's just difficult when half the Council seems to want me dead," Liv stated.

"As I said before, I believe that if Haro voted for you, he must believe you're capable of the task."

"And Lorenzo?" Liv inquired.

Akio shook his head. "I've known the Rosario family for a long time, and I can't say. Maria keeps to herself, and her brother is unreadable."

"And Bianca and Adler?"

A half-smile crossed Akio's face. "I think we both know those two have a distaste for you."

Liv laughed at the stoic Warrior's bluntness. "At least I know I'm not reading anything into it."

"My point about the falcon is that the mice invaded our property because the hunter had disappeared and wasn't patrolling anymore," Akio said. "My concern is about the demon problem. There is no reason that there should be an influx unless…"

"The falcon has gone missing," Liv said, finishing his sentence. He was referring to Stefan. However, she had seen him hunting demons with her own eyes. Well, mostly interrogating, but he did kill it. Still, Akio was right. There was definitely something suspicious here.

"Are you ready to spar?" Akio asked, taking his position in the middle of the training studio. They had grown accustomed to the routine of training, having practiced several times each week together. Liv liked him as a teacher. He was kind, but strict. Thoughtful, yet stern.

"Yes, more than ever," Liv stated. "I'm going to pretend you're a demon and my job is to slay you."

"Remember your training," he urged. "And more than anything, remember your teachers. That's what will guide you in battle."

Liv nodded, recalling what Akio had said about holding her earliest teachers, her mother and her father, in her heart while fighting. She unsheathed Bellator and stood at the ready, reminding herself that the sword was an extension of her.

As before, Akio came at her strong and fast, his sword slamming into hers and nearly knocking it out of her hands. She spun to the side, trying to get her balance before his next attack. It came like a rush of wind, fast and nearly tangling her in knots as she tried to block all of his attacks. She felt close to asking for a timeout, needing a break from his relentless pursuit. However, in the back of her mind, she heard a voice, one she hadn't heard in a long, long time.

"Fight with love, not vengeance," she heard her mother say. It was a line she'd said to Ian many times while they trained, Liv sprawled out reading a fantasy book on a training mat nearby. How had she forgotten this memory? She'd always been present for Ian's training since they were both odd-number children who could become Warriors one day.

Fight with love, Liv thought, avoiding another of Akio's attacks. That's not at all what she was doing. She was reacting out of fear. Self-preservation. But what had Akio said?

"We rarely can persevere for self-preservation alone. However, when we remember the ones who made us who we are? Well, we become unstoppable ."

Liv pictured Akio as a demon. Her hand tightened around Bellator and she spun, ducking attack after attack. When she'd gotten a good distance from Akio, she felt her heart expand and her arms lengthen as if she'd suddenly grown. In one rapid movement, she brought Bellator across Akio's sword, knocking it to the mat and leaving him weaponless.

He bowed slightly, a look of appreciation in his eyes. "It appears that you've learned an important lesson."

"That if I need a haircut, I should come to you?" she joked.

He shook his head. "The desire to survive is miniscule compared to the need to protect. Just now you fought me not to win, but rather with an urgency to defend. Take that into battle against any demon, and you will slay them."

CHAPTER TWENTY-EIGHT

The moment Liv stepped onto Rory's property, her feet were swept into the air, suspended by something invisible, and her head was upside down, her fingertips inches from the ground.

"What the hell?" Liv growled, trying to pull herself up to see what had her feet trapped. She tried several times to do a crunch, but was unable to right herself.

"Looks like you need to do more crunches," Plato stated matter-of-factly, watching her attempts with mild interest. He stood next to her, unaffected by whatever had her upside-down.

"Seriously, now isn't the time to remind me I need to work out more," she complained, grunting as the blood rushed to her head.

"Okay, later, then."

"Why don't you help me and tell me what's got me trapped?" Liv urged.

"Magic," Plato answered plainly.

Liv tried to gain momentum by swinging. "Wow, you're so much help."

Plato's eyes followed Liv as she swung back and forth, trying to catch her feet. "It appears you've triggered some sort of trespassing spell."

"Bloody hell!" Liv complained. "Rory could have told me about this when he invited me over."

"Hey, Liv," Rory's voice called casually from behind her as he strode from the house. "I put protective wards on the property, and if you trigger them, you'll be trapped."

"Got it! Thanks!" Liv yelled, trying to twist around to see the giant. "Can you let me down?"

"I can," he said simply.

"Will you?" she asked, her irritation building.

"Sure."

Nothing happened.

"I think you were remiss in not specifying when you'd like to be released," Plato imparted.

"Seriously, do you want me to kill you both?" Liv grimaced, looking at the lynx's upside-down face. "Rory, will you let me down now?"

"Yes, once you say the magic word," he replied.

"Giant stew!" she yelled.

Rory came around so that she could see him, shaking his head and suppressing a grin. "That's two words, and I hear we taste awful. Very gristly."

"Oh, look who finally has some jokes," Liv countered. "Will you please let me down, grandma? And thanks for the etiquette lesson. Whatever would I do without you?"

"You'd remain stuck like this for a long, long time," Rory stated, swiping his hand in a circle.

The grip around Liv's feet released and she crashed to the soft earth head-first. Rolling over, she brushed off her arms and looked up at the giant with a scowl. "You enjoyed that way too much."

He extended a hand to her. "I admit that I did. You look even funnier when you talk upside-down."

Liv took his offered hand and allowed him to help her up. He nearly threw her across the yard when he pulled her to a standing position.

"So what's up with the new security measures?" Liv asked, rolling out her shoulder, her arm having nearly been pulled out of the socket.

"The elf has been trying again to get onto my property," Rory explained.

"And you got tired of continuously putting out fires?" Liv asked, noticing the many scorch marks on the lawn.

He nodded. "That was only supposed to be a short-term solution until I had time to up security. I know now that this thief must be using a spell that tracks the sword."

"How do you know that for sure?" Liv asked. "Maybe he just knows that you and I are connected, and has therefore concluded that you have the sword? I mean, you *are* a giant and all."

"Yeah, that's a reasonable explanation, but remember when I told you where my house was?"

Liv thought back. That felt like eons ago, rather than a few weeks. "You gave me a piece of paper. The address only appeared when I set off for your house, and Plato said that no one but me could read it."

"That's right," Rory affirmed. "And the address would have disappeared afterward. You see, only those I invite can even see my house. Otherwise, this lot looks like a disorganized junkyard."

"What about Plato?" Liv pointed to the feline. "He can see your house, and he wasn't invited. He just followed me here."

Rory lowered his chin and regarded Plato with a considering stare. "Yes, just like he can follow you into the House of Seven. The same principles of magic don't apply to lynxes. For instance, he didn't set off the alarms, and therefore wasn't trapped the same way as you."

"Yeah, and why is that?" Liv asked, glancing at Plato.

The lynx casually shrugged. "Let's say it's because I'm soft-footed."

"You can see how lynxes are considered untrustworthy creatures, can't you?" Rory asked Liv, acting as though Plato wasn't present. "There's no way to guard against them trespassing."

"I'm glad you're my friend rather than my enemy," Liv told the cat with a wink.

"Lynxes have no friends," Rory growled, striding in the direction of the house.

Liv gave Plato a sideways look. "I don't believe that's true."

"What you believe is all that matters," Plato replied.

"With you and our friendship?" she asked.

"With everything," he answered.

Liv followed Rory into the house, and when she crossed the threshold, she was unsurprised to find that Plato had disappeared. The kittens were playing in a box in the middle of the living room floor.

"Say, you wouldn't be keeping these kittens around

because you know Plato doesn't like them and therefore won't come around while they are here, would you?" Liv asked, picking up Samson and cuddling the orange kitten in her arms.

Rory avoided eye contact, pacing in front of the fireplace, where Turbinger hung above the mantel. "I don't know what you're talking about."

"I think he does," Liv said to the kitten, who had his eyes closed and was enjoying the belly rub and not listening.

"The wards I have protecting the sword won't hold much longer," Rory said, thinking. "I need something stronger."

"What can I do to help?" Liv asked. She figured he'd say nothing because she couldn't remember a time that he'd ever asked for help.

To her surprise, Rory turned around, a questioning expression on his face. "Will you keep watch over the sword tonight? I need to go and do something and don't think I should leave it to chance. This elf is tricky, and keeps getting around my security measures."

"Of course I will," Liv answered. "Where are you going?"

Rory shook his head, taking the kittens out of the box one by one and setting them to the side. "Nowhere."

"For some reason, I don't believe him," Liv said to the purring kitten.

When the box was empty, he pointed, and it filled with what Liv thought were medical supplies. He folded the lid over the top before she could get a better look.

"You're going to be gone all night?" Liv questioned.

Rory nodded.

"Are you going to your girlfriend's house?" Liv teased.

"Yes," Rory answered at once, binding the box closed with tape.

"Is she a giant too?"

He ignored her.

"Do you two Netflix and chill?" she continued.

"There's food in the refrigerator," Rory said, pointing to the kitchen. "Don't go into the backyard."

"What's in the backyard?" she asked.

"Giant stuff," he replied.

"Like tractors and bulldozers?"

He rolled his eyes.

Liv slapped her leg, laughing at her own joke.

"So that's why you asked me to come over?" she asked. "We're not going to train?"

"Have you read *Mysterious Creatures* all the way through three times yet?" Rory questioned.

"Not even once. I've been busy, but I browse through it when I have time."

Rory was looking around as if trying to determine if he'd remembered everything. He directed his gaze to Liv. "You don't have a case you need to work tonight, do you?"

"I do, but it can wait," she answered. "I'll study up on demons tonight, so I'm prepared for the carnage tomorrow."

Rory, who was still absentmindedly looking around, did a double-take at her words. "Demons? You've been assigned to hunt down demons?"

"Yes and I'm sure that like the fae, you think I have to do it," Liv said with a yawn.

Rory shook his head of curls. "Absolutely not. I had faith that you'd figure out how to deal with Queen Visa, but she can be reasoned with. Demons are the vilest creatures on Earth. You can't go after them."

"But I have to," Liv argued. "I don't have a choice."

"You always have a choice. You just don't like the consequences if you don't do it," Rory stated.

"Yes, because my family gets kicked out of the House of Seven," Liv stated.

"They are just going to keep bullying you." Rory gave her a cold look, his resentment showing. "Have you ever considered that it's not worth being a part of the House of Seven? It's a bureaucracy that will never see the other magical races as equals."

Liv set Samson down. "Have you considered that if I give up, there's little chance for change? Yes, I have to face deadly stuff and ridiculous challenges, but if I survive, I can find out what the House is hiding. I can find out what really happened to my parents and my siblings. If I give up? Well, then I'll just be some girl in LA with no powers and no chance of uncovering the truth."

Rory considered this and nodded. "That was the right answer, although I wish you didn't have to face demons. That doesn't make me comfortable at all."

"Well, any words of advice?" Liv asked.

He shook his head. "Find someone to go along who runs slower than you."

"Ha-ha," Liv said, watching as Rory lifted the large box like it was a tiny carton of Chinese takeout. "Is there a bedroom at the back where I can sleep? Some cozy pjs I can wear, since you didn't give me a heads-up on this sleepover with the kittens?"

He looked her up and down. "No. The couch is comfortable, although it might have fleas."

As he set off for the door, Liv called, "Thanks. You're an incredible host. Please consider opening a bed and breakfast."

CHAPTER TWENTY-NINE

Liv's eyes were closing of their own accord before the sun had even set all the way. She blinked and tried to clear her head, the heat from the fireplace making her feel like she was in a coma. After hours of reading, she'd learned that the most effective ways to kill a demon were to burn it alive or to cut off its head. Neither seemed very easy to do, since also according to the book, demons were incredibly strong and agile and also resistant to fire. They could literally walk through flames without being harmed, so they had to actually be trapped in the fire for it to end them. And then there was the incantation, which was listed in *Mysterious Creatures*:

Metuendas Dcemonis violentias, dimittere unam animam de amicae tuae involasti, permittens eos tandem requiem. Ad infernum, a quo factum est tibi in sempiternum in ipse comburetis.

Which meant:

Demon, release the soul of the one you stole, allowing them to finally rest. Return to hell, from which you came, where forever you shall burn.

That was the only way to fully sever the demon from the soul it had latched onto. Liv had also learned how demons came to be, spreading a deadly virus that took over magical creatures. They had been around since the beginning of time, but Bermuda said their numbers had always remained static—which begged the question why all of sudden there was an incursion.

Liv's stomach growled, reminding her that she was still human. She pulled the sleeping kitten from her lap, laying him on the sofa, and trudged for the kitchen. It wasn't that she wasn't curious what was in the backyard that Rory didn't want her to see as much as she was pretty sure he'd have wards that would throw poison darts at her if she dared to sneak a peek.

She shrugged off her curiosity and opened the refrigerator.

"Oh, dear God," she said at the sight. Liv didn't remember her grandmothers, who had died before she was a baby, but if she had spent any time with them, this was what their refrigerators would have looked like. It would be bursting with casserole dishes and covered pie tins. In Rory's refrigerator, there was no shortage of food. She pulled out a pan of lasagna and went to work slicing a large piece when she heard a strange sawing noise.

Pausing, Liv looked around, watching the kittens scurry around, trying to catch each other's tails on the kitchen floor.

The sawing got louder. Liv knew that Junebug was a master at getting into things, but she couldn't fathom what he'd be doing making that sound.

"June?" she called, negotiating around the other kittens, a spatula in her hands from the lasagna tray.

The sawing got faster and more intense. Liv retraced her steps to the living room, where the sawing was originating. When she stepped around the corner, what she saw took her several seconds to understand.

A single arm was suspended in the middle of the living room, feeling around like a blind man trying to find his way.

Liv blinked, not understanding what she was seeing. Why would half an arm be floating in mid-air in Rory's living room? Was this something that happened often? A visitor from the giant's realm? And then she saw it.

The scar! It ran along the length of the pale arm, black spider veins spreading away from the gaping wound.

Liv threw her hand forward, the spatula leading the way like the worst sword ever. The utensil did absolutely nothing to the elf trying to break into Rory's house.

She tried to attack him with magic, but it dissipated, not having the usual effect.

He pulled his arm back through a moment later, though, and Liv thought she'd done something to frighten him away. Then the front half of a saw peaked out from seemingly nowhere, going back and forth as the noise continued. He was trying to saw his way through Rory's wards from a different dimension or another place or something. She'd never seen magic like this. The saw cut deeper, making a bigger hole.

Liv threw the spatula to the ground, nearly hitting one of the kittens. She directed all of her attention to the hand that reached through a moment later, trying to force him back, but her magic had little effect. He must have done something to the space to weaken her magic. That meant that she had to take him out before he got through.

Sprinting across the dining room, Liv threw a kick at the arm reaching through the space, thinking she'd knock him back to where he'd come from. However, a shock radiated through her foot, knocking her to the ground. She sprang up, but her knees were weak. Whatever enchantment he was using was preventing her magic from operating at full strength and was protecting him.

Both hands were reaching through the invisible door. Liv looked around, not knowing what to do. Rory had trusted her to protect Turbinger but she was helpless as the long fingers started to roll back the invisible door, making more of the elf's body visible. She didn't have much time. Once he got through, she'd have to deal with him, and with no magic and his strange defenses, she worried he'd win this time.

Liv made an impromptu decision. Picking up a duffle bag beside the door, she began scooping up the kittens. They didn't seem to mind being corralled into the bag. Actually, Junebug came springing from the kitchen and leapt into the bag like it was a game. Liv used the last of her magic reserves to pick up the three remaining kittens and deposit them into the bag, sealing it at once. Whatever the elf had hit her with had gone straight at her magic, limiting it.

The elf's shoulder came through the door, then his foot. His leg. She didn't have much time.

Liv sprang in the direction of the fireplace, jumping up on Rory's chair and grabbing the sword. It was heavier than she remembered, bringing her to the ground with a thud, the blade cutting into the hardwood. Immediately she connected to the strange feelings and memories flowing through her from the sword, just like the first time she'd held it. Blocking them out, she yanked it up and considered using it to fight the elf. However, she felt the static electricity as she neared the elf, slowly inching his way through the opening.

No, if she dared to use Turbinger on the elf, whatever enchantments he was using might electrocute her. Instead, she ran for the duffle bag that was squirming by the door and slung it carefully over her shoulder.

When she flung open the door, she was careful to peer around the darkened yard to ensure there was no one waiting for her there. It appeared empty. Liv turned back briefly to spy the elf's face coming through the opening, a vengeful expression adorning it. He caught sight of her as she bounded out into the yard, Turbinger and the kittens in her arms. As soon as she was a safe distance away and could use her magic fully, she opened a portal to the only place she could ensure safety.

CHAPTER THIRTY

The House of Seven was quiet when Liv slipped through the door, Turbinger in her hands and the kittens squirming in the bag. She hadn't known where else to go. The elf obviously knew about John's shop, which made that the wrong place to escape to. Furthermore, she couldn't put him in danger by drawing the deranged elf there. Also, she hadn't had a chance to put any wards on her apartment, which didn't make that a good option either. So with little time to think, Liv decided to flee to the refuge of the House where no one but a royal could enter. Well, besides Plato.

She halted in the entrance, listening to ensure she didn't walk up on anyone. With a quick nod at Turbinger, she sort of disguised it as a magician's sword, although it was a poor attempt, the language of the giants still present around the hilt and on the blade. Something told her that it would be really difficult to hide completely.

At first, Liv considered sneaking up to Sophia's and Clark's residence. However, if she was caught, they'd be in trouble too. She didn't want to risk that. Clark was hopefully making progress with investigating the canisters of magic, and Liv didn't want to ruin that for them. Therefore, she put a quick disguising spell on her and the kittens, making them blend into their surroundings as she sped up to the library. There was no safer place in the world, she thought, taking the steps two at a time.

When she'd finally made it to the couches next to the wall of symbols, Liv set down the bag and sword and checked on the kittens. They must have enjoyed the ride because they were all snuggled together, some of them mewing but many of them fast asleep.

Liv let out a sigh of relief. "Okay, it's not Rory's house, but we're going to stay here tonight. Try to act right." She pointed to the kitten with bright blue eyes, giving him a look of warning. "I'm mostly talking to you, Junebug."

He yawned loudly at the order, lying down next to his brothers and sisters, ready to sleep for the night. Exhausted from the strange and sudden events, Liv laid down on the sofa, finding herself yawning too. She tucked the sword under one arm, covering it with her cape, and nodded off at once, falling straight into dreams.

A sharp cough awoke Liv, making her crack an eye open. When she was a child, if she fell asleep in the library in the House of Seven, she'd awake in a different place. That's how the strangeness of the library worked. For that reason, she wasn't surprised that she was snuggled up in a window seat, a row of books and paintings she didn't recognize surrounding her. Actually, she didn't recognize anything around her except for the figure standing a short distance away. He was blurry until her eyes adjusted, but she recognized his frame and pale face.

"Good morning, Liv Beaufont," Stefan said with a smirk on his face, his arms folded and his feet crossed as he leaned against a bookcase.

Liv stopped herself from bolting up and acting as if the position he'd found her in wasn't precarious. She had known when she'd passed out in the library that there was a chance others would stumble upon her, but as exhausted as she was, it had been worth it.

She stretched her hands over her head and yawned. "Hey, what's up?" she replied, pretending like the bag of kittens mewing on one side of her and the sword on the other weren't anything to be concerned about.

"Well, I'm not sure where to begin," he said with a coy smile.

She tried to nonchalantly cover the sword with her cape. Its disguise had faded, and now it just looked like a giant-ass sword which was made by a giant and probably owned by a giant.

Liv stroked her belly. "Is anyone hungry?"

Stefan pointed to the bag of kittens. "I'd say your litter is hungry."

Liv blushed. "Oh, these aren't mine."

"Whose are they?"

"Well, I'm watching them for a friend."

"Your lynx?" Stefan asked.

Liv shook her head, unzipping the bag and checking on the kittens. Junebug immediately tried to jump out, but she caught him. She looked up at Stefan. "Do you have any meat?"

He smiled, withdrawing something from his robes. "I happen to keep beef jerky on me at all times."

He handed her a pouch and she reached in, grabbing the pieces of meat and sprinkling them into the bag for the kittens to fight over. "And no, these kittens don't belong to my lynx. Different friend. Really, it's a boring story. Seriously lame."

"I'm already nodding off, wondering why you're sleeping in the library with a dozen kittens and a giant's sword beside you," he said.

"There are only ten," she corrected.

"Say what?" he asked.

"There are only ten kittens in this bag." She pointed.

He nodded like this made sense. "Of course. You'd need a bigger bag for more than ten."

"Thanks for the food," Liv said, grateful that the kittens were happy. She'd have to get them back to Rory soon. Actually, she had to find Rory and explain what had happened to him before he got too worried.

"Well, although I want to know why you are fostering ten kittens for someone, I'll cut to the chase," Stefan said. "I heard about the demon case from Raina and came back as soon as I could."

Liv's head jerked up from the kittens. "You what?"

"Liv, you can't go after demons on your own," he said in an urgent voice.

She nearly growled at him. "Why, because I'll fail?"

He nodded.

"But you did it," she argued.

He shook his head. "And I would have failed too. However, I had help. The Council didn't know about it. Well, Raina did, but she doesn't count. Anyway, I had someone to teach me how to fight the beasts, and you will too."

Liv considered him for a moment. "Are they trying to take me out?"

He nodded. "Most likely. Well, not the majority, but Adler for sure. He did the same to me and roped the others in with him. He doesn't like nonconformists, and he assigns the cases in a way that serves his agenda."

Liv nodded, zipping up the bag of kittens. Once she'd stood up, she stretched, trying to hide Turbinger, which was lying on the cushions behind her.

"So how about I go along with you on this mission to Florida?" Stefan offered.

Liv considered him, conscious that the kittens were trying to crawl over her boots even while confined in the bag. "Don't you have your own cases?"

"I do," he agreed. "But I don't see what harm it would cause to take off a few days."

"That begs the question: if you're doing your job as a demon hunter, why is there an influx?" she asked.

He shrugged. "I've been busy."

She knew that wasn't true. He'd been hunting demons, but there was another reason he wasn't working his cases, or at least why he wasn't keeping the demon population in check.

"Well, what if I did need help?" Liv asked. "What do you want in return?"

He gave her a roguish smile. "The only thing I want in

return is to find out exactly what you don't want to tell me." He pointed to the bag of squirming kittens. "Once we slay the demons, all you have to do is tell me who these adorable beasts belong to."

Liv's eyes slid to the sword sitting in plain view before connecting with Stefan Ludwig's unwavering gaze. She held out her hand. "You have yourself a deal."

CHAPTER THIRTY-ONE

Liv wasn't sure if Rory was more relieved to have the kittens back or Turbinger. He'd met her at her apartment and picked them up while she grabbed her sword. If Stefan hadn't awoken her earlier in the library, she might not have been able to slip out before anyone saw her.

She was worried when Rory stated he was going back to his house, but he couldn't be deterred. He kept saying, "There's something I'm working on. It's the only way to protect the sword."

He was a lot less on edge when she confessed that Stefan was going to help her with the demon case. They parted ways, each concerned about the other but knowing that the danger they faced was part of the job.

After stepping through the portal, Liv waited for Stefan. She'd had to create the portal since no one could know that he'd accompanied her to the wetlands of Florida.

Stefan stepped through, his boots sinking into the mud, a considering look on his face.

"So how do we track down these soul-suckers?" Liv asked him in a hushed voice.

She caught a pair of familiar reflective eyes in the distance. It instantly made her feel better to know Plato was close by, watching her.

Stefan sniffed the air, gazing at the swamp and trees dripping in vines. "I know how to find them."

"Cool, but how do *I* find them?" she asked.

He started forward, looking over his shoulder at her. "You follow me."

Liv rolled her eyes, hurrying to keep up with him. "That won't help me when I need to track and slay demons on my own."

He stopped abruptly, his face filled with silent apprehension. "You shouldn't kill them on your own. For as long as the Council assigns you demon cases, I'll be with you to help."

"Although that's appreciated, I'm sort of used to working alone. And you learned how to find and kill them from someone, so I'd like you to teach me."

Stefan's eyes were large and tragic. "Hunting demons isn't something you should be doing. You're too good for this. The Council will see that and outvote Adler and Bianca, and you'll move onto something worthier of your talents."

Liv didn't know what to say to that. It was a compliment wrapped up in mystery. "Shouldn't keeping the balance between good and evil be at the top of the list as far as worthy cases go?"

"Yes, and it's my job." Stefan kept walking, constantly scanning the dark wetlands.

So, was this an ego thing? Liv wondered. Did Stefan not want her pinching his territory? This didn't make sense.

They'd walked a fair distance, easily keeping a steady pace, when they came to a clearing with a small house. Stefan spun in a circle, looking momentarily disoriented. "Where did you go?"

"I'm guessing you're referring to the demon you're hunting while I collect wildflowers," Liv joked.

Stefan's eyes fell to Liv's hands, which were hanging loosely by her sides, as if expecting to see her holding a bouquet of tulips. He shook his head. "The demons know we're here, and they are playing games with us."

"I didn't get the invite, so I'm not playing the same game."

Liv knelt and grabbed up a bit of earth, letting it run through her fingers.

"What are you doing?" Stefan asked.

"I'm tracking the demons," she lied.

"How's that going for you?"

She shrugged, standing and dusting her hand off. "I don't know. I've just seen them do that in the movies."

He gave her a sideways look. "You're very strange."

"You should see me on a full moon."

"Do you turn into a werewolf?" he asked, curiosity written on his face.

"Oh, no. I decoupage."

Liv realized it was a horrible joke. That was the whole point. However, Stefan could have at least rolled his eyes instead of narrowing them at her, pure vengeance filling his face.

In a swift movement, he pushed her to the side and

whipped out his sword, swinging it at the demon who had materialized behind her. In a clean movement, he severed the head, spraying black blood over the leaves and ground.

Liv's heart was racing from the adrenaline rush. She spun around, searching the area for the other demons, but Stefan waved her off.

"They aren't here right now," he stated confidently.

"How do you know?"

"I just know," he said, getting close to the demon's severed head and rolling it over with his sword.

"I like how when I ask questions, you give me bullshit answers," Liv fired back, holding her breath against the odor. This demon smelled worse than the one in Amsterdam. Maybe that was because it was in Florida where hardly anyone bathed, she thought with a morbid laugh.

"Oh, you like that, do you? We'll get along just fine, then."

"Ha-ha," Liv said, withdrawing the bag she'd brought.

"You're the one who likes secrets so much," Stefan related. "I'm just playing your game." His eyes widened when she neared him, crouching by the disgusting head. The demon's black eyes were still open. "What are you doing?"

Liv used magic to bag the head, tying the sack tightly. "I'm taking a souvenir. I've never been to Florida, and I need something to remember it by."

"Most people just get a magnet for the refrigerator," Stefan said, disgusted.

"Where are the other two, demon whisperer?"

Stefan nodded in the direction of the abandoned cabin. "They are waiting in there, I believe."

"Not that you're going to answer this question, but how do you know that?"

"Pull out your sword," he ordered, fury flaring in his eyes.

Liv dropped the head of the demon on the ground, and it landed with a thud. She did as she was told, turning to face the tiny cabin.

"Whoa, where did you get that?" Stefan asked, his eyes wide as he regarded Bellator.

"Same place you left all the answers to my questions," Liv said.

He nodded, a slight smile flicking to his eyes. "Well played, Liv Beaufont. But please note this is not the first time I've seen you with a giant-forged sword." He added, "Today."

Liv feigned ignorance, regarding the sword with awe. "This is a giant-made sword? Well, I'll be. I got it at a flea market from a guy named Leonard. Short fella. Definitely not a giant."

He snickered slightly, facing the cabin. "Well, thankfully, if you do come up against one of the demons in there, you've got an extra advantage. Usually, there are only two ways to kill a demon."

"Fire and beheading," Liv supplied.

Stefan nodded. "Yes, but I've heard a theory that giant's swords are deadly to demons."

Liv lifted Bellator, eyeing it with appreciation. "Let's test that theory." She started forward, but Stefan caught her by the shoulder, spinning her back around.

"Let me go in first," he suggested. "You should go

around the back to keep a lookout, and cut them off if they try and flee."

"That sounds like a bullshit plan where you get to have all the fun and I stay out of harm's way," Liv said.

He nodded. "I agree that it's a brilliant plan. Thank you. We'll meet out here after I'm done with them."

"What if I insist that we go in together?"

"Then I'll insist you tell me why you were cuddling with that sword that was stolen from the Natural History Museum," he countered.

"You know, I think checking out the back of the cabin sounds great," she said with a slight laugh.

He winked. "I thought you might."

Liv watched as Stefan soundlessly moved to the front of the cabin, his cape flying behind him. She stealthily moved around to the back of the building, where she was unsurprised to find no back door. She didn't like that Stefan had taken over this case, but she needed his help and didn't need him asking too many questions. It was just one case, and then she could go back to working alone. Also, she hoped to learn more about him, specifically what he was hiding. So far, though, he had been a tightly-sealed vault.

As Liv slid next to the cabin, she heard scratching from within. That was Stefan's problem. She was the lookout. The backup. That wasn't going to do, and his whole attitude around his territory of demon hunting was annoying. After this was over, she was going to realign the framework of their relationship, ensuring she was standing even with him. She realized that as a newbie warrior she had a lot to learn and he was in a position to teach her, as Akio was doing with combat. However, Stefan hadn't shared any information yet.

After Liv slipped around the back of the cabin, a loud thud made her jump. It had come from inside the building. Something had been thrown against the wall, making it shudder.

"Looks like someone is having fun," Liv said dully to herself.

Another assault hit the wall, making her think it would splinter.

She took another step, sinking deep into the mud. "Damn it to hell." Liv tried to pull her boot out but realized she was sinking. *Seriously, this is a thing? I thought quicksand was just a plot device for movies.*

She was about to use her magic to unstick her boot when she heard a voice clear and loud in her mind. Plato's. *Watch out!*

Liv looked up as something leapt off the building and crashed on top of her. The demon yanked her out of the mud, propelling her into a forward roll. She dropped her sword in the fall but rose to her feet as soon as she could. The demon had too and was hunched over, growling at her, its hands touching the ground. The beast was by far the ugliest thing she'd ever seen, with its small horns protruding from its cheekbones and brow. Its black eyes didn't blink as it regarded her with a vicious stare. It took a crouching step toward her, dragging its other leg behind it.

Liv didn't look directly at her sword, which was a few feet away, slowly sinking into the mud. A few weeks ago she'd have been dead at this beast's hands. However, her training with Akio had been a good idea. Now was the time to make him proud. And her parents. She remembered them, but more than anything, she remembered the training they'd instilled in her.

Fight with love, not vengeance. The words wrapped around her heart, making Liv feel stronger than she was alone, a cumulation of the people who mattered most in her life.

The demon lunged at her, drooling. She moved faster than she ever had, the way Akio moved—like a phantom, there and gone. She slipped behind the demon, making it spin around. She was already on the other side of him, moving so fast that her feet didn't even sink into the mud.

The beast screamed, making its frustrations known. Liv confused him again, taunting him by appearing at his back twice more. She picked up Bellator just as it was about to disappear into the mud. Swinging the debris off of the sword, she splattered the demon. It screamed again, showing rows of sharp teeth, its long pointed tongue stretching out of its mouth.

With Bellator in her hands once again, she noticed immediately that she didn't move as fast, just as Akio had warned.

"We gain and we lose when we hold a weapon. They make us deadly, but often slow us down. Never forget that wielding a weapon isn't always the right approach. It depends on the battle."

She knew exactly what he meant now, but she also knew that Bellator was the right approach. She could run circles around this demon, but that would only disorient him. The means to the end was in her hand.

The monster dove for her. Liv rotated, bringing Bellator around, slicing it through the abdomen. It crumpled at once, writhing in pain and gripping its stomach. The scream that left its mouth was like the ones she'd heard in Amsterdam, searing her ears.

Liv brought Bellator over her head, trying to remember the Latin that would free the soul within it.

"Metuendas Dcemonis violentias, dimittere unam animam de amicae tuae involasti, permittens eos tandem requiem," she intoned as the beast tried to reach for her boots, its claws finding only mud. Gripping her sword, she dug deep for the courage to do the next seemingly impossible thing. She'd never killed anything, even something so evil. Still, no matter what it was, killing wasn't natural. It shouldn't be, and she knew that. It should come at a great price so that it never became easy. She sucked in a breath. *"Ad infernum, a quo factum est tibi in sempiternum in ipse comburetis."*

With force fueled by a passion she wasn't acquainted with, the sword came down, slicing the demon's head off cleanly. Liv backed away from the body, not believing what she'd done. It wasn't an act she hadn't ever thought she'd be proud of, and yet, she was. She'd freed a soul, and rid the world of a horrible entity.

The scream of another demon echoed from the cabin. The walls shook. Fueled by instinct, she ran around the side of the building, halting once she was in the entrance. She froze, having déjà vu. The scene before her looked very much what she'd seen in Amsterdam. Stefan had pinned the demon to the wall with a series of knives. Black blood was dripping from the cuts, staining the wall. However, the demon didn't appear to be in pain like the one she'd just slaughtered. This demon, uglier than the rest, lifted its head, its body pulled down by the weight but still pinned to the wall.

If demons could smile, that was what this one did, its greenish teeth sawing back and forth and making a horrid sound.

"How dare you come after one of your own?" The demon hissed the words, its gaze flicking to Liv, who was standing in the doorway.

Stefan looked over his shoulder at Liv, swallowing hard before swinging around to face the monster again. "Get out of here, Liv," he urged.

She didn't move, just studied the scene. Stefan had pinned the demon. Granted, he didn't have Bellator, which made her job much easier, but this looked like it was personal. Like he wanted to punish this demon.

"Oh, she doesn't know, does she?" the demon sang, its voice not at all melodic.

"Delirium has set in. It doesn't know what it's talking about," Stefan said over his shoulder to her. "Get out of here. There's another one left."

She shook her head, holding up Bellator, which was soaked in black blood. He nodded roughly, something catching in his throat.

Stefan lifted his sword, holding it even with the demon's neck. However, he didn't take this opportunity to end things. Instead, he hesitated as if he were unsure he should kill the monster.

"I know you are a man right now, but you're destined to become a demon just like me," the beast spat, seeming to play with Stefan.

"No, I'm not!" Stefan roared, slamming his elbow into

the demon's chest, blood squirting out from its wounds onto his face.

The demon gurgled on a scream that turned into a choking laugh. "Yes, I can smell it on you. You've been kissed, and soon you'll be just like me."

Liv sucked in an audible breath, remembering what she'd read about demonism in Bermuda Laurens' book. She'd called it a kiss too, but remarked that it was more like a bite. The demons affectionately called it a kiss because it was what kept them prowling the Earth.

"How long do you have?" the demon asked, sniffing the air like it smelled something tantalizing. "Maybe not long. And then you'll be one of us—the ones who will inherit this planet."

"No! That will never happen! Never! Never!" He brought his sword around, slicing the demon's head off cleanly. It landed at his feet, its black eyes staring up at him and a grin on its face.

When Stefan turned to face Liv, his face was splattered with black blood and he was vibrating with a hostility she'd never before witnessed. It didn't scare her. At that moment, she knew with absolute certainty that Stefan Ludwig was in danger of becoming a demon. He'd been bitten by the very thing he hated most, and she was going to help save him.

CHAPTER THIRTY-TWO

"Make it a double," Stefan said. He laid a wad of cash on the table they'd taken at a bar in Venice, a local joint that was dark and not filled with hipsters.

The waiter nodded, giving Liv an expectant look.

"I'll take the same," she replied, pointing to Stefan, who looked like he'd just fought a gang of demons, although he'd taken the time to wipe the blood off his face. The brooding hostility was still brimming in his eyes as if something dark in him was begging to escape.

Liv waited in silence until they had their drinks, thinking that they probably both needed them to continue the next inevitable part of the conversation. When the waiter returned with two whiskeys, sliding the glasses in front of them, Liv and Stefan weren't saying a word but rather staring off uncomfortably.

Once the waiter had left them, Liv took a sip of her drink, the whiskey burning her throat but instantly making her feel better. She drank half of it before setting it down and looking at Stefan directly. He appeared to be a hollow man, simply going through the motions.

"Do you want to tell me about this demon-bite business?" she asked.

He cut his piercing blue eyes at her. "Oh, no. Kittens first. That was the deal. I help you with the demons, you tell me why you have a bag full of kittens."

Liv laughed, finishing her drink and flagging down the waiter. She was going to need more drinks for this conversation. Scratch that. She was going to need all the drinks.

"Bring the bottle," she said to the waiter when he was almost to their table. He nodded, heading back to the bar.

"So, on the side, I volunteer at the animal shelter," she began. "Would you believe that during my shift—"

Stefan slammed his glass down with a blunt force, giving her a "no bullshit" glare. "Here's the deal. If you're straight with me, I'll be the same with you. The moment you close up, so will I. But you should know, Liv Beaufont, that I'm not your enemy."

Liv considered Stefan for a long moment. The earnestness in his blue eyes was hard to ignore, but how could she trust someone just because they told her she could? Wasn't trust something people earned? One of her biggest problems was that she didn't know who her enemies were. The Council was a major pain in her ass, and the deranged elf was definitely no friend of hers. But who was behind all that? Who was behind her parents' and siblings' deaths?

Slowly she nodded, swirling the remaining whiskey in her glass. "The kittens belong to a friend of mine. Someone broke into his place the night before you found me in the library."

"To get the sword, I gather," Stefan guessed as the bartender brought over the bottle of whiskey.

Liv's instinct was to divert, but she couldn't keep doing that if she wanted Stefan to cooperate with her. Yes, she'd thought he was up to something, and it appeared he was—trying to survive a demon bite.

"Yes," she finally answered, "I panicked and took the sword and the kittens to the House of Seven."

Stefan laughed, refilling their glasses. "You definitely had to have some balls to bring that sword into the House. I can only imagine what would have happened if Adler had caught you, or someone else."

"I'd have thrown a kitten at them and run away," Liv joked.

Stefan ran his fingers over his stubbled chin. "Kitten bombs; not a bad idea."

"Yes, they are so adorable that they momentarily disarm the enemy, allowing me to escape."

The smile dropped from Stefan's face. "The next question is, why did you steal the sword, and what did you do with it?"

Liv shook her head. "You said I only had to tell you why I had a bag of kittens. The sword was not part of the deal."

Stefan held up his hands as if in surrender. "You're right. So then, please continue about the kittens. What did you do with them?"

Clever approach, Liv thought. He was mostly referring to the sword, probably realizing that the kittens and weapon went together. "I returned them to my friend."

"And do you think the little felines are still in danger?"

Stefan quickly added, "From whoever tried to break in before?"

"I'm certain they are."

He nodded. "So what does your friend plan to do with ten kittens, especially with criminals posing such a danger to them?"

"That I don't know," Liv answered, knowing all too well that they were really talking about Turbinger. "I suppose I'll need to continue to help him protect them, although I'm not sure what that will involve."

Stefan took a drink. "Do you need some help?"

Liv arched an eyebrow. "Actually, I think you're the one who needs help. How long have you been infected?" She pointed to his right arm.

"How do you know where the bite is?" he asked, looking impressed.

"You're drinking using your left hand, although you use your right to swing your sword," Liv explained. "I'm guessing in battle it doesn't bother you, but otherwise you favor it."

"And here I thought you hardly noticed me," he said with a wink.

Liv snapped her fingers, an impatient expression on her face. "Out with the story, Stefan. I've got to get to bed on time since I'm opening the store tomorrow morning."

Stefan cracked a smile. "I think you're the first Warrior in the history of the House of Seven to have a side job."

"Yeah, but you go to college on the side, right?" Liv asked. "You're majoring in avoidance."

"Double major, actually," Stefan corrected. "Avoidance, and the art of distraction." He poured another drink for himself, looking to have loosened up considerably since they had sat down.

"So this demon that bit you. His name is Sabatore, right?" Liv threw him a curveball. "You're trying to track him down, aren't you?"

On cue, Stefan's mouth fell open. "How do you know its name?"

Liv took a drink. "I'm much better at following you than you are at trailing me. You never even knew I was there."

A dark shadow fell across his eyes as he lowered his chin.

Liv waved off his sudden seriousness. "Hey, it's only fair."

He shook his head. "No. You asked me to stop following you, and I did."

"Well, if I'm completely honest—"

"As you should be," he interrupted.

"Yes, as I should be," she continued, "the Council is suspicious of you. Clark related that to me. Said he thought you were hiding something. Since I don't trust anyone, I had to check things out for myself. I followed you the night you went to Amsterdam."

Realization dawned on him. "And you saw me questioning that demon about where Sabatore was?"

Liv affirmed his guess. "I didn't know then that you'd been bitten by a demon. Not until tonight when that demon said you'd been kissed. How would he know, though?"

Letting out a weighty breath, Stefan closed his eyes for half a beat. "The demon could smell it on me. Sense it in me. Demons share a common bond with one another, and he knew I'm not completely human anymore."

Liv tensed, feeling the severity of the matter suddenly. There was no hiding behind jokes anymore. "How long do you have?"

Stefan drained his glass. "It's hard to say. Each case is different, and most are not documented."

"Because the person who was bitten doesn't tell anyone, and therefore no one knows until they've disappeared and turned into a demon?" she suggested.

He nodded. "Yes, something like that."

"But why are you tracking down Sabatore?"

"Because that's the only way to create the antidote," Stefan explained. "I need his blood."

"Tonight when you were tracking those three demons, how were you doing it?" Liv asked, believing she already knew the answer.

"We're connected, like I said before. I can feel them."

Liv covered the shiver tracing its way down her spine. "Then why can't you find Sabatore?"

"It must be a part of the system of conversion," Stefan said with a sigh. "I think I'm blocked from him."

"Otherwise, everyone who was ever bitten would track down the demon who did it and get the antidote," Liv guessed.

Stefan assented with a nod.

"But if you've been on the hunt for Sabatore while tracking down demons, why is there a rise in their numbers? I saw you kill that one the other night."

Stefan ran his hands through his chaotic black hair, making it look much worse. "I've neglected my job in my attempts to find Sabatore. Yes, I've been going after some demons, but only specific ones who I think would know his whereabouts. That takes time. And it's getting harder to kill them, as well. Sometimes... Well, sometimes, I don't."

"Tonight you didn't seem to have a problem," Liv said, trying to be encouraging. The melancholy dripping off the other Warrior was nearly suffocating her.

"You were there," he admitted. "And it depends. I killed the demon in Amsterdam, but the day before, I let a few go, unable to finish the act."

"Because it feels like you're killing one of your own?" Liv guessed.

Stefan pushed her drink toward her with his forefinger. "Your drink is getting cold."

She smirked at this and swallowed the rest, pouring them another round. "Hester knows. Does anyone else?"

Stefan raised an eyebrow. "That's why in the library you asked me if I'd been bitten by something, isn't it?"

"Yes, she let it slip to me," Liv admitted.

His laugh broke the tension. "I kept wondering how you knew I'd been bitten. It definitely added to your mystery." He leaned forward, looking across the table at her. "I believe you've been bitten on the leg by something. Care to elaborate on that one?"

"Damn kittens," she said at once. "The little shits don't know their own strength."

Stefan laughed again. "And to answer your question, Hester is the only one who knows, besides you now. The Council can't know. No one can. If they did, well, I'd be..."

Liv lowered her chin, giving him an intense stare. "I know you think I'm going to infer the rest of that sentence, but it's incredibly important that you finish it. We can't have any confusion on this subject."

"Liv, protocol dictates that when a magician is bitten, they are 'disposed of.'"

There was that word the Council loved to use: dispose. It was a polite way of saying "kill."

"I don't understand how they could do that when you obviously haven't turned," Liv argued, heat flaring in her chest. "You have time, don't you? To find Sabatore and create the antidote?"

"Maybe. I mean, yes. I hope so." Stefan didn't sound at all sure of himself. "But I won't deny the logic. The demon's impulses are getting stronger. I'm able to control them, but I'm not sure how much longer that will last. And like I said, there is no way to know when I'll turn. It could be fast or gradual."

The man sitting across the table from Liv didn't resemble the demons they'd slain in Florida. His cheeks were flushed with color, and there was passion radiating from his eyes. However, if the demon's venom circulated in his blood, it was only a matter of time until he changed into a beast full of evil intent and malice.

"So you need help finding Sabatore," Liv stated.

Adamantly, Stefan shook his head. "No, I need you to stay out of this."

"Too late," she argued. "I'm already in it."

"Liv, the reason I went with you tonight is that you don't belong fighting demons. It's not a pleasant job, and the risks are high. I figured if I helped you with this case, you could return to the Council and they'd give you something different; something more in line with your talents."

"Although I appreciate the sentiment, I'm a little tired of everyone telling me what I should be doing."

"I didn't mean it that way," he cut in.

"You did, but let's move on from that. You need help," Liv countered. "And I have Bellator, which makes my job fighting demons easier."

"Bellator?" Stefan rolled the word around in his mouth, something sparking to the surface. "The sword you bought off the guy at the flea market—"

"Leonard," Liv supplied.

"Right, Leonard at the flea market sold you a sword named Bellator, which means 'warrior' in Latin," Stefan said.

"Yeah. Totally strange and awesomely random, huh?"

He nodded. "Uncanny, really. You'll have to take me to this market where you find such treasures."

"It's closed until spring."

Stefan snapped his fingers. "Damn my luck."

"Speaking of your luck," Liv began, "I've agreed to help you track down Sabatore."

The light expression dropped from his face. "No. I don't want your help."

"Stefan, this really isn't about you," Liv said, leaning forward. "Tell me, who replaces you if you become a demon?"

He hadn't expected the strange misdirection. "Well, no one. There are no other eligible Ludwigs in line to take the role of Warrior."

Liv nodded, having sensed this. "That means Raina would be booted off the Council. I'm sure Adler will have her replaced by someone more like Bianca and Lorenzo, who vote the way he wants them to. So, as you can see, this really isn't about saving your ass as much as keeping Raina, your lovely sister, in her current position."

His eyes danced with a hidden grin. "Well, when you put it that way…the answer is still no."

Liv knew the rules of reciprocation. It was how relationships worked. All she had to do was play this exactly right to get what she wanted: his consent. Because honestly, she was going to hunt down Sabatore whether or not Stefan agreed to it. She still wasn't sure, but after their day together, she sensed he was a good person. Magicians like him didn't deserve to become demons, preying on the weak and innocent. That would tear his already tarnished soul to pieces. That was the reason she made the impromptu decision.

"I was bitten by a lophos," she said in a rush.

Whatever Stefan was expecting Liv to say next, it wasn't that. He blinked at her in surprise. "How the hell did you encounter one of those? I thought they were incredibly rare."

"They are," she affirmed, then told him bits and pieces of the canister story.

When she concluded, he drummed his fingers on his lips, a speculative expression in his blue eyes. "Okay, you can help me."

"Wait, what?" Liv asked. "That's it? You aren't curious, or have questions or insights or anything?"

"Oh, I have all of that. Well, no insights, actually," Stefan said. "However, I think you're on to something. I've been suspicious since we were invited into the House of Seven, but I've never found anything like this. I'm going to accept your help in tracking down Sabatore, but in return, I want to help you."

Liv considered him for a moment. "I'm not asking for your help."

He grinned. "And I didn't ask for yours."

"Well played," she said.

"Honestly, I'm not sure what help I can provide," he stated. "I'm more of a Warrior than you."

Offense jumped to Liv's face. "I may be new, but—"

He held up his hand, pausing her. "Liv, Warriors are soldiers sent to do the Council's bidding. That's not you, though. You act on your own, and figure out things for yourself. You're more of a detective than a brute force, which I'd wager to say makes you more dangerous than the strongest of us."

Liv relaxed, softening her face. "Fine. Nice save."

"Now, I don't suppose that while we're building all these bridges, you're going to tell me why you stole that sword from the Natural History Museum?" Stefan asked.

Liv finished her drink and grinned. "Sure. I have a liking for antiques."

CHAPTER THIRTY-THREE

It was obvious from the moment Liv stepped through the Door of Reflection that most of the Council were surprised to see her. If anyone was curious what she was carrying, they hid it well. She took her place next to Stefan, careful to keep her eyes focused ahead.

As usual, Adler paused the lecture he was giving to regard Liv with mild contempt. "Ms. Beaufont, why are you here? The demon case—"

"It's done," she said simply, interrupting Adler. It was their thing. A cute little game they played.

Adler let out an audible sigh. "Ms. Beaufont, it takes Warriors weeks to track down demons, maybe even longer in your case since you're inexperienced. You can't expect the Council to believe you hunted down three demons all by yourself in a couple of days, do you?"

"Call it beginners' luck." Liv tossed the bag of demon heads into the middle of the chamber floor. They rolled out, their black eyes looking up at the Council. Bianca shrank back, as did the white tiger. Adler and Haro leaned over the bench, staring down at the heads as the crow swooped down, pecking one of the demons in the eye.

"Ms. Beaufont, are you making a mockery of these meetings?" Adler asked.

"I do believe you doubted whether Liv had in fact completed the case," Clark said, his tone laced with pride. "She's only providing proof." He looked at Hester and then Raina. "That seems perfectly reasonable to us, doesn't it? Considering that she completed the case in record time, and there would be skepticism on our part without such proof."

Hester agreed with a nod. "I don't think there is any way we can doubt Warrior Beaufont now."

"How?" Adler said with a growl, his eyes narrowed on Liv.

She rocked forward on her toes and back on her heels. "I cut off their heads."

This seemed to make him fume more. "No, how did you track down three demons in the middle of southern Florida so fast?"

"Well, although everything in Florida smells pretty bad, demons are the worst, so I followed my nose," Liv stated. "And I found a few tracking spells that sped up the timeframe. Oh, and they were really hungry, so I bought a herd of goats from a rancher to use as bait."

"Goats?" Bianca questioned.

"Yeah," Liv answered. "They are these farm animals. Some have horns. These didn't, because they were baby goats. Don't worry, none were harmed in the slaying of the demons."

"I know what goats are, Olivia, I was simply questioning why you'd use them on this case," Bianca said, her expression severely pinched.

"Because my name is Liv," she said dryly, so tired of correcting her on this one.

"It was a good idea," Hester said at once. "Although not common knowledge, goats are good bait for hungry demons."

Liv hadn't known that bit of uncommon knowledge until Stefan had shared it with her while they were planning how this whole thing would go down. He'd told her that most of the Council wouldn't believe she'd slaughtered the three demons on her own so quickly, so they'd constructed a scenario no one could doubt.

"Well, it appears that you, Mr. Ludwig, could take a page out of Ms. Beaufont's book," Alder said, leaning back as he grimaced at the crow pecking at the demon head. "Maybe if you were doing your job better, the rise in the demon population wouldn't be happening."

Stefan nodded. "Yes, sir. I'll work harder to control it."

"You do that," Adler said, scrolling through his tablet. "I guess you're ready for a new case, Ms. Beaufont. We had something come in today that would suit you, and although the Council hasn't voted on it, I'm sure they'll all agree it's perfect for you and—"

"I want to keep hunting demons," Liv interrupted.

All of the councilors looked up at Liv, surprise evident in their stares. Clark was the one leaning forward the farthest. He looked like he was about to topple over the bench.

"It's just that I am good at it, and there's a need," Liv stated. "And maybe if Stefan and I tackle them together—"

"I assure you that's not necessary," Stefan said, injecting ego into his voice.

"I only meant that there is so much a newbie demon hunter could learn from you," Liv said.

While the Council considered this, Hester gave Liv a discriminating stare that said, "Do you know what you're doing?" She knew Liv was partnering with a magician who could turn into a demon at any moment, putting her at ultimate risk, but the councilor also knew that if Sabatore wasn't caught, Stefan would be lost forever.

Stefan turned and gave Liv a contemptuous glare. "You'll only slow me down."

"Stefan," Raina scolded from the bench.

Adler held out his hand, seeming to enjoy this. "Actually, after what we've learned today, it appears that you, Warrior Ludwig, would be the one to slow *her* down. How many demons have you slain this month? Two?"

"Two and a half," Stefan corrected.

Adler raised a discerning eyebrow. "How is there a half?"

"I severely injured one," Stefan explained. "I think it will be easy to track it down and finish it off."

"Well, good," Adler said, looking pleased. "I think that Ms. Beaufont's help will be what you need here. Maybe get you out of your rut."

Stefan glared at Liv, doing an excellent job of looking like he hated her very existence. "I work alone."

"You work with who we assign you," Adler stated.

He probably thought that he'd be getting rid of two nuisances at once, not even realizing he was being played.

"I don't particularly want you in my sandbox either," Liv told the Warrior.

"Fine, then we'll hunt demons separately," Stefan said with a tired sigh, his arms behind his back and his chin lifted.

"You will do it together," Adler said with finality.

Liv grunted with disapproval.

Stefan lowered his eyes.

Adler cast his eyes left and right down the bench, checking for agreement. "All in favor?"

The councilors all consented, Hester showing the least enthusiasm.

Liv could hardly believe they'd played the Council so well. Maybe she and Stefan Ludwig would make a good team after all.

CHAPTER THIRTY-FOUR

"Well, that settles it," Rory said, deboning a salmon as the kittens mewed at his feet. "You've lost your damn mind."

"What do you mean?" Liv asked, checking the dining room when she heard a noise. It was only Junebug crawling into a teacup on the dining room table. Spread across the surface was a floral print tablecloth. On top of it was a polished silver tray that held a teapot, creamer, sugar, and a tray of cookies. "Why does it look like you're about to have the queen over for afternoon tea?"

"What?" Rory called from the kitchen. "Oh, that? I always have that sitting out. It's decoration."

Liv lifted the lid off the teapot, steam rising from it. "And you always have freshly brewed tea, too. That's impressive."

"It's nothing," Rory said. "I just like to have some tea sometimes."

Liv observed that there were two place settings at the

table and shook her head. "Are the kittens joining you? If so, you need to set out some extra teacups."

Rory shook his head at her when she reentered the kitchen. "The kittens are having salmon. They don't drink tea."

"Right," Liv said, drawing out the word. "Thanks for clarifying. And you do realize that stores sell these cans of food? Cats love it, and it's easier than deboning fish."

Rory grimaced. "You don't feed that stuff to Plato, do you?"

"He likes it," she argued.

"He just doesn't know any better."

Liv rolled her eyes. "Plato has been around a lot longer than me, and he knows what he likes. If he wants something different, I suspect he'll tell me or go get it himself."

He shook his head at her, using his shoulder to push the hair out of his eyes. "You still misunderstand so much about lynxes."

"It's hard to learn much from the book about him," Liv stated. "At first it wasn't so bad, because every time I opened it, somehow it was on that chapter dealing with lynxes. However, now when I crack open the book, it's always a different chapter, and I can't find the one on lynxes."

"That's because the book tries to tell you what you need to know about most," Rory explained. "At first you didn't need to know that much, but with your growing responsibilities and challenges, your knowledge base needs to expand."

"So what do I misunderstand about lynxes?" Liv asked, thinking back to the wetlands in Florida and firmly believing that if it hadn't been for Plato's strange warning, the demon might have taken her out.

"You're his human," Rory said, sliding the bones into the trash and arranging the fish on a decorative plate. "A lynx only attaches itself to one human at a time. The scope of their world becomes his, so even if he can go off to eat the finest foods in Paris or wherever, if that's too far from you, he won't risk it. He'll confine himself to your vicinity and eat the junk you feed him because that's part of your world."

"For someone who seems to loathe Plato, you just said a lot of things to the contrary," Liv stated.

"I never said there weren't some redeeming qualities to lynxes," Rory reasoned. "It's only that you must ask yourself why he's attached himself to you. At their core, lynxes are self-serving. They hide the truth and guard secrets."

Liv couldn't argue with any of that. These had been her concerns about Plato, but she wasn't getting rid of him, no matter what. For whatever reason, her instinct told her to trust him the same way she had with John when they'd met, and now Rory. And maybe even Stefan. If everyone were as pure and perfect as little Sophia then choosing to trust them wouldn't be so hard, but as people grew up, things weren't so black and white. Liv hoped she and Sophia always had a relationship where the trust was blind and the bond unwavering. It was the easiest part of her life. She never doubted her loyalty to the little girl, or to Clark either, really. *Familia Est Sempiternum.*

"Back to the matter at hand," Rory said, setting the plate of fish on the floor, the kittens tripping over themselves to get to it. They lined up around the plate, gobbling up the food. "You can't work with someone who has been bitten by a demon. Actually, the Council should know about it. Stefan is a danger to himself as well as others."

Liv shook her head. "I'm not going to rat on him, and he's aware of the dangers. So am I, and he needs my help."

"Liv, I get that you want to be the hero here—"

"But I don't," Liv cut in. "I'd be happy working in the repair shop for the rest of my life, but that's not an option for me anymore. John is moving on, and my family needs me. And for that matter, Stefan needs me. If you got bitten by a demon, I wouldn't stop until I had tracked down that beast and helped you create the antidote. That's not acting as a hero, that's being a friend."

Rory washed his hands, drying them on a pressed kitchen towel. "Yes, but Stefan isn't your friend."

"No, he's not, but he doesn't have anyone else he can rely on. And isn't that how we, the disadvantaged loners of the world, haphazardly make friends? We fall into need, and someone helps us? That's how you and I came to be whatever we are." Liv motioned between them.

"You're a thorn in my side," Rory said.

"Yes, I like that better than friend too," Liv said with a wink. "But my point remains. If I hadn't had my magic unlocked and was about to destroy WeHo with it, I wouldn't have asked for your help, and we wouldn't be here now."

Rory glared down at the kitchen floor and scowled. "And there wouldn't be mud tracked all over my floors. Were you raised in a barn?"

"A hidden magical house, actually," Liv said, swiping her fingers to the left and making the dirt disappear.

"Sorry, the mud in the wetlands is awful to try to get out of the grooves in my boots." She pointed at her boots, removing them and stationing them outside the front door. "And then there's John. I never would have met him if I hadn't been lost and alone and looking for work. He took me in and gave me a job, and now? Well, he's the best."

Rory's face softened. "Yes, John is a good man. I'm sorry to see him go."

Liv found it hard to swallow. "My point is, we have to rely on each other, and Stefan needs me. I'm not sure I can help him find Sabatore, but I've got to try. I think you'd do the same thing in my position."

Rory rolled his shoulders, looking at the cuckoo clock on the wall. "It's time for you to go."

"What?" Liv asked, surprised by his abruptness. "But I just got here, and we were supposed to discuss the elf. Did he take anything? Search your place? What wards have you put up to ensure he doesn't get back in here?"

"That's why you have to go," Rory stated. "I have someone coming over who might be able to help with what I'm working on."

Liv ducked her head into the dining room to look at the tea service. "Oh, is this... Are you having a lady friend over?"

Rory didn't look at all pleased with her. He was glaring at the back door, its window shade tightly closed. "I'm working on something, and need you to leave."

"Oh, that thing in the backyard you didn't want me to see?" Liv asked. "I didn't sneak a peek, by the way. I'm good like that."

"I know you didn't," Rory said. "You still have all your fingers."

Liv held her hands to her chest protectively. "Damn, you're a warped and strange giant."

"I'm much nicer than most," he assured her.

"Fine, I'll get out of your curly afro," Liv said as the doorbell rang. It was a low, chiming noise that went on for a while. She swung around to gauge Rory. "Do you want me to portal out of here?"

He shook his head. "You can't." He looked at the back door and then the front, apparently trying to decide what to do with her. Resigning he trotted toward the front door. "Fine, follow me, but don't say anything dumb. Actually, don't say anything at all."

Liv nodded, pretending to zip her mouth shut. "Im-mana-preden-I-cat-halk."

"Don't do that," Rory warned.

When Rory opened the door, another giant stood on the porch, wearing a dress full of greens and blues. On the woman's head was a large hat adorned with flowers and fake birds. She leaned under the archway to the door, stepping through and hugging Rory.

"Well, look at you," the woman said, her voice much more shrill than Liv would have expected given her size. "You're every bit as handsome as you were the last time I saw you, my dear little boy."

"Little boy," Liv muttered to herself.

The woman looked at Liv, releasing Rory. "And who do we have here? A friend of sorts? Is this why you called me over?" The woman looked at Rory and Liv, anticipation on her face. "Have you decided to settle down? Not with a magician. Oh, please, no."

Rory's face blossomed into an awful shade of red. "Oh, no. Liv? No." He shook his head. "No. That's not why I asked you over. It's not like that. Liv is no one."

"I'm flattered," Liv said dryly.

The woman studied her. "Well, she's a bit puny, I agree. And her features are not at all handsome, but I'm sure there are other redeeming qualities to her."

"I can hear you," Liv said loudly.

The woman who shared Rory's large nose and green eyes elbowed him in the side. "On the plus side, she has excellent hearing. That's always good. We should never take these things for granted. Your father lost his hearing working in the mines with the gnomes. I swear, I would shout his name until I was blue in the face and he wouldn't hear me." She placed her pinky to her chin, considering this notion as if something new had occurred to her. "Come to think of it, he always came home when supper was ready, so maybe it was selective hearing loss."

Liv pushed out her cheeks, feeling exceptionally uncomfortable. "Well, I'd better be off. Sorry to interrupt your tea party."

The woman waved a gloved hand at Liv. She looked fit for a Sunday church service. "Don't be ridiculous. Please join us."

"She can't," Rory said at once.

"Oh, Rory, stop being that way and introduce your friend to your mummy." The woman extended her large hand to Liv. "I'm Rory's mum. You can call me—"

"Bermuda," Liv interrupted.

The woman blushed. "I see you've heard of me, and I was going to say 'Mrs. Laurens.' We're a bit new for first names, wouldn't you say?"

Liv wrung the woman's hand, feeling like she was… well, shaking hands with a giant. "Yes, of course. My apologies, Mrs. Laurens. I'm simply surprised to meet you. Rory didn't tell me you were stopping by."

"Stopping by?" Bermuda asked Rory. "You requested I drop everything to get here. Said it was supremely important. I used my transport stone to get here, which will be causing tremors all over the city, I suspect."

"Yes, thanks, Mum," Rory said. "It is important, and we have much work to do. I'll explain everything."

Bermuda clapped her hands together, a smile springing to her face. "Well, it looks like all those years of finishing school served you well. You set out tea for me."

"Finishing school?" Liv mouthed behind Bermuda's back as she admired the dining room table.

Rory shook his head at her, discouraging her from saying any more.

"Well, let's not let it get cold," Bermuda said. "Please sit, children, and then you can tell me everything that's been going on, Rory, and about your new friend. I'm sorry, I didn't catch your name."

"Liv," she answered. "Liv Beaufont."

Bermuda raised an eyebrow as Rory covered his face with his hands. "And there we have it. My son has made friends with not just a magician, but a royal."

"I'm a Warrior, actually," Liv supplied, which made Rory groan again.

Bermuda nodded curtly. "A Warrior. How very charming, Rory. Just wait until your family hears about this." The tone in her voice made it seem like it would not be welcome news.

"Well, look at the time," Liv said, glancing at her wrist although she wasn't wearing a watch. "I better get going. I've got gnomes to slay and demons to arrest. I mean, demons to slay and...never mind."

"Don't be silly," Bermuda said, pulling out a chair. "I'm sure if my son is tolerating your company, it's for a good reason. Or..." She looked at Rory suddenly, grief covering her face. "You haven't caught that evil virus you had when you were a baby that affects your cognitive functioning again, have you?"

Liv cupped her hand to her ear. "What? Oh, I think I hear my cat calling me. I better go."

Bermuda giggled. "Everyone knows that cats can't call you. Now, a lynx? They could call you from a fair distance, but only someone mentally unstable would keep a lynx around."

Liv nodded, half-enjoying the panic streaming across Rory's face. "Right, and who would do that?"

"No friend of my son's," Bermuda said with a giggle, pulling off her gloves. "Now, take a seat. I want to learn all about you. I'm sure you're not as despicable and self-serving as my notions lead me to believe."

Liv stalled, not sure what to say for a moment. "I would, but I have bowling practice."

Rory closed his eyes tightly.

Bermuda paused in the middle of reaching for a cookie. "Bowling practice? You mean that sport with the balls and slippery shoes?"

"That's the one," Liv said, looking down at her bare feet. "And I'm late. Although I'd love to stay and watch Rory age ten years, I'd better be off. It was nice to meet you, Mrs. Laurens."

"Well, I'm not sure I'd exaggerate so much about our first meeting, but okay. Nice isn't the word I'd use," she said, waving to her with a pleasant smile. Then the giantess saw something over Liv's shoulder and her smile faded. She pointed. Looked back at Rory. Did a double-take at the fireplace. "Rory, is that…"

He gulped. Nodded. "Yes. That's the reason I asked you to come here."

Bermuda nearly pushed Liv over, striding by her and over to the fireplace, where Turbinger hung above the mantel. With an agility Liv wouldn't have guessed she possessed, she picked up the sword and swung it lightly, appreciating the weapon in her hands. When she looked up at Rory, her eyes were brimming with tears. "My dear son, how did you get this?"

Rory let out a breath, his chest rising and falling greatly with the act. He pointed at Liv. "The runt. She recovered the sword for me. For us."

Bermuda's eyes widened in shock and then narrowed with a strange appreciation. "You got back my father's sword, did you?"

"Well, I was… I met a brownie…and yeah, it was me."

Bermuda acted as if she hadn't heard Liv stuttering as she swung the sword again; not much, but enough to test the balance. "It has been a long time. I didn't think I'd hold this sword again in my lifetime. I didn't even think my son would hold it one day. It's been a long, long time." Holding the sword still, Bermuda bowed slightly to Liv. "I appreciate any danger you faced to return this to us. I do not know the extent of your relationship with my son, but I'm more hopeful than before that he's not squandering his time with useless aristocrats."

"Thank you?" Liv said, drawing out the word, uncertainty laced into the two words.

"You're very welcome." With a deep sigh, Bermuda returned the sword to its place above the mantel and clapped her hands, turning back around to face them. "Well, we have much to discuss and celebrate. Shall we sit down for tea?"

The look on Rory's face screamed no.

Liv coughed. "I'd love to, but like I said, I've got to get to bowling practice. Those pins aren't going to knock themselves over."

The annoyance was heavy on Rory's face when she backed toward the front door.

"Well, if you must," Bermuda said, not looking sad to see her leave. "But again, thank you for returning that which belongs to the giants. I appreciate the gesture, even if it was probably your own who stole it from the giants in the first place."

"Right. I sort of don't know what to say to the blatant prejudice, so I'll just bid you both farewell," Liv said, realizing that her shoes were parked outside the door.

"Yes, yes, farewell to you," Bermuda said, striding over to the table, not at all concerned about wishing Liv goodbye. "Please say hello to the treacherous magicians you share the House of Seven with. They won't remember me or mine, but we think of them often when confined by their rules."

"I'll pass that along," Liv said with a forced smile, waving to Rory as she slipped out the door onto the porch.

She shook off the strangeness of that interaction as she picked up a boot caked in Florida mud. Liv was just about to slip it on her foot when she caught a spark at the corner of her vision.

From the side of the porch, a fire appeared to erupt. Liv worried that the security system had been set off again, although she immediately remembered that Rory had upgraded it. Her eyes adjusted to the light of dusk, and she noticed a rectangular outline like that of a door etched in firelight. She stalled, trying to understand what she was seeing, when the fabricated door swung open and the deranged elf stepped through.

Liv did the only thing she could think of at that moment and threw her boot at his head, hitting him in the face. He fell back, momentarily confused by the assault, but when he shook it off, he glared at her, fear and frustration in his eyes. He hopped to his feet and sprinted in the opposite direction of the house. Liv didn't hesitate, running shoeless after him into the streets.

CHAPTER THIRTY-FIVE

The pavement under Liv's feet was hard and punishing. She hardly noticed it as she raced after the elf, who moved in a zigzag fashion ahead of her like he was constantly changing his mind about which direction he should run.

He darted toward an overgrown yard, then, after checking over his shoulder, swerved across the street and went down a side alley. A gang of kids playing on the sidewalk watched with amusement as the elf streaked by, Liv following and gaining on him.

Not only was she able to catch up because he wasn't taking a direct path, but he also appeared to be limping. Additionally, his arms dangled strangely by his sides. Something wasn't right with the elf. Liv imagined that it had to do with the poison from Turbinger. It was making him crazy, and much more, she could tell. Running at an even pace, she was sure she'd catch up with him by the end of the cramped alley.

A pile of broken glass was strewn across the pavement.

She noticed almost too late and leapt, not completely clearing it. Bits of glass sank into her feet, but Liv didn't slow down, knowing she couldn't allow the elf to get away yet again. He was the key to whoever was behind trying to get to Turbinger. She'd already worked out that he wasn't the culprit. The elf worked for someone. He'd said as much at the National History Museum.

She recalled his desperation as they fought over the sword: "They will kill me if I return without it," the elf had yelled, his voice tearful. He had reached out. "You might as well murder me."

Whoever the elf worked for hadn't murdered him, though. Why?

Liv pushed herself harder to try to gain on the elf, but the glass in her feet was slowing her down. Then hope spread in her chest. The elf had halted, and he cast a nervous glance at her over his shoulder before turning around to face her directly. She thought he was about to surrender, his face hollow and eyes full of darkness.

However, to her disappointment and surprise, he opened a portal and stepped through quicker than she thought he could in his condition. Liv pushed forward, feeling the glass sink in deeper with each step. She held out her hand, sending a beam out and trying to stop the portal from closing before she got there.

The portal folded in on itself, shrinking toward the center.

No, no, no, Liv thought, not giving up, like a doctor doing heart compressions, unwilling to accept that the patient on the operating room table was gone. She couldn't lose the elf again. He'd be back, and his trespassing would cause even more danger. She was tired of running from the elf. Tired of protecting Turbinger from him. This ended now.

When the portal was almost closed, it exploded into blue and green lights, shining so brightly Liv was forced to halt and shield her eyes. It glowed blindingly before fading slightly, hovering above the ground, unwavering.

Liv let out a breath of relief, hurrying again despite the pain in her feet. Undeterred by whatever was on the other side of the elf's portal, Liv stepped through into the unknown.

To her surprise, Liv recognized the street where the portal spat her out. Downtown LA. They weren't far from where they'd been in Rory's neighborhood.

She stepped onto the sidewalk as mortals strode by, hurrying for the intersections. To them, she would appear as though she'd been in that spot all along. Portal magic made it so that entering highly trafficked areas was not seen as suspicious. Mortals never saw them for what they were and explained away any peculiarities.

Ahead on the bustling sidewalk, Liv spotted the elf. He'd slowed to a walk, swaying like he was drunk. He hadn't noticed Liv slip through the portal. Hadn't even considered that as an option. Rory had stated it was a trick not many knew about. There was apparently a common misconception that portals could only be closed or stalled by the person who had made them. It was that misconception Liv had capitalized on.

Pushing past mortals on the sidewalk, the elf appeared to get angrier as he progressed, yelling at an old woman and kicking a homeless man's shopping cart. The crowd moving in his direction shrank away from him, giving him enough space to pass them without suffering his wrath.

The elf stopped at a building that towered above the rest and brought his chin up, staring at the skyscraper. Even from halfway down the block, she could tell he was muttering to himself, whipping around a couple of times like he expected someone to attack him from behind.

Liv slid into an entrance to a pharmacy, trying to hide in case the elf looked back.

"Where are your shoes?" a bum asked her. He was sitting against the building, counting the change in a worn baseball cap.

That question brought the pain to the surface of her mind. Lifting her feet, she examined the many cuts in the soles. Even though the mortal was looking directly at her, she pointed to her bare feet, pulling the glass out, which brought instant relief. There was nothing she could do about the cuts right then, but she could prevent infection. She summoned her boots from Rory's yard, and they appeared and laced around her feet seconds later.

The mortal blinked at the sudden appearance and nodded. "Oh, I didn't see them before."

Liv smiled at him, peeking around the corner as the elf slipped into the building, looking back and forth as he did.

She was about to hurry after him when a voice in her head stopped her. *Sword. Summon it,* Plato said from somewhere inside her head.

Liv halted, closing her eyes briefly. She hadn't tried

summoning anything so difficult as her sword before. Clothes and shoes were apparently easy, especially because she'd been wearing them earlier. However, weapons were supposedly much more difficult. For that reason, Liv was surprised when she opened her eyes to find Bellator in her hands. She hadn't even realized it was there until she looked at it. Only then did she feel the weight of the sword.

"That's a pretty umbrella," the homeless man said, staring at the sword. *So that's how he sees Bellator,* she realized. "I don't think it's supposed to rain, but at least you'll be prepared if it does."

Liv nodded, sheathing the sword at her waist. Maybe it was the connection between her and Bellator that made it easier to summon. She realized that she'd used more energy to retrieve her boots than the sword.

The bum began humming an odd tune as Liv slipped around the corner, hurrying toward the entrance to the skyscraper where the elf had disappeared. She pushed through the revolving door and ducked behind a group of elderly ladies at once.

The elf was arguing with a security guard, who looked unwilling to let him into the elevator.

"He's waiting to see me!" the elf yelled, his hands waving wildly over his head.

"I have to see him. I need his help!'

The guard shook his head. "He specifically stated that you weren't to come up to his office."

"But I need to talk to him!" the elf complained.

Who was this man the elf needed to talk to? Liv wondered, walking in a crouched position behind the elderly ladies as they chatted and heading in the direction of the elevator.

"If you don't leave now, you'll be escorted from the building and refused entry ever again," the guard said, towering over the elf.

He held up his fist, his lips parted and his yellow teeth clenched in a sneer. Although Liv expected him to argue, he backed away, holding up his hands. "Fine. I don't want any trouble. I'll leave."

The guard nodded as the elf retreated.

However, Liv caught the gesture and evil twinkle in the elf's eyes as he held up his hand, water spraying from it, directed at the elderly women nearing the elevator. They covered their heads, screaming.

"A pipe must have burst on the first floor again," the guard said urgently, reaching for the women before they fell.

Liv slipped away from them in the chaos of the moment, following as the elf sprinted across the lobby to the door on the far side of the stairs. In the chaos of the sudden appearance of the water, the guard didn't even notice the elf slip away, too busy trying to help the women to safety.

Liv hung back until the elf disappeared into the stairwell and then followed. She pulled Bellator from her hip before inching the door back and peering through. When she didn't hear racing feet on the stairs, she knew something was askew. A hand reached through, grabbing her wrist and yanking her into the stairwell.

Liv found herself face to face with the deranged elf. This close, she realized that his entire face was covered in black spider-like veins. His eyes were red, and blood was dripping from one of his nostrils.

Throwing her weight straight into him, Liv slammed him up against the wall, bringing Bellator to his throat. Easily she restrained his arms, realizing that he had little strength.

He winced, his bad breath hitting her straight in the face. "If you just gave me the sword, this would all be over."

Liv placed the blade against his throat, shaking her head. "There is no way to end your suffering. The sword can't help you."

The elf's eyes grew large and tragic. "What? No! I was told that if I got the sword, it would fix me."

Liv shook her head. "They lied to you. Tell me who you work for and I'll do what I can, but no promises."

He tried to shake his head, but it made his throat rub against the sharp blade. He halted. "I can't. They've sworn me to secrecy."

"Whatever they're doing to you, my punishment will be way worse," Liv threatened.

The elf looked undeterred. "You don't understand. I *can't* tell you. Kill me if you must, *please* kill me. But I can't tell you who I work for."

He's been enchanted not to tell, Liv realized.

The elf pushed forward, his throat pressing into the blade. He was trying to get her to end things. Slit his throat.

Liv stepped back, shaking her head at him. "You can't tell me, but you can take me there." She pointed up the stairs with Bellator. "Go!"

The elf's eyes swiveled to the door at their backs, defeat on his face. He wasn't strong enough to fight her, and they both knew that. There was no way he was getting out of this.

Clenching his teeth, he swung around and started to climb the stairs. Liv allowed him to get up to the next landing before following him. The elf smelled like rotting flesh and sickness, a combination that made her stomach rumble uneasily. If possible, it was worse than the demons, because the smell made her realize how sick he was. The elf was dying from Turbinger's mark. Each step seemed to cost him great effort.

As they continued the trek up another flight of stairs, Liv found herself feeling sorry for him. He was just some pawn used to secure Turbinger, but people weren't expendable in her book. And worse than these realizations was the one that she'd marked him with the sword. Although she hadn't meant to, while battling with Turbinger and trying to misdirect the giant sword, it had cut the elf—a fatal blow that was worse than death. Rory said a wound from Turbinger brought madness and pain, which inevitably ended in death, but only after great suffering.

"You should kill me," the elf said after a long moment of silence, almost like he'd read her sympathetic thoughts.

"I'm afraid I already have," Liv said morbidly, listening to their footsteps.

"Then finish the job," he urged, grief constricting his voice. "If there is no saving me using the sword, then end this for me."

Liv shook her head. "I can't do that."

She knew very well that she could. She'd brought Bellator across the demon's neck, ending its life. She didn't think of herself as a murderer, but she was starting to believe she was a killer. Was there a difference? She liked to think there was.

Liv hadn't realized how high they'd climbed until the elf doubled over from exhaustion, his hands on his knees and his breath rattling. She stopped short of him to give him space. They were on the twelfth floor.

"Let's take the elevator from here," Liv suggested, pointing to the door to the floor.

Liv sheathed her sword as the elf opened the door, pushing as if the weight of the stairwell door was almost too much for him. She grabbed it before it crushed him, holding it open.

The floor they exited onto was empty. It appeared to be under construction, some of the areas were covered in white plastic. Paint cans and supplies were stored in the corner ahead. Overhead, exposed wires sprouted out of the canned lighting.

The elf stopped abruptly in front of her, giving her just enough time to halt before running into him. She was shocked to find tears streaming down his cheeks as he turned and regarded her with a tragic look.

"I can't go up there," he said, his voice quivering with fear.

"Can't you see that he did this to you?" Liv argued. Whoever *he* was.

The elf opened his mouth, saliva stretching between his lips. "It doesn't matter. I have to end it now. I only persisted because he said the sword would fix me, but if what you say is true, I'm doomed." He was shaking when he stretched his hands up. He took a step and jumped into the air, grabbing onto an electrical wire

Liv was about to react when she heard a piddling sound. She'd thought the elf had peed himself until she realized that water was streaming from his other hand, pointed toward his feet. It puddled there, covering his shoes.

For a moment Liv couldn't understand what was happening, then he moved quicker than she'd seen him do all day. He grabbed the wires, pulling off their capped ends and holding on tightly.

The elf erupted in sparks, electricity ripping through his body. His eyes bulged unnaturally, and steam rose from his head. He vibrated violently as the electrocution ended him. Liv shielded her face, backing away from the elf, not wanting to watch what would most assuredly be his final moments.

The smell of burning flesh assaulted her nose as the overhead lights dimmed. Then the elf fell backward in a crumpled mess, the water he'd created steaming around him.

He was dead.

CHAPTER THIRTY-SIX

Before the authorities were called, Liv ducked back into the stairwell, taking the steps three at a time.

The elf was gone, and with him the one chance she'd had to determine who was behind stealing the sword. She couldn't ignore the dull ache that erupted in her belly because of the obvious defeat. Watching the elf fry had been horrible. It had been one of the most jarring scenes she'd yet to see, and even though she hadn't processed it yet, she knew it would stay with her for a long time. However, the elf was gone now, no matter what. He'd decided to end things on his terms, and she couldn't really blame him. Someone had lied to him. Told him if he got the sword, his suffering would end. How devastating to learn that it had been a lie and there was no hope.

The desperation was infectious, wrapping around Liv's heart. As long as this person was out there, Rory and Turbinger were in danger. How had she come so far, only to lose this lead?

When Liv came to the bottom floor, she was surprised

to find that the lobby wasn't in turmoil. Apparently, no one had figured out that a death had happened on the twelfth floor. They would, though, and she wasn't sure she should be around for it.

She halted in the middle of the lobby, looking at the bank of elevators with people filing in and out of them. She may not know much, but she knew that somewhere on one of these fifty floors was the person behind the plot to steal the sword. However, she had no idea how to find him.

For an instant, she considered taking the elevator to every floor and investigating. However, that could take a long time, and time wasn't something she had plenty of. She'd promised Stefan that they'd start searching for Sabatore soon, and she needed to get back to the shop and check on John. Disappointment and heartbreak made her head drop. She had to start packing.

The janitors moved around her, mopping up the water she hadn't even realized she'd stepped into. They didn't seem to mind her, but Liv moved out of their way, trying to find dry ground. When she was standing in front of the elevators, something on the directory of the building caught her eyes. At first, she wasn't sure why. She couldn't place the names, but they struck a chord in her mind.

Usher and Usher Law Firm

It was listed as having offices on the top floor.

Where have I heard this before? Liv wondered. Then a recent memory streamed across her consciousness, bringing with it uncomfortable feelings.

"My name is Wayne Grimson. I work for Usher and Usher law firm. You might have heard of us," said the man who had delivered the news to John about the fate of his repair shop.

Liv's eyes focused on the placard with the words Usher and Usher Law Firm on the directory. Could it be just a coincidence that this was the law firm behind John's shop? She didn't think so. She stepped onto the elevator and took it to the top floor.

CHAPTER THIRTY-SEVEN

The law office was buzzing with secretaries hustling between cubicles when Liv stepped off the elevator. She hadn't realized she was dressed so differently from them until she'd gotten three strange looks. If she had thought about it, she would have changed into a pencil skirt and blazer like the rest of them. However, she thought that showing up in her black cape with her sheathed sword might be better. More of an impact.

"May I help you?" the woman behind the receptionist desk asked.

Liv was just about to respond when she recognized the back of a man's head. It was Mr. Grimson, heading into a back office.

"I'm good," Liv said, sweeping by the woman.

"Miss, unless you have an appointment, you—"

"I have an appointment," Liv said, lacing her words with magical intention.

The secretary was easily brainwashed, shaking her head and turning around. "That's right. Of course, you do."

Liv kept her chin high as she breezed past the other offices, earning many curious stares. When she arrived at the largest one at the back, she halted in the entrance. Mr. Grimson's office was much like him, stuffy and lacking any personality.

"Michelle, just put the files on the table," he said, sitting behind his desk and focusing intently on a report in front of him.

Liv strode into the office, pulling Bellator from her hip. She angled the sword and thrust it into the top of the lawyer's desk, piercing the report he'd been reading. He didn't jump back as she had expected, but rather calmly looked up at her, blinking dully.

She knew then that he was behind all this. He had to be. Anyone else would have freaked the moment he was nearly impaled with a sword.

"Oh, it's you," he said, no enthusiasm in his voice.

Liv tilted her chin, making the door at her back slam shut and lock. "Yes, and I know that you're behind the elf who has been trying to steal Turbinger."

Mr. Grimson raised an eyebrow, not at all looking deterred. "Ms. Beaufont, my client simply wants returned to them what is rightfully theirs."

Liv grabbed the hilt of Bellator and yanked it from the desk, keeping the tip directed at Mr. Grimson's unyielding face. "Who is your client?"

The lawyer actually smiled. "Intimidation won't work on me. I'm prohibited from speaking, no matter what form of torture you use." He laughed coldly. "I'll even pretend to like it. I'm not quite sure I can pull that off, but I know I can't talk."

Just like the elf, this man was charmed not to speak and disclose information.

"Why are you forcing John out of his shop?" Liv asked, still pointing the sword at the uptight lawyer.

He shrugged. "My client believes that if you're not willing to give up what belongs to them, you should suffer."

Damn it, Liv thought, a crushing feeling assaulting her insides. This was all her fault. She'd put John in a horrible position. As she feared, her enemies had become his, taking out their anger at her on him.

"You will drop this case against John and leave him alone," she said, injecting the same persuasion she'd used on the receptionist into her voice.

Wayne Grimson simply smiled. "Brainwashing won't work on me. My client has assured that much."

Damn it, damn it, damn it, Liv thought, gripping Bellator tighter.

"What exactly does your client want?" Liv nearly yelled.

"I believe it is quite clear," he answered casually. "They want the sword."

"And?" Liv asked, expecting more.

He raised an eyebrow. "That is all, and quite enough."

Someone was trying to open the door at their back. Mr. Grimson kept his focus on Liv, not distracted.

"In return for the sword, my client is willing to drop the injunction against Mr. Carraway, allowing him to keep his shop," Mr. Grimson continued.

"What?" Liv asked, disbelieving this. "Your client is insane."

His eyes flicked to the point of the sword, which was still directed at his Adam's apple. "My client knows what the shop and Mr. Carraway mean to you. Those are the terms of the agreement. If you don't give me the sword, the case will go forward, and there is nothing Mr. Carraway or you can do."

"I can slaughter you," Liv threatened.

He nodded easily. "You can, but my client will simply hire another lawyer for the case, and I'm sure that will make them angry. Who knows what will happen to Mr. Carraway then? Probably something worse than forced retirement."

Liv's worst nightmare was coming true. The vision from the Door of Reflection of John lying helpless in a hospital bed because of her played in her head.

Lowering her sword, Liv regarded the lawyer from hooded eyes.

"If you bring me the sword, you have my word that the case will be dropped." Mr. Grimson said.

"What good is your word?" Liv asked bitterly.

He blinked at her, appearing more like a robot than a man. "I am bound by oath. If I say I'll do it, it will happen."

"And your client?" Liv inquired. "Will they leave us alone altogether?"

Mr. Grimson gave her a cold look. "It's hard to say. I think that all depends on what you do, and how much you continue to snoop where you're unwelcome."

CHAPTER THIRTY-EIGHT

Rory thundered across the living room floor, his hands in his hair. "Of course it was a threat."

"But I don't understand," Liv said, doing her own pacing. "I stole the sword for you—"

"And I'm sorry that it's gotten you and John into this mess," Rory interrupted.

She shook him off. "No, it's just that whoever is behind this, they think I'm snooping. Do they know about the other things at the House of Seven I've been researching? The ring? The founders' language? The message Reese left us?"

Rory shook his head, careful to step gingerly over the kittens as they raced underfoot. "Maybe. It's hard to know at this point, but you have to back off."

Liv halted, regarding him like he'd just eaten one of the kittens. "Hell, no. I'm not backing off."

"Liv, whoever is behind this, they are dangerous and powerful," Rory stated. "I haven't seen in decades the enchantments the elf used to try to get into my house.

Those aren't easy spells, and I suspect the elf didn't use them on his own but rather was given them."

"That's even more reason for me to keep searching," Liv stated. "Whoever is behind this is powerful, and who knows what they are trying to hide or control?"

"You shouldn't get mixed up in this, Liv," Rory said, warning in his voice. "It's bigger than you."

She agreed with a nod. "Yes, and it might be what killed my parents. It might be what killed Ian and Reese. They knew something was going on, and they left us clues. I can't ignore that."

Rory stopped abruptly, peering at the back bedroom. "We should quiet down. Mum is sleeping."

"Oh, I thought you had gnomes sawing wood in the backyard," Liv joked, plastering a serious look on her face. "Is that what you've been hiding in the back? Do you have a workcamp of gnomes? If so, I'm under obligation to bring you in."

Rory dismissed her with a shake of his head. "Well, I can't make you stop what you're doing."

"About damn time you wised up," Liv said with a wink.

"However, I *did* get John into this mess, and I'm going to get him out." Rory strode over to the mantel and removed Turbinger from its resting spot.

"What? No!" Liv realized she had said that too loudly as soon as Rory cast a punishing glare over his shoulder at her.

"Rory, you can't give them Turbinger. Your family has been parted from that sword for too long," Liv stated. "And I'm going to keep poking my nose into whatever I see fit.

It's better if John gets out of this mess. They'll just use him as a way to get to me."

"That's true," Rory stated, holding the sword up and appraising it. "That's why we've got to ensure he's protected. Once they drop the settlement, we've got to pool our strength and work to protect the shop. Maybe you brainwash a board member from the city. I can hire someone to trail John and ensure he's safe at all times. Then we set up wards around the shop and his apartment building to keep magical beings who aren't us away."

"Are you listening to yourself?" Liv asked, unsure she could even believe what he was saying.

He nodded. "You, as I suspected, aren't going to back down. That means this isn't going to stop. Whoever is behind this will continue to retaliate if they suspect you're snooping or stepping onto their territory."

"I don't even know what their territory is," Liv complained.

"I realize that," Rory stated. "I asked you to get the sword, but that's somehow raised red flags, and I don't know why."

Liv crossed her arms over her chest. "Well, it doesn't matter. I'm not going to allow you to give them the sword."

"Don't you want John to keep the shop?" Rory asked thoughtfully.

Liv gawked at him. "Of course, I do."

"Do you want John to move to Mexico?"

Liv was about to reply but stopped herself, unsure of the answer. "I want John to be safe."

Rory lowered his chin and regarded her with a sincere

expression. "I assure you the best way to do that is to keep him near us. If he's far away, we can't protect him."

"But Rory, this is your grandfather's sword. Your mother, who already loathes me, will pound me to bits if you give up Turbinger."

A smile lit Rory's eyes. "Haven't you been wondering what I've been working on in the backyard?"

Liv faked a yawn. "Not in the slightest."

He rolled his eyes and reached forward, holding out the sword. "Take it."

Liv gave him a cautious expression.

"You remember what it was like the last few times you held Turbinger, right?"

She nodded.

"Then take this," he encouraged.

Liv did as she was told, expecting to feel the strange emotions and memories that flowed through her when she held the ancient sword. Her fingers wrapped around the hilt of the blade, the cold metal heavy in her hands. There was nothing. She felt a twinge of energy like before, but not the flow of centuries of wisdom and battle. The sword felt strangely like a regular weapon.

Liv looked up in surprise. "What did you do to it?"

Rory's eyes danced with delight. "I made a replica." He snapped his fingers, and in his hands appeared another sword that looked exactly like the one she was holding. "This is the real Turbinger."

"That's what you've been working on in the back?" Liv asked, lowering the replica, taxed by her battles and not wanting to strain herself by supporting the heavy sword.

Rory nodded. "Yes. I figured that whoever was after the

sword wasn't going to quit until they had it, so I made the replica, which should fool anyone except a giant. In the last hundred years, you're the only magician to hold the sword and therefore the only one to know why this one is a fake. Otherwise, it should fool any other magician or magical creature."

"But the real sword…what will you do with that?" Liv asked.

The lightness on Rory's face disappeared. "I'm afraid it isn't safe here. They have a tracking spell that will find it if it stays close by. That was why I asked my mum to visit. She's going to take Turbinger back with her."

"Will it be safe with her?"

"Yes, because she lives on the other side of the world in a remote giants' village where outside magic and spells aren't allowed," Rory explained. "They won't be able to easily find Turbinger there. But more importantly, if they have the replica, they won't even think to look."

Liv ran her eyes over the real Turbinger and then the replica, amazed that they looked identical. "I can't believe you were able to make this."

Rory let out a forced laugh. "It wasn't easy. Also, this one has none of the magical qualities my grandfather put into Turbinger."

"Okay, so we give the dumb lawyer the sword, and they let John keep his shop," Liv said, her heart starting to expand with hope.

Rory nodded. "And we work together to quickly put into place the measures I talked about to protect John, just in case."

Liv smiled, suddenly very grateful that John was going

to stay and the shop would be okay. She hadn't realized how long it had been since she had last breathed in fully. She had stopped that day that Mr. Wayne Grimson had stepped into the shop.

"There's one more thing," Rory said, an edge to his voice.

"Yes?" Liv replied.

"I haven't had a chance to recover the memories buried in Turbinger," he began. "I think they may be a part of the mystery you're trying to uncover."

"Me, too," Liv agreed.

"I've been busy creating the replica," Rory stated. "But if you give me one more day, I'll try to unearth them. Then you can take the replica to the lawyer and Mum will leave with Turbinger."

Liv nodded. "It sounds like a plan."

Rory regarded the sword in his hands with quiet appreciation. "Good, because the timing has to be perfect."

CHAPTER THIRTY-NINE

Beatles music streamed from an old jukebox that Liv had gotten working for just that occasion. Shane, the regular customer who owned the pawn shop down the way, had sold it to her for a hefty price. She didn't care. She'd pay three times that to get something she'd known John had wanted for a long time.

Shane wasn't in attendance at the party that evening. As she and John had agreed, he was the only mortal in the shop that night. It was safer that way. Besides, there was someone coming who Liv wanted to ensure was extra safe. No mortals. No outsiders. Only those she thought she could trust. The number of people on that list was growing, and that scared Liv. Who was she when she had so many around her she trusted and cared about? The thought made her feel vulnerable, and she realized the brutal aspect of trust and why it had been so hard for her. Trust equaled love and vice versa.

"She's a beauty," John said, slapping his hand on the top

of the jukebox and smiling widely at her. “I can’t believe you got this for the shop.”

“I got it for you, John,” she corrected.

“Well, you didn’t have to,” he reasoned. “First you saved the shop, and now this.”

“I didn’t save the shop,” she said, looking around. “Rory did it. I just was the middleman.” That afternoon she’d taken the replica of Turbinger to Usher and Usher law firm, hiding it from prying eyes until she gave it to Mr. Grimson in his office. From that moment on, John’s shop had been free from danger.

“You seem to be waiting for someone,” John remarked as she scanned the shop again.

“I’m just looking forward to Rory getting here so we can thank him together,” Liv lied.

The door opened, and a familiar face came through. John pointed. “Looks like that pretty boy is back to see you.”

Liv shook her head. “I call him Poo Poo Face, and I invited him because I need to ask him something. I hope that’s okay.”

John smiled and reached down to pet Pickles. “Fine by me. I’m going to go melt the cheese for the nachos. Do you want jalapenos?”

“What do *you* think?” she asked with a grin.

“I’ll make it double, as usual.” John trotted to the table of snacks, which was piled high with Cheetos and pizza and quesadillas. Really, all things involving cheese.

“How is the love of my life doing?” Rudolf asked, sidling up next to Liv.

"I haven't been to the pet store lately to ask the guinea pigs," Liv replied. "I'll let you know when I do."

"Oh, you scorn my heart with your constant rejections." He clutched his chest, looking crestfallen.

"Have you made any progress?" Liv asked him as Plato jumped up on the closest workbench and blinked at them.

"I have," Rudolf replied.

"Really? That's great!" Liv said excitedly.

"Yes, I think so, too. Thanks for the enthusiasm." Rudolf turned in a circle, showing off his burgundy tunic, his wings glamoured not to show.

"What am I looking at? And why are you making my eyes bleed?"

"It's my newest tunic. Beautiful, isn't it? You asked about my progress, and I just got this back from the tailor."

Liv scoffed. "No, I was referring to the ring. Have you been able to uncover the memory tied to that?"

He deflated. "So you don't like the tunic?"

"I think it would look better with your blood on it," she threatened.

He shrank away, clutching his tunic protectively. "I've been working on it. Shouldn't take me much longer, but nothing yet."

"Much longer?" she questioned.

"Like a week or so," he answered.

The door chimed again, and the person Liv had been longing to see entered alongside Clark. "Okay, then keep your word, Jerkface."

"Where are you going?" Rudolf asked, sounding disappointed.

"Away," she answered over her shoulder.

"But what will *I* do?" Rudolf asked.

"Play with the cat," Liv replied. "He loves knock-knock jokes and when you do babytalk at him."

"Oh, then I'm your man, little lynx," Rudolf said, turning his attention to Plato. "Knockity-Knock."

Plato looked unpleased as Liv squatted in front of Sophia. "You came," she exclaimed.

The little magician wrapped her arms around Liv's shoulders, hugging her tightly. "Of course. I wouldn't let you down. Clark didn't want to risk it, but I told him he was stuffy and mean and he loosened up."

Liv looked up at Clark appreciatively. "Thank you. I know you took a risk to bring her here."

He shrugged, looking around uncomfortably. "It's fine. I knew how much it meant to you."

She nodded, pointing at the table of food. "Go get the cheese dip before Rory gets here. There won't be anything left after that."

Clark didn't look pleased about being at a party with a giant, and his disappointment grew when he spotted Rudolf chatting up Plato by the jukebox. "You invited that fae?"

"Yes. He's sort of an ally now," Liv said.

"'Ally?'" Clark questioned.

"Well, maybe a friend, but if you tell him I said that, I'll deny it vehemently," Liv stated with a wink.

"Fine. You make the weirdest friends, dear Liv," Clark said, striding toward the refreshment table.

Liv turned her attention to the little girl, who was wearing a yellow and white checkered dress, her expression sympathetic. "Did you hear the news?"

Sophia nodded. "I know you're not moving into the House of Seven anymore."

Liv swallowed. "And are you okay with it?"

The little girl squeezed her sister's hand with more force than Liv had known she possessed. "I want you to be happy. That's what family does for each other. If living where you are and working here makes you happy, then I'm happy." She looked around the shop, her eyes blazing with excitement. "And this place seems completely magical."

Liv pulled her close and kissed her head. "Thanks, Soph. And it totally is. Just a different brand of magic than you're used to."

The girl giggled, unleashing true happiness in Liv's heart. Blinking away tears of joy, Liv stood, pulling her little sister away.

"There is someone you have to meet." Liv didn't stop until she was standing at John's back. She coughed to get his attention. He'd set up a crockpot of creamy queso on a workbench. When he turned to them, he was wearing a smile. If possible, it broadened when he took in the sight before him.

Dropping the ladle onto a dish beside the crockpot, John knelt, offering a hand to Sophia. "Well, you must be the famous little sister I've heard so much about. I'm John."

Sophia blushed, giving John her hand and curtseying slightly. "I'm not famous at all. I haven't left the House of Seven since I was a baby."

John laughed, looking up at Liv. "She has your sense of humor. I bet she has your brains, too."

Liv shook her head. "Oh, she's much smarter than me."

John winked at her. "I think you two are a dynamic duo, destined to take over the world."

Sophia looked at Liv with a smile that could only be described as being full of happiness. "That music—I like it. What do you call it?"

John laughed. "That's the Beatles. Have you never heard of them?"

Sophia shook her head, then pointed at the row of old cameras John had on the shelf. "And what are those?"

"Those are cameras. I collect them. Do you want to test one out?"

Sophia shook her head. "I don't know how."

John waved her forward. "I can show you. They are really fun. I'm working on fixing one right now. You can help."

Sophia looked at Liv for permission, and she encouraged her with a nod. The little magician took the hand John offered, and the two strode over to a far shelf to explore the old cameras.

"You know, John would not have been happy in Mexico," Rory said, suddenly appearing at Liv's side.

She turned, hiding her surprise. "Why is it that, for a giant, you move like a mouse?"

He looked around, not answering her question.

"And I'm certain that John would have found some happiness with the waves crashing next to his bungalow and enjoying an afternoon beer on the beach every day," Liv countered.

Rory pulled his gaze away from Rudolf, who appeared to be explaining to Plato the complexity of knock-knock jokes. "No matter what the landscape, John wouldn't have been happy there."

"Well, he loves his electronics, so I'm guessing that over time he would have opened another shop," Liv said. "Then he would have been happy."

Rory looked down at her. "Liv, he loves *you*. *You* make him happy."

Liv didn't know what to say to that, so instead, she watched as her favorite mortal explained to her magician sister how cameras worked. Sophia's face blossomed with surprise when the film popped out.

"The handoff went okay?" Rory inquired.

Liv nodded. "And your mum? Has she taken her prejudice back to the remote isles?"

He nodded. "I won't apologize for what she said."

"It's fine," Liv stated.

"But that's how most giants feel," he continued. "Now you know."

Liv watched Clark regarding a Cheeto like it was a strange piece of nuclear technology. "You are one of the few giants who live in society, aren't you?"

He nodded. "I'm one of the only ones."

"That must make dating a bitch," she related.

"It makes life in general different," Rory confided. "However, I don't agree that we should live separately, but I'm also not good with living alongside others. So I definitely don't have things figured out."

Liv looked around the room at the mortal, magicians, fae, lynx, and giant and smiled, her heart full for the first time in a long time. "I don't think many of us are good at living together, but we're trying, and that's what counts."

"You know, when I found out you were a Warrior for the House of Seven, I had my doubts," Rory said.

"And now?" Liv asked.

"I still do, but in spite of everything, I think you might be what that institution needs," Rory said.

Liv was speechless again. Rory's visit with his mom seemed to have humanized him somehow. "Would you like to meet my little sister?"

Rory nodded and then shook his head. "Yes, but first I have something to tell you."

Liv paused. Sucked in a breath. "Go on."

"It's about Turbinger," he related.

"You found out the memories it was holding?" Liv asked.

He ran his hands through his hair. "I don't think I fully understand it yet, to be honest. I saw so many things, and I'm still trying to piece them together."

"At least you did it before the sword was taken away," Liv said hopefully. "Maybe in time, it will make sense."

He nodded. "I think that's where you come in."

Liv looked up at him quickly. "Really?"

"Well, before I told you to back off and not pursue leads," Rory began. "I was worried about you and John and whoever was behind the elf. However, I realize now that we need answers more than ever. Something has been covered up that none of us can explain. There is a history that has been erased, and although I can only see bits and pieces of it, I think that uncovering it fully will change everything."

Liv stiffened. "Rory, what did you see?"

He gave her his full attention and spoke in a whisper.

"Liv, a long time ago, there was a war between magicians and mortals. It didn't end well, and from everything I could see, I can't tell you who won."

Liv sucked in a breath. "What? I've never heard of such a thing. How do we not know about this? It sounds monumental."

Rory agreed. "I think it was, and I believe everything has been rewritten so that we forgot the past."

Liv looked around the room, a chill running down her spine. "Then it will be our mission to uncover everything. Whatever has been lost will be found." She looked at Rory, giving him a meaningful expression. "Whatever has been broken will be mended."

He almost smiled at her. "Then maybe we can all live as one again."

SARAH'S AUTHOR NOTES

MARCH 1, 2019

Thank you to you, the reader, for reading the books and supporting the series. I'm still so thrilled you all have connected with Liv, Rory, Sophia and the gang. I've gotten a huge outpouring of attention for Rudolf. Can you believe that this fae wasn't even a part of the regular cast? He just showed up on the page one day, insulting Liv and making awesome jokes. Since then, I've been reluctant to let him go.

I found myself in Las Vegas on holiday between books two and three. That's when I came up with the idea for the Fae Kingdom. I was looking out at the Vegas strip and thought, *what if the fae owned all of this?* Then the idea started to unravel as I had a drink at the Chandelier at the Cosmopolitan. That bar is totally whimsical and the perfect backdrop for the sexy fairy creatures. I knew I wanted to modernize the fae in this series, making them edgy and not carrying flowers or wearing kilts. Vegas seemed like the perfect place for these deceptive creatures. However, what I didn't realize until after starting book three was that there would be a ton of layers to these seemingly superficial fae.

As some of you've read about in other books, I often enlist Lydia, my daughter, to name characters. One day, we were sitting at our favorite Indian restaurant, discussing the next book. We often do that at this place and then Lydia draws scenes from the book on the paper covering the nice table cloth. While she was drawing, I asked her what the queen of the fae should be called. She told me Queen Visa and that she'd have a pet bear named, Bruiser. I have to admit that I forgot about Bruiser when I wrote about Queen Visa, but there's time to include him in later books. It was a good idea for the queen to have a pet bear and Bruiser, a small black bear, is Lydia's favorite stuffed animal. He has an alter ego that we call "Own Bear." In the morning he jumps around the bed and says, "I'm my ooooown bear. You don't own me! Don't tell me what to do."

If I ever wonder why my daughter rebels later, please remind me of this bear's alter ego which I absolutely created. Anyway, Bruiser will show up in another book, I'm sure.

But Lydia got her wish about naming Queen Visa. She's pretty much named half the cast at this point. Funnily, Michael was reading the outline for the book and saw the name Queen Visa and made a note that said: "King Mastercard? Prince American Express? Lol. (Sorry, it was so easy…)."

Okay, it was easy and he's right. I deserved that. I allowed a seven-year-old to name a character and she has no idea what a Visa is, but probably heard it somewhere.

However, when she named this queen who owned the Vegas strip Visa, I was like, you're a freaking genius.

My question to Michael is, what are you doing living in the fae kingdom? And what have you done with Bruiser? And are you and Queen Visa trying to take over the world?

Oh! And where are my BBQ nachos? I finished another book!

MICHAEL'S AUTHOR NOTES

MARCH 3, 2019

THANK YOU for not only reading this story but these *Author Notes* as well.

(I think I've been good with always opening with "thank you." If not, I need to edit the other *Author Notes*!)

RANDOM (*sometimes*) THOUGHTS?

Have you ever hoped for something wonderful, and it was just that much more precious because you were able to be a part of it for someone else?

That is my life right now.

The success of Liv's stories has been a wonderful surprise, and watching Sarah's reaction to the success has been particularly satisfying. I've had more than one opportunity to either chat with her in Slack or on the phone when she admits she still feels like pinching herself.

<Pinch away Sarah, I'm sure you will blame me somehow for the black and blue marks, and I'll assume the Fae in Vegas did it to you. You have NO idea how the

Cosmopolitan is a den of inequity. I bet you don't even remember being asleep, do you? Yup, you went down up to the Fae penthouse…>

Joking aside, (really, not really) I would like to convey how your support of this series has made the beginning of 2019 cause Sarah's eyes to glow, her lips to smile, and an easy chuckle cross her lips.

Wait, I'm sorry…she was looking at a hipster and making a comment.

My bad.

Ok, joking aside, your reading of these stories has made 2019 a special time in my life as I watch a wonderful collaborator succeed with these characters far beyond what we expected.

Thank you.

AROUND THE WORLD IN 80 DAYS

One of the interesting (at least to me) aspects of my life is the ability to work from anywhere and at any time. In the future, I hope to re-read my own *Author Notes* and remember my life as a diary entry.

DFW Airport, on an airplane...

Those joining me for the trip out of town are almost finished boarding, and it will be time to scoot down the runway and lift off towards fair Samarkand.

Or as we like to call it, Las Vegas.

I live in Las Vegas, just a few short steps from the Cosmopolitan Sarah mentioned in her notes. She is right—if there was a location for the Fae on the Strip, one of the courts WOULD probably be right there in the Cosmopolitan.

Interesting fact about the Cosmo—it doesn't belong to any other players' club. When you go to the Cosmopolitan and get a player's card, the big "C" is the only casino which you can play using that card.

Just like I would suspect some non-sharing fae to operate.

In the car (middle floor only) they have a drink that has a bud of a plant on the top. You are supposed to chew the bud, then drink the liquor. When you do this, the plant (which is horribly nasty in my opinion) will numb the crap out of your mouth, tongue, (and if you try to spit it out, like yours truly) your lips.

Who would concoct such a nasty drink?

Fae, I tell you. I bet they laugh at the mundanes who come into that place all the time.

Like me.

FAN PRICING

$0.99 Saturdays (new LMBPN stuff) and $0.99 Wednesday (both LMBPN books and friends of LMBPN books.) Get great stuff from us and others at tantalizing prices.

Go ahead. I bet you can't read just one.

Sign up here: http://lmbpn.com/email/.

HOW TO MARKET FOR BOOKS YOU LOVE

Review them so others have your thoughts, and tell friends and the dogs of your enemies (because who wants to talk to enemies?)... *Enough said ;-)*

Ad Aeternitatem,

Michael Anderle

ACKNOWLEDGMENTS

SARAH NOFFKE

My favorite part of writing any book is creating the acknowledgements page. It reminds me that writing a book is not a solo task. I might sit alone and write, but the finished product is a result of the support and encouragement of a tribe of people.

Thank you to the readers who buy the books, read them, review and recommend. YOU are the one who keeps us writing. I'm always inspired by the messages I receive from readers. Thank you supporting the books and offering so much richness to my life.

Thank you to my LBMPN family for all the support. Steve, Michael, Lynne, Moonchild, Jennifer and so many others who help champion the book to publication and beyond.

Thank you to the beta readers who offered so many valuable insights early on. Thank you to John, Chrisa, Kelly, Martin and Larry.

Thank you to the JIT team for all the awesome feedback. A new series is always exciting and nerve-wracking.

Michael and I thought we had a great idea for a new world, but we don't really know until we get objective feedback. What would I do without all you awesome readers?

Thank you to my friends and family. Writing is a strange profession. I work weird hours, talk to myself, have a strange diet, get antsy about deadlines. But the wonderful people in my life continue to show their encouragement and thoughtfulness no matter what. It is never lost on me because I know that I wouldn't be doing what I love without all you amazing people, cheering me on.

And as with all my books, the final thank you goes to my muse, Lydia. I wrote my first book so that I could make my daughter proud, and it's never stopped. I write every book for you, my love.

BOOKS BY SARAH NOFFKE

Sarah Noffke, an Amazon Best Seller, writes YA and NA sci-fi fantasy, paranormal and urban fantasy. She is the author of the Lucidites, Reverians, Ren, Vagabond Circus, Olento Research, Soul Stone Mage, Ghost Squadron and Precious Galaxy series. Noffke holds a Masters of Management and teaches college business courses. Most of her students have no idea that she toils away her hours crafting fictional characters. Noffke's books are top rated and best-sellers on Kindle. Currently, she has thirty-three novels published. Her books are available in paperback, audio and in Spanish, Portuguese and Italian. http://www.sarahnoffke.com

Check out other work by this author here.

Ghost Squadron:

Formation #1:

Kill the bad guys. Save the Galaxy. All in a hard day's work.

After ten years of wandering the outer rim of the galaxy, Eddie Teach is a man without a purpose. He was one of the toughest pilots in the Federation, but now he's just a regular guy, getting into bar fights and making a difference wherever he can. It's not the same as flying a ship and saving colonies, but it'll have to do.

That is, until General Lance Reynolds tracks Eddie down and offers him a job. There are bad people out there, plotting terrible things, killing innocent people, and destroying entire colonies. **Someone has to stop them.**

Eddie, along with the genetically-enhanced combat pilot Julianna Fregin and her trusty E.I. named Pip, must recruit a diverse team of specialists, both human and alien. They'll need to master their new Q-Ship, one of the most powerful strike ships ever constructed. And finally, they'll have to stop a faceless enemy so powerful, it threatens to destroy the entire Federation.

All in a day's work, right?

Experience this exciting military sci-fi saga and the latest addition to the expanded Kurtherian Gambit Universe. If you're a fan of Mass Effect, Firefly, or Star Wars, you'll love this riveting new space opera.

**NOTE: If cursing is a problem, then this might not be for you.*

Check out the entire series here.

The Precious Galaxy Series:

Corruption #1

A new evil lurks in the darkness.

After an explosion, the crew of a battlecruiser mysteriously disappears.

Bailey and Lewis, complete strangers, find themselves suddenly onboard the damaged ship. Lewis hasn't worked a case in years, not since the final one broke his spirit and his bank account. The last thing Bailey remembers is preparing to take down a fugitive on Onyx Station.

Mysteries are harder to solve when there's no evidence left behind.

Bailey and Lewis don't know how they got onboard *Ricky Bobby* or why. However, they quickly learn that whatever was responsible for the explosion and disappearance of the crew is still on the ship.

Monsters are real and what this one can do changes everything.

The new team bands together to discover what happened and how to fight the monster lurking in the bottom of the battlecruiser.

Will they find the missing crew? Or will the monster end them all?

The Soul Stone Mage Series:

House of Enchanted #1:

The Kingdom of Virgo has lived in peace for thousands of years...until now.

The humans from Terran have always been real assholes to the witches of Virgo. Now a silent war is brewing, and the timing couldn't be worse. Princess Azure will soon be crowned queen of the Kingdom of Virgo.

In the Dark Forest a powerful potion-maker has been murdered.

Charmsgood was the only wizard who could stop a deadly virus plaguing Virgo. He also knew about the devastation the people from Terran had done to the forest.

Azure must protect her people. Mend the Dark Forest. Create alliances with savage beasts. No biggie, right?

But on coronation day everything changes. Princess Azure isn't who she thought she was and that's a big freaking problem.

Welcome to The Revelations of Oriceran. Check out the entire series here.

***The Lucidites Series*:**

Awoken, #1:

Around the world humans are hallucinating after sleepless nights.

In a sterile, underground institute the forecasters keep reporting the same events.

And in the backwoods of Texas, a sixteen-year-old girl is about to be caught up in a fierce, ethereal battle.

Meet Roya Stark. She drowns every night in her dreams, spends her hours reading classic literature to avoid her family's ridicule, and is prone to premonitions—which are becoming more frequent. And now her dreams are filled with strangers offering to reveal what she has always wanted to know: Who is she? That's the question that haunts her, and she's about to find out. But will Roya live to regret learning the truth?

Stunned, #2

Revived, #3

The Reverians Series:

Defects, #1:

In the happy, clean community of Austin Valley, everything appears to be perfect. Seventeen-year-old Em Fuller, however, fears something is askew. Em is one of the new generation of Dream Travelers. For some reason, the gods have not seen fit to gift all of them with their expected special abilities. Em is a Defect—one of the unfortunate Dream Travelers not gifted with a psychic power. Desperate to do whatever it takes to earn her gift, she endures painful daily injections along with commands from her overbearing, loveless father. One of the few bright spots in her life is the return of a friend she had thought dead—but with his return comes the knowledge of a shocking, unforgivable truth. The society Em thought was protecting her has actually been betraying her, but she has no idea how to break away from its authority without hurting everyone she loves.

Rebels, #2

Warriors, #3

Vagabond Circus Series:

Suspended, #1:

When a stranger joins the cast of Vagabond Circus—a circus that is run by Dream Travelers and features real magic—mysterious events start happening. The once orderly grounds of the circus become riddled with hidden threats. And the ringmaster realizes not only are his circus and its magic at risk, but also his very life.

Vagabond Circus caters to the skeptics. Without skeptics, it would close its doors. This is because Vagabond Circus runs for two reasons and only two reasons: first and foremost to provide the lost and lonely Dream Travelers a place to be illustrious. And secondly, to show the nonbelievers that there's still magic in the world. If they believe, then they care, and if they care, then they don't destroy. They stop the small abuse that day-by-day breaks down humanity's spirit. If Vagabond Circus makes one skeptic believe in magic, then they halt the cycle, just a little bit. They allow a little more love into this world. That's Dr. Dave Raydon's mission. And that's why this ringmaster recruits. That's why he directs. That's why he puts on a show that makes people question their beliefs. He wants the world to believe in magic once again.

Paralyzed, #2

Released, #3

Ren Series:

Ren: The Man Behind the Monster, #1:

Born with the power to control minds, hypnotize others, and read thoughts, Ren Lewis, is certain of one thing: God made a mistake. No one should be born with so much power. A monster awoke in him the same year he received his gifts. At ten years old. A prepubescent boy with the ability to control others might merely abuse his powers, but Ren allowed it to corrupt him. And since he can have and do anything he wants, Ren should be happy.

However, his journey teaches him that harboring so much power doesn't bring happiness, it steals it. Once this realization sets in, Ren makes up his mind to do the one thing that can bring his tortured soul some peace. He must kill the monster.

Note This book is NA and has strong language, violence and sexual references.

Ren: God's Little Monster, #2

Ren: The Monster Inside the Monster, #3

Ren: The Monster's Adventure, #3.5

Ren: The Monster's Death

Olento Research Series:

Alpha Wolf, #1:

Twelve men went missing.

Six months later they awake from drug-induced stupors to find themselves locked in a lab.

And on the night of a new moon, eleven of those men, possessed by new—and inhuman—powers, break out of their prison and race through the streets of Los Angeles until they disappear one by one into the night.

Olento Research wants its experiments back. Its CEO, Mika Lenna, will tear every city apart until he has his werewolves imprisoned once again. He didn't undertake a huge risk just to lose his would-be assassins.

However, the Lucidite Institute's main mission is to save the world from injustices. Now, it's Adelaide's job to find these mutated men and protect them and society, and fast. Already around the nation, wolflike men are being spotted. Attacks on innocent women are happening. And then, Adelaide realizes what her next step must be: She has to find the alpha wolf first. Only once she's located him can she stop whoever is behind this experiment to create wild beasts out of human beings.

Lone Wolf, #2
Rabid Wolf, #3
Bad Wolf, #4

BOOKS BY MICHAEL ANDERLE

For a complete list of books by Michael Anderle, please visit:

www.lmbpn.com/ma-books/

All LMBPN Audiobooks are Available at Audible.com and iTunes

To see all LMBPN audiobooks, including those written by Michael Anderle please visit:

www.lmbpn.com/audible

CONNECT WITH THE AUTHORS

Connect with Sarah and sign up for her email list here:

http://www.sarahnoffke.com/connect/

You can catch her podcast, LA Chicks, here:

http://lachicks.libsyn.com/

Connect with Michael Anderle and sign up for his email list here:

Website: http://lmbpn.com

Email List: http://lmbpn.com/email/

Facebook: www.facebook.com/TheKurtherianGambitBooks

www.ingramcontent.com/pod-product-compliance
Lightning Source LLC
Chambersburg PA
CBHW031621100726
47898CB00006B/1895

9781642021462